THE
THREADS
REMAIN

THE
THREADS
REMAIN

Glenn Shapiro

BRANDYLION
PRESS

Trade paperback ISBN: 9798998501517
eBook ISBN:9798998501524

Typeset in Garamond by Andy Barr
Cover by twenty-five design

Printed and bound by IngramSpark

Für Mutti: For Mom

CHAPTER 1
VERSTECKEN: HIDING
1944

He had created chaos, and he was enjoying it. Friedrich jabbed the point of a short stick into an ant hole in the Platz (square) in front of his home. He knew that his Mutti (Mama) was watching from the third-floor railing in front of their apartment, two floors above the piano store that stood at ground level, as she always did while he played in the small patch of land. The square was outlined by one-lane roads in a sleepy part of München Gladbach. It was mostly grass-covered with some bare patches and a few scraggly bushes on each corner that were perhaps decorative at some point but now seemed to make the square look bleaker on this gray, cool November afternoon. Allied bombs had hit two of the dozen or so buildings that surrounded the square and were hollow shells of their former selves, with jagged edges of brick, looking paper-thin, almost defying gravity to stay upright. One still smoldered, giving the air a faint smoky scent that might have been pleasing if not accompanied by the image of wreckage.

Friedrich was six months past his third birthday. He was slim and tall for a boy of that age, with a narrow face and olive skin. His dark eyes were lined with lush, thick black lashes which gave him an angelic look that every woman he met commented on. He wore a drab gray stocking cap and a brown wool coat that was missing a button on the front and had a small hole in the arm. A few wavy black locks of hair escaped the stocking cap and hung down his forehead.

The ants poured out of the hole as he jabbed the stick at the opening with the typical lack of coordination of any three-year-old child. He began to trace the pinwheel-like shape that he saw on the banner across the square from his apartment. That shape was everywhere. Soldiers wore it on their arms, bright flags bearing the shape streamed from buildings all over town. Even the piano shop at the base of their building displayed that shape in the window. He liked it. As he traced it over the ant hole, the ants scurried in every direction. The boy watched, curious, studying, transfixed. He heard and saw nothing around him as he focused on the chaos he had created. Then his body lurched as his arm was yanked, and he rose violently into the air.

Friedrich looked up and realized he was slung under Mutti's right arm. Renate Brunst was a tall, slender woman, but she was wiry and strong. She easily ran across the street and bounded up the steps, two at a time, all the way to their third-floor apartment while carrying the boy like a grocery sack. Friedrich was disoriented by the jostling and began to whimper halfway through their ascent. As they reached the apartment, Renate swung the door open, then closed and locked it with one hand, still carrying the boy under her right arm. She lifted him onto the table in the kitchen and knelt before him. Friedrich was glassy-eyed, his lips puckered and trembling, making him look even more angelic than usual. Renate leveled her gaze on him and held both of his cheeks in her hands, which were moist with sweat. She had a strong, masculine jawline but kind eyes. "Friedrich, my dear," she said softly with a quiver in her voice. "You must listen to me carefully. You are going to hide, and I need you to stay completely quiet for a very long time. You are not to come out or make a sound until I come to get you. You must promise me."

A tear escaped his eye and rolled down his left cheek as he nodded slightly.

Sliding her hands down to his shoulders, Renate gripped him firmly. "Do you remember the stories in *Struwwelpeter* my dear?" She nodded for him. "And do you remember the *Grimms' Fairy Tales*?"

Friedrich nodded. The stories scared him. Each tale ended with some horror visiting a child who did not obey. One story in *Struwwelpeter* haunted him. It was about a boy who sucked his thumb, so a demon came and cut the boy's thumb off with shears. The image on the page of the smiling lanky demon with shears and blood pouring from the boy's thumbless hand gave Friedrich nightmares and had cured him of ever sucking his thumb again. He looked back at his Mutti. He had only known love and gentility from this woman. Now, her face was twisted with a fear that penetrated his own chest. He made no reply.

"I need you to say that you understand, that you will hide quietly until I come for you."

"Yes, Mutti," he squeaked out over a trembling lower lip.

Now tears escaped Renate's eyes as she saw the fear and pain on his face. She hugged him closely. "I love you, my son. I always will." She turned to the back wall of the kitchen, placed her hands firmly in the center of the paneling, pushed in, and then slid it to the left. The panel fell forward against her hands. There were the sounds of heavy footsteps on the stairs outside that caused them both to look toward the front door. She closed her eyes and drew in a deep breath. As her eyes opened, she smiled softly and spoke quietly. "My love, I am sorry. I wish we had time to help you understand. I wish I could hide with you, but there is no room and if I am not accounted for ..." she trailed off and shook her head. "You are such a good boy, such a brave boy. I know you can do this. Not a single sound, no matter what you hear. Do you understand?" She forced another smile and nodded gently.

Friedrich blinked and said again through trembling lips, "Yes, Mutti."

The moment he agreed, she hugged him tightly one more time, placed him into the opening in the wall, and replaced the paneling.

Everything went pitch black. Friedrich trembled and began to cry but did so silently. He had never known darkness like this. There was no light. He felt the rough back of the paneling against the backs of his hands as they hung by his sides. He tilted his head forward just a few centimeters until his nose felt the same rough surface. He was in a box, between wall studs on each side, the building siding behind him and the paneling before him. In complete blackness.

There was a bang at the door of the apartment. He heard

men's voices and his own Mutti's, but they sounded strange to him, shrill and angry. The men's voices rose, followed by a loud crashing which sent vibrations through the wall that Friedrich could feel against his nose. His mouth opened to scream but no sound came out as he remembered his promise.

The unfamiliar man's voice rose again and sounded closer now. The words were foreign to Friedrich, *harboring*; *witnesses*; *enemy*. His Mutti's voice responded, "He's gone. Yesterday. You will never find him, you devil." The final word rose to a shriek. There were two loud bangs, so jarring that Friedrich let out a startled yelp and then held his breath. He heard two men now, arguing. Then the room was silent.

After a long silence, there were footsteps around the room. He heard a clatter of things falling or being thrown around. Friedrich continued to cry silently. He said to himself, *I must stay quiet until Mutti gets me.* The door closed and the house was silent again. He waited.

Friedrich could not know how long he had been inside the wall, but he knew he was hungry and had to use the toilet. The fairy tales were not kind to children who didn't eat their supper or who made a mess. They were also clear on obeying your parents, so he felt torn. He was going to break one or more of these rules and surely be gobbled up by a witch or meet some other grisly end. He hoped his mother would open the panel soon and let him avoid that fate. But she did not come.

As time passed, he propped his body against the wall stud to his right. He had been standing for so long his legs were numb. With his weight shifted, and somewhat supported, he drifted to sleep. He awoke to sounds in the home and a terrible smell. He had messed his pants. He began to cry, thinking of what would happen to him. Is it a demon or a witch in the house now, come to claim the bad child who messed his pants?

A man's voice spoke softly in the house. "Little boy. Where are you?" It was no voice he knew. *A demon*, he thought, and he stayed silent.

CHAPTER 2
TREFFEN: MEETING
1928

Biermann Variety Store was located on busy Kaufingerstrasse (Kaufinger Street). It was in an ideal location within Munich, with stores up and down the road that drew steady foot traffic. Max and Dora Biermann established the small store before World War I and had run it continuously since then with no employees, other than immediate family. Max, a slightly hunched, gray-haired man who looked older than his sixty-two years, was skilled at getting bulk deals on merchandise, particularly closeout items or excess stock from factories, so the store's identity changed weekly. Max wore the same outfit to work every day: a white shirt with a loosely fitting button-down black sweater and a brown burlap apron on top. It made him appear as if he were manufacturing the goods in the back of the store that he later sold in the front.

Dora was the beating financial heart of the operation. She

kept the books, watched their accounts, and gave Max approval for any purchases. She also operated as Max's last resort on negotiations. He would toss a glance back toward his wife and shake his head, signaling that she would not go higher. She wore a gray frock that hung over her shoulders off of the front of her breasts, loosely away from her body. She had short-cropped gray hair and looked all of her sixty years.

The small store's shelves were piled high with a mishmash of goods in no particular order. A well-priced, fine steel pot might sit beside a box of wool socks. The chaotic storage-shed feel of the place added to the sense that deals were there to be had, and the store did steady business with loyal customers who returned to browse for hidden treasures.

Max and Dora had one child; a son also named Max. They had struggled to conceive for years before Dora became pregnant twice in her thirties, losing the baby within three months each time. Then, shortly after her fortieth birthday, she was pregnant again, to their great surprise. They held no hope that the child would be carried to term, and the doctor all but assured them that their pessimism was warranted.

With each passing month, they pushed back the hope that crept up in them until the hope overwhelmed them after seven months of pregnancy. Their boy, Max, was born a month early and weighed just five pounds, but he was strong and healthy. He had been their entire world ever since.

Young Max Biermann had worked in the variety store since the day he graduated from primary school. He was short, though slightly taller than his father, perhaps due only to the older Max's hunched shoulders. He had thick, curly black hair with a yarmulke flattening a circle in the center. His beard had been growing since he was sixteen years old; now twenty, it was mostly full, with a few scraggly spots, symmetrically placed on each lower cheek, just to each side of his chin. He wore a warm, bright smile and had a kind word for every customer or supplier, most of whom would seek him out, preferring to haggle with him versus his father.

It was the third Friday in June 1928. A bright, sun-filled day was beginning, filling the downtown merchants with optimism for a busy day on the streets. The door opened, ringing the small chain of bells hung at the top on the inside. It was a welcome sound, the sound of commerce.

A short, slender young woman walked in, holding a wooden crate in front of her with both hands. She was attractive, with olive skin and dark eyes, surrounded by thick, lush lashes.

The elder Max shuffled forward and asked, "May I help you find something here, my dear? Perhaps some cookware, or fine linens?"

"No, sir. I've actually come to sell some things." She paused. "Some things I have made."

Max frowned. "I'd rather be selling than buying today, but let's have a look." He stepped forward and peered down into the crate. Inside he saw on one side four crocheted animals made from cellulose fiber. There was a bear, a rabbit, a sheep, and a dog. Each was wearing an intricately woven outfit, custom made to fit the little animal, with buttons on the back, so the outfit could be put on or taken off. On the other side of the crate were two knit sweaters. Both were children's sizes.

"I'd be happy to take these off your hands," Max said, shaking his head and shrugging slightly. "But I'm afraid the value is not very high."

The young woman looked dejected. "I've worked quite hard on these. I think you will find the workmanship excellent."

The elder Max drew in a breath to speak but was interrupted by his son who had been watching intently, unseen from the aisle to their right. "Let me handle this, Papi." The two men held each other's gaze for a moment, then Max Sr. smiled, nodded, and shuffled away.

"May I take a look, please?"

"Of course."

"My goodness, the work is exquisite. You have such a gift. What is your name?"

The woman smiled shyly, looking down and then back up, her dark eyes meeting his. "I am Gerda Karelitz."

Max noticed her delicate features, her cheeks tapering gently to her jawline, then cascading to the defined point of her chin. As she smiled, a slight dimple appeared by the left corner of her mouth.

"I am Max Biermann. This is my store," Max said, realizing immediately that he sounded pompous as he tried to make an impression. "What I mean is, this is my family's store. But I will take over the store soon, and what you have made is exactly what I want more of here. We have too much clutter and the toys do so well. In fact, toys make up only ten percent of the inventory but account for nearly twenty percent of the sales. I know exactly how I want this place to look. No more clutter, a place where children and adults immediately feel happy." He stopped himself, realizing he was speaking quickly and may have even sounded crazed, but as he looked at Gerda, she was smiling gently, appearing to enjoy his enthusiasm.

"Well, I can make much more of what you see here if you like it." Pausing, she added, "If it will make people happy."

"I do like it very much. We will take all of it." From the back, he heard his mother clear her throat.

Gerda looked at him questioningly. "We have not agreed on a price."

Max looked back at his mother while responding to Gerda. "We will pay what you think is fair, Fräulein Karelitz. My mother will give you the money." He gave his mother a wink, which earned him a veiled smile and a reluctant nod in return.

* * *

Gerda Karelitz stepped out of her front door on Monday morning with a crate full of her handmade goods. She descended the single flight of stairs to the ground level of her apartment building and saw Max Biermann, the young man she had sold her goods to three days prior, standing directly across from the bottom of the stairs, hands behind his back.

"Good morning, Fräulein Karelitz. It's good to see you again."

Gerda paused, registering confusion on her face. "Hello, um, what are you doing here?"

"Well, I clearly did not want to bother you on the weekend, so I waited here since six o'clock this morning. I did not know what time you typically left home."

"You've been standing here for three hours?"

"Yes, about that."

"Why?"

"To see you, of course."

Gerda paused, then responded, "Okay." But it came out more like a question.

"I owe you more explanation, of course," Max said. "I was quite taken by the quality of your work. Stunning, really. You recall, I told you my plans for the store. I see it so clearly. It will be a place of joy for anyone who enters. Your beautiful animals and knitted and crocheted goods will be perfect there."

"So, you came to my home and waited three hours to tell me you would like more of my products for your store." She paused, adding, "Someday when you take over?" She gave him a skeptical look, along with a hint of a smile.

"Well, perhaps I had some interest in the person who made those beautiful things as well," Max replied, returning a wry smile. "Would you join me for tea?"

Gerda nodded.

It was a breezy morning with blue skies and a few wispy clouds. Gerda wore a thin yellow sweater she had knit herself. She had knit butterfly shapes around the neckline in the same color yarn as the base sweater, so that one could only make them out at close range. Max wore a brown long-sleeved shirt with black buttons. As they began to walk, he kept his hands clasped behind his back.

"My parents quite liked you, you know?"

"Did they? I couldn't really tell. I think they both felt you overpaid for my goods."

"They think we overpay for anything. I suppose it makes them good businesspeople, and of course I love them dearly, but I don't think they have a vision for what the store could be." Max became animated again. "There is no place in the downtown where children, and adults who remember what it's like to be young, can just explore and play. My parents see individual transactions; I see an experience."

"Well, I suppose you do have to make money on your sales, don't you?"

"Of course, but the money will come when people find joy. They will want to come back again and again."

"It sounds wonderful."

"It will be, you will see."

Gerda gave him a curious look at his last statement.

They arrived at a small bakery with four tables outside. Max guided Gerda to an open table and walked into the bakery. He emerged with two cups of tea and two slices of Bienenstich (bee sting) cake. The moist, honey-drenched cake was still warm, and the scent of honey and cream filled the air.

"How did you know that I love Bienenstich?" Gerda asked.

"I think I know a great deal about you, Fräulein Karelitz."

"Oh, I am quite interested in what you think you know about me, Herr Biermann," Gerda said with a hand to her chin, tilting her head to the left to peer at him questioningly through her right eye. "You know, perhaps I'll allow you to call me Gerda if you tell me enough truths."

"I accept the challenge." Max leaned forward, looking closely at Gerda, as if studying her. She giggled slightly at his theatrics. "Here is one truth about you. You like beautiful things but prefer not to draw attention to yourself." He leaned back and smiled confidently.

"What does that mean?"

"I'll give you an example. You have woven butterflies into your sweater. They are beautiful and show incredible skill, but you made them the same color as the sweater. It is enough that you know they are there. You have no need of anyone else knowing about them or complimenting you on them."

"That's not bad, but you are just across the table from me. It seems easy to spot the butterflies and make an assumption about me."

"So, you want another truth to prove my powers are real?"

"I do."

"I'll do better than that. I will give you two more. First, you love animals. You probably have at least one pet, but I am guessing more." Max rubbed his beard, thinking. "I will say two pets. Yes, two."

Gerda looked surprised. "Did you look in my window?"

"I promise I did not," Max said nervously. "I am really just guessing."

She laughed. "I have a cat and a dog, and I love them dearly. Well done. How did you know?"

"The cellulose animals that you brought to the store were made with such love and care, I knew you loved animals. You even dressed your creations in fine clothes. It also tells me that you are kind, but that is not the other truth, it is just an easy observation." Max looked excitedly at Gerda and added, "The last truth is that you do not suffer from pride. I have two examples as proof. First, in the store when my father suggested, as part of his negotiation, that your goods were not worth much, you did not protest. Most people with your skill would have taken insult, but you showed none." He paused and flushed red.

After a long pause, Gerda prodded. "You promised two examples and only gave one." She looked across at the man who had been so confident but now seemed lost.

Max's fingers fidgeted as he looked down at the table. "The real truth is that you are the most beautiful woman I have ever seen, but you don't seem to know it because you agreed to spend this time with me."

She took in a breath and held it, looking at the kind face opposite her. After a moment she exhaled, reached both of her hands across the table and held his. Their fingers interlaced in an easy weave. She looked at their hands and smiled. "I suppose you can call me Gerda now, but you may have been wrong about something."

Max followed her eyes to their connected hands, then gazed up at her, looking stunned and momentarily speechless.

She continued without waiting for a response. "I'm not really sure if it is pride but it feels something like it when I make my creations." She smiled, still looking down at their hands. "It may be what you feel when you talk about the toy store you imagine creating, a place of joy you called it. I start with bare threads, cellulose fiber for the bodies, dyed wool for the clothes. They look like nothing. If I left them alone, these would be scraps, eventually discarded. They would have no life, but when I weave them into a small creature ..." She cut off her thought and shook her head, looking embarrassed. "I sound silly."

Max squeezed her hands gently and looked into her eyes. "You absolutely do not. Please continue."

Gerda blushed, but his look encouraged her. He appeared not only interested but eager to hear. She took another deep breath and closed her eyes. "I guess I imagine their life, the places they will go. I hope they will bring joy or even comfort. I think, perhaps, if I make them well enough, these threads will go on beyond me." She opened her eyes and looked back at Max, who held his serious gaze on her. "I suppose that sounds something like pride."

Max shook his head slightly. "It sounds more like love to me."

CHAPTER 3
MUTTI: MAMA
1957

There was a bustling energy in the Academic Hospital Schwabing Munich. Busy doctors and nurses hustled by the door. The sounds of gurneys rolling past, patients calling for assistance and discussions between medical staff filled the air. The vitality of the place stood in stark contrast to Minna Becker, who lay motionless, almost lifeless in her bed, a small stream of drool escaping the left corner of her mouth.

The once energetic woman who filled every room with her laughter and constant chatter had lost half her weight to the cancer that ravaged her body. She was months away from her forty-ninth birthday but looked twice her age with baggy skin and hollow cheeks. Asleep, she looked as if the cancer had already taken her last breath, but during her increasingly rare and fleeting bouts of consciousness, she still flashed her smile and acted as if she would be up and about soon. Her husband and son knew it was an act but played along.

Friedrich Becker sat close by her side on a small swivel-topped stool that the doctors used when they came in to examine his mother. He held her hand and spoke to her, fighting the urge to weep. He came every day after class at Gymnasium, the top-level primary school in Germany. He excelled in academics and music; Minna had seen to that.

The tall, lanky sixteen-year-old had a mop of dark hair to match his dark eyes and thick lashes. His thin face wore a serious expression most of the time but could produce a friendly smile when he allowed for one.

He knew he was losing his mother, so he spent every free moment here with her. This woman had made him the center of her world. She taught him mathematics before he entered school. He learned to read while still short of his fifth birthday.

As he held her frail hand, he thought of their most precious time—the time seated at their piano. These hands, now so small and fragile, had seemed so large to him as they lay atop his own hands as a child, teaching him notes and chords. Her favorite composer was Beethoven, and her favorite song was "Für Elise". She would say, *It may have been written one hundred forty years ago but it is still the most beautiful music today*. Now, her hands looked skeletal; the slack skin shriveled, hanging over brittle bones.

Standing against the wall, two meters back and centered on the foot of the bed, Dieter Becker was stick-straight and expressionless. Dieter was a man of few words. His stiff posture, square jaw, and intense eyes told the world he was a serious man. He and Minna married in 1930 when he was twenty-five and she was three years his junior. Minna would tell people that she was his first girlfriend, which Friedrich assumed was true, but Dieter never commented.

The prospect of life without Minna was terrifying to Friedrich. He had always been at her side. He had few friends and would choose piano lessons with his mother over any opportunity to mingle with people his own age. Dieter would tell him that he needed to *make more associations,* in his typical overly formal way of communicating. *You don't want to be a mother's boy forever.* Now, with Minna leaving him, he suspected his father had been right.

"Goodbye for now, Mutti," Friedrich said as he stood up, leaned over her, and gave a long kiss to her forehead. Her mouth curled up in the corners with the hint of a smile in her sleep. Dieter walked forward and put a hand on Minna's leg, paused for a moment, then turned to leave.

The two walked down the hall with its gleaming linoleum floor, hearing again the bustle of the hospital. Friedrich was slightly taller than Dieter if both stood straight, but with his father's impeccable posture and Friedrich's tendency to slouch, he appeared shorter.

"Father, do you think there is any hope for Mutti?"

"No. The doctor says there is nothing to be done," Dieter replied stiffly, swallowing and clearing his throat. Friedrich noticed his father doing this often when speaking about his wife's condition.

"I don't know what we will do without her."

Dieter stopped walking and faced Friedrich. "What do you mean? You will go to school, and I will go to work. We will eat when we are hungry, and we will do the things that are needed in our home. We will do what is necessary."

German sensibility lived in high concentrations in his father, thought Friedrich. He knew his father was hurting but he had no way to talk with him. Dieter did not talk much and certainly did not entertain discussions about *feelings*.

They arrived home and walked up the single flight of stairs to their second-floor apartment. The home had two bedrooms, a living space, kitchen, and one bath. It was neat and orderly, everything in its place. The couch and chairs surrounded the living room symmetrically, leaving space for the small spinet piano against the wall. A few photos adorned the walls and piano top, all of Friedrich. The apartment conveyed a sense of order and efficiency.

Friedrich went to his room and crawled into bed, still dressed, not feeling he had the strength or will to even change into bed clothes. The tune of "Für Elise" played in his head. He started to drift off when he heard footsteps at the open door to his room.

"Good night, Son." Dieter stood silent, seeming like he had more to say but then he just closed the door.

"No, Father," Friedrich said frantically and sat up quickly. "Remember, I need it open."

Dieter opened the door, let out a sigh, and said, "You will need to outgrow that fear." Then he walked away.

* * *

The school day came to a close, and once again, Friedrich made the two-kilometer walk to the Academic Hospital Schwabing. It was late September, and the weather was unseasonably warm. He ambled up two flights of stairs to the ward where his mother was housed. As he approached her room, number 327, he sensed a change. The light coming from the room looked different to him. He took a step inside the door and saw the curtain that typically divided the room was open. The bed behind it was neatly made. The machines that had monitored his mother were tucked in the corner, their wires coiled neatly. There were no signs of the room being occupied. No water glass, no food tray. His father was not there, as he had been every day.

Friedrich ran to the nurse's station. A nurse with short brown hair and a round face with glasses and a small white nurse's cap did not look up immediately. "Excuse me," he said in almost a whisper.

She raised her head, appearing annoyed at first, then immediately changed her expression at seeing Friedrich. "Oh, it's you. Did you not talk with your father?"

"No. I've come here straight from school." He knew what he was going to hear next but waited to hear it anyway.

"I'm so sorry. I, I thought you would have been told." She stumbled and hesitated, then added, "She went peacefully."

The walk home from the hospital usually took thirty minutes, but as Friedrich approached their apartment building, he felt he had been walking for only moments. He had been so lost in his thoughts that nothing of the walk remained in his memory. How could she be gone? Where was his father? Why had he not been told? These questions occupied the whole of his mind.

Entering the apartment, he saw Dieter sitting in his favorite blue upholstered chair. No one ever sat in that chair other than him. His hands were on his knees, his back was straight, and he stared forward.

"What happened?" Friedrich snapped more harshly than he intended.

"Your mother passed. I see that you learned that already."

"I mean, why wasn't I called? When?"

"It was 10:13 this morning. It just happened at once. She simply stopped breathing, so there was no need to call you."

"No need? No Need?" His voice escalated as he repeated the words. "My mother died, and there was no need to call me?"

"And what would you have done? She died. We knew that she would, and she did. It had already happened. What would you have done, exactly? Come to the hospital? She was no longer there. Come home?" Dieter paused to compose himself, as his voice had begun to rise, then he added in a softer voice, "Leaving school would not have helped. There was nothing to be done."

There it was again, the German sensibility Friedrich had known all his life. Being angry at his father for his cold logic would be like being angry at a rock for being hard. "Are you OK, father?"

"I am OK. Thank you, Friedrich."

Friedrich walked to his room and lay down on the bed. He reached to a small side table and retrieved his bear, Bärli. The small bear was woven of cellulose fiber and wore a beautifully crocheted outfit of gold and white with buttons up the back. Its eyes were two unmatched black buttons, the right larger than the left. He had kept this bear by his bed for as long as he could remember. He knew a toy bear was meant for a younger child and would have been embarrassed if anyone knew that he spoke to the bear at difficult times.

"So, my little friend. What do I do now? I know my mother and a toy bear should not be my closest friends, but it's too late to change that. Father was right, of course, that I should have made more *associations*, but it looks like it's down to just me and you." Tears welled in his eyes, and he gave a quivering smile to the bear, laughing slightly as he added, "But you are not much of a conversationalist."

At that moment, he thought again about his question: *What do I do now?* The answer was suddenly obvious.

CHAPTER 4
BÄR: BEAR
1932

Excitement raced in Josef Zohren's heart as he skipped up the road ahead of his parents, urging them forward. It was his seventh birthday, and his mother and father had taken him to Munich from their nearby home in Freising, which lay to the north of the city. He ran ahead of his parents looking in shop windows in search of his birthday present, which he was being allowed to pick for himself for the first time in his young life. It was a drizzly day with gray clouds hanging low in the sky, providing an atmospheric blanket that made the day unseasonably warm for November.

Josef was the only child of Karl and Ingrid Zohren. His dirty-blond hair was stick-straight and his bright blue eyes shone against his milky white skin. He was tall and broad-shouldered for his age, looking every bit the German stereotype. He took his looks mostly from his father, who shared the dirty-blond hair and blue eyes, though the senior Zohren was more slender-built and walked with a significant limp. A leg deformity kept him from military service, a shame that Ingrid Zohren wore openly and reminded him of regularly. Karl had an easy smile and would nod and brush aside her criticisms.

Ingrid was a stout woman with a serious gaze. Her short-cropped hair and wide shoulders would sometimes cause her to be mistaken for a man from behind. The day's outing had been Karl's idea, with Ingrid protesting, "We spoil that child. We make him soft."

Josef ran ahead and rounded a corner onto Kaufingerstrasse. He was out of sight for a few seconds as Karl and Ingrid walked up to the corner at Karl's limited speed, then Josef reappeared, out of breath, and excitedly exclaimed, "I found the best store."

When they rounded the corner, he was waiting in the doorway of a shop fifty yards down on the right, darting in once his parents saw him. Ingrid shook her head. "Silly child."

Karl patted her arm, "He's a child only once, dear."

Biermann Toy Shop was neatly carved into a wooden sign that hung on a rod perpendicular to the building, above the front door. "Wonderful, a Jew store," Ingrid said with a toss of her head, motioning to the sign.

"It's a toy store, dear. I don't think the toys practice religion." Karl gave a wry smile, but Ingrid just shook her head and walked in. A bell jingled, announcing their arrival.

The store was a carnival of colors and shapes with toys from floor to ceiling. Busy aisles overflowed with handmade toys, boxed puzzles, model trains, and a variety of stuffed animals. Josef was on the floor rolling a wooden train engine, to which he had hooked several cars, trailed by a caboose. He looked up to see his parents approaching. "Mutti, Papi, isn't it wonderful?"

Ingrid nodded. "Very nice."

In an instant, Josef was off to look at kites. A young man approached, perhaps in his mid-twenties. He had dark wavy hair with a yarmulke perched in the middle of his head, which gave him away as a Jew, though his thick black beard would have done so anyway. He tilted his head down in respect and said, "Hello. I am Max Biermann. I'm so pleased to have you in my store."

"Your store? You are so young," Ingrid said with a frown.

"Indeed, Madam. It was my parents' store, and I took over managing it just last year. For years this has been a variety store with a toy section, but since I took charge, we just kept adding toys until there was simply no room for anything else." With that he let out a laugh. It was likely the same story he told every new customer.

Ingrid remained stone-faced, but Karl obliged with a smile and a laugh. "Well, you certainly have captured my son's attention. It's his seventh birthday today."

"How wonderful! I hope he finds something that will create a lifetime of memories."

Behind the counter in the back of the store sat a young woman, also in her twenties. She was a small woman, attractive with olive skin and a pleasant smile. Her dark eyes were surrounded by lush, thick eyelashes. She wore a gray frock but had a crocheted flower pin on the front with bright yellow petals. Josef had made his way near her and was staring.

"Hello, young man. What is your name?"

"I am Josef. What is that?" He was transfixed by what she

was holding. His parents could not see because the counter blocked their view. As they approached, they saw it was a toy bear, made of coarse, tan-colored cellulose fiber and dressed in an intricately crocheted one-piece outfit, with gold yarn at the bottom and over its shoulders and a white midsection. Hand-sewn buttons up the back of the bear allowed the outfit to be removed or put back on. The work was exquisite and detailed. The bear had finer clothes than most wealthy Germans.

Max walked up to the counter and smiled. "This is my wife, Gerda. She is very skilled with knitting, crocheting, or any form of needlework. You have a good eye, young man. That is a beautiful bear, very special indeed. That cellulose fiber will last a lifetime." Turning to Ingrid and Karl, he added, "I met her here when she was selling her handmade goods. I asked her to marry me three months after we met and for the life of me, I don't know what took me so long." He let out a laugh.

Karl smiled. It was clear this shopkeeper told these stories often, but there was something very likable about him.

Still staring at the bear, Josef asked, "What is his name?"

Gerda smiled and held out the twenty-centimeter tall, tan bear with his gold and white outfit and small black button eyes. "You see, that's the thing, Josef. He doesn't have one yet. I just finished his outfit, and I wondered what name he might have. Perhaps only a good friend will know."

Ingrid leaned toward Karl and through gritted teeth said, "He is a boy and will not have a doll for his birthday, for God's sake. A train or kite or popgun, but no doll." She grabbed his arm tightly and added, "He is already too soft."

Karl often gave way to Ingrid but maintained his right to stand firm with her at certain moments. He turned to look straight into her eyes, making clear this was one of those moments. "It is the boy's birthday, and we told him he could pick his present. We will not interfere." He held her gaze as they momentarily had a contest of wills, but it ended quickly when Ingrid shook her head and walked out of the store.

The small bear had a vacant but vaguely kind look with its small black button eyes. Josef crouched to look closely, not yet taking it from Gerda's hands. "I think he will be Bärli." He pronounced the word *Bear-lee*. He spun toward his father, not noticing his mother's absence. "This is the present I want, Papi."

"I knew the moment I saw it, Josef. It's a fine bear, and you will no doubt take very good care of him."

The boy beamed. "I will care for him always." He ran outside with his new toy to show his Mutti while Karl paid the shopkeepers.

CHAPTER 5
EINGEZOGEN: DRAFTED
1941

Gymnasium school was the elite level for German students, offering an advanced education for students who performed exceptionally well on standardized testing for mathematics, reading, and logic in the fourth grade. Those exceptional students were separated into either the boys' or girls' Gymnasium system from the fifth grade onward. Josef Zohren was excelling at school, even amongst the elite students. Either he or his best friend, Günter, would typically achieve the highest score on every test—which were routinely posted for all to see.

At fifteen years old, he was already larger than most of the older boys in the school. He had inherited his father's height and his mother's build. A head taller than most grown men, with broad shoulders and a thick chest, Josef was often mistaken for being much older. His dirty-blond hair had lightened somewhat as he aged, and his piercing blue eyes still shone intelligently from his pale white face.

While Josef excelled in academics, he lagged in physical education. He did not lack coordination, but he was passive, whether wrestling or on the Fussball pitch (soccer field). The coach would frequently yell to him: *For God's sake, use your size, Josef* or, *You must be more aggressive, Josef.*

It was late March, 1941. With World War II in full swing, German pride was soaring. Josef walked out of school, passing several large banners bearing swastikas and one with the likeness of the Fuhrer, Adolf Hitler. It was normal to see military recruiters at the school, and pro-war posters were everywhere, but school lessons had not changed much and neither had most of the students. The last class of the day, Latin, had ended at three forty-five, and Josef was exiting the school when he saw a commotion ahead. Three older boys had surrounded a small boy and were pushing him back and forth between them. Josef planned to just walk past, but as he glanced over, he could see it was his friend, Günter, at the center.

One of the older boys said, "Are you sure you are not a Jew? You sure look like one."

Günter Kimmich was almost a year older than Josef but a head shorter. He had a slight frame and a mop of curly black hair and dark eyes. His face was expressive, and he had a quick wit. His skin was darker than most Germans', causing many people to mistake him for being Jewish.

Günter felt the top of his head and put on an exaggerated, confused look. "Hmmm. No yarmulke. I guess I'm not a Jew." He smiled.

Another boy slapped the back of Günter's head. "You think you are too clever."

"Hey, Günter. It's time to go." Josef stood next to the group. He did not look at any of the older boys, just at Günter.

"Are you sure, Josef?" Günter replied. "You see, I was having quite a bit of fun and wish I could stay." He picked up his bag and placed the spilled books back in it. None of the boys protested, as Josef loomed over the group.

It was not the first time Josef had pulled Günter from a scrape. It was always surprising to him that none of the older boys challenged him. He knew he was large, of course, but he had never been in a fight and truthfully, he was terrified to fight. He hoped that his size would keep him out of fights forever.

As they walked home, the boys talked about their classes that day and laughed about one of the teachers. As they reached Günter's home, he grabbed Josef's arm excitedly. "I almost forgot. I have more pieces for the erector set. We can add to our tower. I think it will reach the ceiling now. You must come in. I'll ask my mother if you can stay for dinner."

The boys hurried into Günter's room. It was an absolute mess, as always, with clothes on the floor, toys spread out, an unmade bed and in the far corner, the metal tower they had been building for a year, adding pieces as they arrived through mail-order.

"You know, Günter, maybe those boys had a point about you. I mean, what German would keep a room like this? We are a country of order and discipline." As Josef said the words, he mimicked the Fuhrer and even held his arm at forty-five degrees in salute—then burst out laughing.

"I am a creative. You can't put limits of discipline on a mind like mine." Günter flashed a smile. Then he pushed his clothes pile away from the base of the tower. It was built using ten-centimeter metal erector bands that had fastener holes in the center of the band at two-centimeter intervals. The bands were fastened together with a short bolt with a nut threaded onto the other side. They had built the building so all of the threaded nuts were on the inside, which gave it a cleaner, more finished look. With the crisscrossing bands, many places had only small openings to reach inside and thread the nuts. Günter had to handle those, with his smaller hands. He would tell Josef, *Those hams on the ends of your arms won't fit.* At the base of the tower, the structure was three bands wide. Every six bands the tower rose in height, saw it narrow by one band.

"With these last pieces, we will make the spire. I measured that we have just enough room for it to be three sections tall. We will start with a square and taper to a point at the top. We will have to bend the pieces up there. That's really why I invited you over—for muscle."

"I see all I am good for." Josef laughed.

They played for hours, as they did several days each week, then Günter's mother called for dinner. She was an attractive woman in her late thirties but looked younger. She was short and slender with dark hair and eyes. It was clear that Günter favored her side of the family. She was a friendly and lively woman, who clearly had affection for Josef as a friend of her son. Günter's father often worked late at his factory job and was rarely home for dinner. Günter's older sister, Liesel, was in the last year at the girls' Gymnasium. She was smart like her brother.

Liesel was taller than her mother, with similar looks. She had dark eyes, shoulder-length black hair, a delicately pointed chin, and dimples on each cheek when she smiled. Josef often found himself speechless around her. He thought about her often and felt guilty for having impure thoughts about his best friend's sister.

Dinner was beef and cabbage. Frau Kimmich scooped some food onto Josef's plate and said, "Günter tells me you had the highest score in Latin and English. Your parents must be very proud."

"Well, Günter had the highest scores in mathematics—again. So, I still need to catch up." He tilted his head down and felt himself blush as he tried to avoid looking at Liesel.

"You are too modest," Frau Kimmich added.

Josef sat silently and then decided to take his boldest step and ask Liesel a question. "What is your favorite subject, Liesel?" He noticed Frau Kimmich smile and glance at her daughter. His stomach sank as he thought to himself, *It's too obvious how I feel.*

Liesel obliged, though. "I like the languages: Latin, French. I like thinking about the different places and hoping someday things will be different here too."

As she spoke, Josef felt inadequate, he knew he could never think of something so clever to say. But he also felt proud for asking her a question, this girl that he had been so afraid to speak to for the past year. As dinner ended, Josef thanked Frau Kimmich, said goodbye to Günter and Liesel, and headed to the door.

Liesel came outside after him. "Josef."

He turned and began to blush again.

"I know you protect Günter. I just wanted to thank you." She leaned in and hugged him.

His entire body became warm as if he were blushing from

head to toe. The entire walk home, he thought of nothing but her: her smell, her warmth, the softness of her body against his. He had never felt this way in his young life.

He entered his home and could not remember any of the walk there. "Hello, Mutti. Hello, Papi. I'm home."

"Why so late?" his mother asked in her usual brisk manner.

"I was at Günter's. I ate dinner, Mutti."

"You need to make more friends. You need more than that one little boy."

"What's wrong with being small. I didn't decide to be big, you know. Günter is the smartest boy in the school."

"You are the smartest. And being big helps. No one will push you around."

"Well, he is my best friend." Josef felt as if he were defending Günter from another bully.

"Well, you need more friends," Ingrid repeated.

Karl joined in. "It's better to have one great friend than ten average ones." He always had a way of saying a great deal in just a few words.

* * *

Despite the war, school time had been kept fairly normal, other than the days when the recruiting office would come and assess the boys. At first, this happened infrequently, but lately, they would come every few weeks and invariably a few older boys would be gone the next day. At this point, the school population was down about a quarter of where it had been the prior year.

It was a Monday in early April and the students had filed into the classroom. Herr Meyer stood in front of the class and the room fell silent. He was a strict but fair teacher who demanded absolute obedience. He was a small, dark-haired man with round glasses. He wore tightly fitted clothes and stood with perfect posture to maximize his limited height. "We are honored with a visit from military recruitment today. You will present yourselves individually. They have set up in the nurse's station." He paused and looked at them all appraisingly. "There is no greater honor than to fight for the fatherland."

Josef felt a pit in his stomach. This was new, different. He looked around the room and saw that the other boys were feeling on edge too, casting their eyes about and then looking away if they made eye contact with anyone. Günter made eye contact with him and did not look away. Instead, he shook his head almost imperceptibly.

Günter was among the first to be called to the nurse's station. It seemed to Josef that he was gone for a long time. He watched the clock and thought about his small friend being pulled into combat. When Günter returned, he was ghost-white and holding a yellow index card in his hand. He did not look up and just shuffled to his desk. Josef stared at him, imploring him, silently, to look at him and then he heard his own name called—*Josef Zohren.*

The school hallway never looked so long and narrow to Josef. His heart beat loudly in his chest. The lights above him flickered slightly and gave off a soft buzzing sound. Had they always done this? He was fifteen. Why would they call his name? They had started last year with the seventeen-year-old boys and moved to sixteen earlier this year. Were they really going to take boys at fifteen? He knew he looked like a man, but he did not feel like one. He secretly still slept with his toy bear named Bärli that he picked out for his seventh birthday.

He kept him in a box under his bed and would take him out and pull him under the covers when his parents were asleep, then return him to the box before even getting out of bed. He was not a man. His body was a lie he told the world every day.

Suddenly, the hallway that had looked like an endless tunnel as he stepped from the classroom ended, and he stood at the door of the brightly lit nurse's station. Josef peered through the door and saw two men sitting, one behind the desk and the other to the side. The man behind the desk had his coat unbuttoned and leaned forward, scribbling notes. The other man held a pad of paper but watched the first man, expectantly.

"Josef Zohren," the man behind the desk said without looking up.

"Yes, sir."

He looked up now and revealed his long, narrow face with a neatly trimmed, thin mustache. He looked to be in his early thirties and wore a serious expression as he looked up and down Josef's tall frame. "You are a large man."

"I'm fif-fifteen, sir." The response felt like a retort, and Josef immediately regretted it.

The man stood up slowly. He was tall, about equal to Josef's height but much slighter. His eyes narrowed as he walked slowly around the desk and faced Josef, who cast his eyes down. "I did not ask you, did I?"

"No, sir."

He grabbed Josef's face with his right hand and lifted his chin so the two of them were nose-to-nose, centimeters apart. Josef felt compelled to meet this man's gaze and did so, but he felt naked. He fought back the urge to cry. As the man gazed into Josef's blue eyes and then up at his blond hair, he said, "You are a proper German for sure. Do you love the fatherland?"

"Yes, sir."

"Do you want to honor your family by fighting for the fatherland?"

Josef knew there was only one answer he could give; it did not matter how he felt. "Yes, sir."

"My papers say your father could not serve. Would you like to make right that shame?"

Anger bubbled in Josef's throat. His father was a good, honorable man. He could not help his disability. But again, there was only one answer. He quelled the anger and said softly, "Yes, sir."

The man stared into his eyes and Josef felt he was being judged. Had this man wanted to provoke anger? Did he see something in Josef at this moment? Did he already assess him as soft? Josef felt exposed and prayed for the moment to end.

"Good boy." The man walked back around the desk and nodded to the younger man seated to the side. The latter quickly wrote some words on a yellow card and handed it to Josef.

CHAPTER 6
VERLASSEN: LEAVING
1941

It had been a long night. No one in the household slept. Ingrid Zohren feigned pride in her son joining the Nazi army and fighting for the fatherland, but her usually stoic demeanor was betrayed by moist eyes and quickly leaving the room whenever emotions crept up in her. The yellow card lay on the desk in the living room and read *Report to Grafenwoehr Training Area, Munich, Tuesday, April 15, 1941.*

"It's wonderful that our family will do its part for the fatherland," she said as her voice broke slightly. She stood just outside Josef's room where he was packing on Tuesday morning. "We will win this war, and you will be a hero. There will be parades for you and your fellow soldiers. It's wonderful."

Josef heard her walk briskly to the kitchen and sob softly. He had packed his bag with the necessary clothes and now reached under his bed for the small box where he kept Bärli. He hid him in the box since the day he found him in the garbage when he was twelve. His mother felt he was too old to sleep with a bear doll and threw it away. He secretly rescued the bear and hid him. Since that day, he never let his parents see Bärli. He would often whisper to the little bear, *Don't worry, I am here to protect you. You won't be discarded again.*

Josef quickly stashed the bear in the top of his pack, gave one last look at his room, and stepped out to say goodbye to his mother. She had decided she was too busy to accompany Karl and Josef to drop him at the training center. Both men knew it was her way of avoiding the pain.

Ingrid was facing the wall when Josef emerged. He saw her straighten her dress and wipe her face before turning to him. She walked briskly forward and placed two hands on his face, pulled him down to her level, and kissed his forehead. "Make us proud." She then snatched his pack, saying, "Let's make sure you have everything. I can't trust you boys to remember."

Josef had no time to protest and just blurted out, "Mutti, no," as she opened the bag and saw Bärli.

"What is wrong with you? How do you still have that wretched doll? What do you mean to accomplish, bringing this to war?" She left no time for responses. Her voice became shrill, and she yelled, "You need to be a bear, not play with one, if you are to come home to me." A flood of tears erupted from Ingrid's eyes as she clutched the bear so firmly in her grip, she looked to be strangling the small animal.

Josef had never seen his mother cry this way and stood in stunned silence. Karl walked to her and wrapped his arms around his wife, her body quaking. "Let me deal with this, my love. I'll talk to him." With that, he pried the bear from her grip and slipped it inside his coat.

The train ride to Munich was silent. Josef looked at his father, a kind man with an easy smile, and saw pain. His Papi looked lost in thought, perhaps searching for the words to say when they parted.

As they exited the train, they saw the table that had been set up to receive the new recruits. Karl pulled Josef in the opposite direction and walked him around the corner of the station. He looked to his left and right, assuring himself that no one would hear what he had to say. "You are a good boy, and I am sorry for what you will have to do in war. No matter what they say. No matter what they try to convince you of, this war, like all wars, is evil. Remember that not all you are told is true and only you can decide what is true and what is not."

He took Bärli from his jacket, turned his son around, and placed it in his pack. "You will see a lot of ugliness, I'm afraid. It won't do any harm to have something to remind you that there is beauty in the world."

Karl Zohren kissed his son's cheek and walked away.

CHAPTER 7
HASSEN: HATE
1934

Shards of glass stuck out like teeth from the window frame of Biermann Toy Shop. Max rushed to the door, unlocked it, and pushed it open. The bells barely jingled as the door opened slowly, pushing through debris on the floor. Gerda followed him into the store, and they began to survey the damage. Tables had been overturned, display cases toppled, half of the inventory either taken or damaged and unsalvageable. On the surface of the desk that Max's mother dutifully sat at for years, ringing up sales, a swastika was crudely painted in black paint, still wet. Grooves from the paint brush bristles crisscrossed at the jagged edges of the symbol and thick black paint bled from the corners.

On the floor were drops of blood, trailing back to the shattered window. Someone had cut themselves jumping through the opening to steal toys or vandalize the store. It was the third such attack on their store in less than two years since Adolph Hitler surged to power, brandishing anti-Jewish rhetoric.

Max bent down, pulling a small object from under a display case tilted against the side wall of the store. It was a Steiff stuffed tiger, wearing an intricately crocheted outfit with Zebra stripes on it. The store had become known for its beautifully dressed animals with clothing made by Gerda. She and Max would dream up combinations that made them laugh. A tiger wearing zebra stripes had been Max's idea and it delighted Gerda. They had sold several, so she kept making more. The tiger's head was torn partially off and the buttons on Gerda's zebra outfit were missing.

"Why must they destroy such beautiful things?" Max asked, almost under his breath.

"We will make more beautiful things, my love."

"Will it matter? Sales are half of what they were two years ago. Every few months we have to rebuild, fix displays, replace windows. It's too much."

"It's only too much if we allow it to be," Gerda said, placing her arms around Max.

"I will never understand this hate, but I also will never understand how I ended up with such a wife. So, I guess it more than balances out." Max gave Gerda a sad smile.

Max and Gerda Biermann had grown the sales of his parents' store by more than triple in their first two years owning and running the little shop on Kaufingerstrasse in Munich. They married in 1929 and took over the operation of the variety store in 1931. At the time, the toy section was a single window display and one aisle inside the store. Their love of toys and children had them buying more and more inventory of toys until they changed the sign that hung outside in early 1932 so it would read Biermann Toy Shop.

They had no children, though not for lack of wanting. Much like Max's parents, it simply had not happened in the earlier years of their marriage. Now, in 1935, it seemed irresponsible to even consider it, given the anti-Jewish climate in Germany.

The store bustled until 1933, when Hitler took his seat of power, and then the boycotts began. Jewish businesses were picketed and a fair number of reliable customers stayed away, either due to their own feelings toward Jews, or fear of being seen as sympathizers.

While business dropped sharply, they survived by cutting expenses and living on the bare minimum they needed to survive. Max would say, *It will pass, it must.*

They began the arduous process of cleaning up, reflecting on how they had become more efficient through practice. Gerda started with the painted markings, using paint thinner and a rag. Max got a broom, shovel, and garbage barrel to clear glass and debris. After two hours of work, the store started to resemble itself. Display tables were set right side up and any salvageable toys were stacked in the corner to be cleaned before returning to the displays for sale.

The familiar ring of the bells on the door alerted them to an arrival. Max turned to see a boy who looked about twelve, with light brown hair and freckles. He wore new-looking black shoes that had been recently polished, along with blue pants and a white shirt.

Max smiled. "I'm afraid we have a little bit of a mess here, young man, but if you tell me what you are looking for, I might find it."

The boy looked at Max, then at Gerda but didn't reply. He then gazed over at the pile of toys in the corner and walked to look closer. He removed a popgun that was covered in dust but otherwise undamaged.

"A good choice, young man. That is beechwood, very nice quality."

The boy ran to the door and began to leave.

"Young man, you have not paid."

He turned, with a sneer on his face, spat on the floor, and said, "I don't have to pay a dirty Jew."

Max ran to the door, but Gerda grabbed his arm. "There is nothing to be done here. If you catch him, what then?"

She was right, but that did not ease the pain and insult. Max turned back to Gerda and said, "I know this is not the right thing for me to say, but I was happy to see the blood on the floor today. At least someone paid some small price."

* * *

Shortly after lunch, a slim man in his thirties walked into the shop, which jingled the bells at the inside top of the door. He was dressed in brown work clothes and carried a toolbox in his right hand. "Hello, Max," the man said softly, with his hands folded and eyes lowered.

"Herr Schiffers. You are timely as always."

"Just Hubert, please. I am sorry that your business is so regular for me, Max," he said, as he looked over the window he would be replacing.

Max replied, "At least someone will prosper." He let out a good-natured laugh.

"You know it is not the way I want to make a living."

"Of course, my friend. I only jest so I won't cry."

Hubert's face became serious, and he placed a hand on Max's shoulder. "Have you considered replacing your sign, rather than your windows?" He saw Max's confusion, so he added. "I know it isn't right, but if you did not have a Jewish name on the store, you would be a less likely target."

Max looked thoughtful, rubbing his beard, shaking his head slightly. "My father and mother built this store from nothing. My father negotiated hard but always treated people fairly. My mother watched every penny to be sure they could provide for me. When I took over the store five years ago, I made some changes, but the spirit remained. Everything I have done has been to preserve their legacy." His lip began to quiver, and he paused for a moment. "My father passed two years ago. The only blessing in his death is that he did not have to witness this." Max held his arms out, showing the hate-fueled vandalism of his parents' store. "I cannot bury his name so soon after burying him. I will not."

CHAPTER 8
WAISE: ORPHAN
1957

The house had been quiet since Minna went into the hospital. Now that she had passed, stillness and silence hung like thick black curtains between Friedrich and his father. Her illness and recovery had been among the few topics in which Dieter and Friedrich could readily engage. Now, there were perfunctory questions about school and little else.

During the week, a quiet breakfast would be mercifully followed by Friedrich needing to rush off to school and Dieter heading to his job as an engineer with the German government. He specialized in road and bridge design. Even now, twelve years after the war had ended, there were countless projects to rebuild the country's infrastructure.

Today was a Saturday, so there was no easy escape from the silence. After breakfast, Dieter sat in his favorite chair and read a newspaper. Friedrich paced in the kitchen, working up the nerve to speak to his father about something real. It would be his first attempt at discussing something meaningful with his father. That was Minna's role.

Working up his nerve, he strode into the living room and stood across from his father. Dieter lowered the paper. "Father, I have something to ask you." Dieter folded the paper, placed it neatly on the side table, and crossed his hands, giving his full attention. Friedrich wished he could talk to him behind that paper. The scrutiny of his father's serious gaze felt too intense. "I want to take on a research project," he started, knowing that this framing would intrigue his father. He was right.

"Indeed. What is it you would like to research?" Dieter looked as interested and excited as his stoic manner would allow.

"My history."

Dieter's brow furrowed. It was an open secret that Friedrich was adopted but something they never discussed. Friedrich knew nothing of how the adoption came to pass or where he came from. "What of it?"

"I want to learn about my ..." He paused and lowered his eyes, looking at the floor. "... birth parents." He had thought through these words carefully. He knew the phrase *real parents* would have been hurtful. Dieter was a man of facts and science, so the term *birth parents* should not be offensive.

"They are dead. There is nothing to be done." He picked up his paper, unfolded it, and began to read. Friedrich lingered a moment until the silence became too painful, then left the room.

* * *

Two weeks had passed since Minna's death and more than a week since Friedrich attempted to talk with Dieter about his goal to learn about his birth parents. The silence in the home had reached a new plateau as Friedrich refused to answer even basic questions about school.

Dieter finished his eggs and took the Saturday paper with him to sit in his chair. He stopped as he left the kitchen and made one more attempt at conversation. "You haven't played the piano since …" He paused.

"Since my mother died?" The words came out sharper than Friedrich intended. He was angry. How could his father not understand his need to find his original family? He saw a hint of pain on Dieter's stolid face, a slight clench of his square jaw, and a momentary break in eye contact. His father left and sat in his chair with the paper.

Friedrich buried his head in his hands, feeling the guilt of having hurt his father, a man he was not sure could be wounded. He stood and walked into the living room and sat at the piano. He did not need sheet music to play Minna's favorite song. His hands touched the keys, and he imagined her hands on top of his, the way she had taught him in his earliest memories. He pressed on the keys to the familiar beginning of "Für Elise": A–E–A–A–E–A–C. He played it slowly, at half tempo, which gave it a haunting beauty. Tears streamed down his cheeks as he thought of the woman who loved him so fully.

As Friedrich ended, he sobbed softly. There was silence behind him, so he peered over his right shoulder toward the blue chair. Dieter sat, still clinging to his paper, but it was crumpled on both sides, as his hands had balled into fists. His eyes were wet. Friedrich had never seen him show emotion like this and it was frightening.

Dieter stood and walked behind Friedrich, placing both

hands on his shoulders. "That was very nice, Son." He turned to walk from the room but stopped at the door without turning and said, "We adopted you from Munich Municipal Orphanage on Waisenhausstrasse (Orphanage Street) On May 2, 1945. It was the greatest day of our lives." Then he walked from the room.

CHAPTER 9
DAS MÄDCHEN: THE GIRL
1957

The school day dragged on. Friedrich watched the clock, urging the minute hand forward. When it finally ended, he walked in the opposite direction of home, toward Waisenhausstrasse. He had no idea what to expect. Would he find answers at all after more than twelve years? His adoption coincided with the loss of the war. Would they even have records?

As he approached the building, he stood momentarily and took it in. It was a magnificent structure, four stories tall, lined with windows evenly placed along each side. A fifth story of sorts sprung from the roof line with dormers placed at the same interval as the windows below. The massive building absorbed an entire city block and had the grand feel of a monastery with its clock tower at the center of the roof, cupola on the far end, and carved stone figures atop the fourth-floor facade. The sight intimidated him. He would surely be sent away and perhaps chided for wasting their time.

He took a deep breath and walked on, scanning the exterior for the main entrance. When Friedrich came to the main entrance, he laughed at himself for thinking he would have to discover it. It was a grand doorway with a high arch above. It looked like an entry to a place of reverence. He stepped in, hands folded in front of him as if he were at a church service, head bent down. He was relieved to see a girl close to his own age at a desk just inside the entryway. She had a round face and shoulder-length brown hair. She wore a yellow sweater over a white blouse and had a hairpin holding back the hair on her left side as she read a book intently.

"Hello," Friedrich said, barely more than a whisper. He was glad he spoke so softly because even his timid greeting echoed in the stone hall.

The girl looked up, startled, then smiled broadly. "Hello. My name is Sigrid Yorck. How may I help you?" She had a bubbly tone that almost projected as singing her words.

"I don't know, really." Friedrich looked down and shuffled his feet.

"Aaah," She gasped. "I know that look. You were adopted from here and you want to find your real parents." She jumped to her feet with excitement.

"Yes, but how did you …"

"Once every few months, someone comes in. I can spot the look now. It's very exciting. I love to help look, though I must tell you, we most often don't find the parents. I did it at least once last year, and it was amazing. They ended up being in Poland." She spoke fast and flailed her hands, moving to the words like a conductor with an orchestra.

Friedrich stood silent for a moment, then asked. "How do we start?"

"Well, tell me your name and everything you remember." She looked up at the clock and held a hand up. It was 3:55 in the afternoon. "I am off in five minutes."

"Oh, I see." Friedrich's heart sank. When can I come back?"

"No, silly. I mean, in five minutes, we can get started. I would not miss this for anything. Just wait for me outside."

Friedrich walked outside, still unsure of what was happening. In exactly five minutes, Sigrid emerged.

"Let's sit on the wall here and get started," she directed. The investigation won't be easy, but the more you tell me, the better chance we will have. Do you understand?"

"I think so."

"Let's start with the easy part. What is your name? When were you adopted? It's OK if you only have an estimate."

"I am Friedrich Becker. I was adopted on May 2, 1945, by Dieter and Minna Becker."

"Well, that is a promising start. I will know exactly where to look. Now, what else do you remember?"

"I, I don't really remember anything. I was just past my fourth birthday. So, I …"

Sigrid jumped in excitedly. "You know your real birthday? That is unusual and will help us as we check birth records. How do you know it, exactly?"

"I'm not sure. I have just always known. My parents, Dieter and Minna, said I told them my birthday."

"Extraordinary." She looked at the tall, lanky boy and seemed to be assessing him. "So, you are just sixteen now? You look older. I will turn eighteen in January, but people think I look younger."

Friedrich had never known anyone who spoke this fast

and frenetically. He wondered if this young girl, still seventeen, would have the authority to do all she claimed. "Can I ask you a question?" She nodded and smiled. "How long have you been here?"

"Well, in a way, I have already told you." She paused, appearing to enjoy his puzzlement. "It will be eighteen years in January."

Friedrich looked confused. Understanding crept over his face as he realized her meaning. "So, you are an orphan as well?"

"Yes. It seems we were here at the same time. Do you know how long you resided here before you were adopted?"

"I am afraid I don't."

"It's OK. Tell me anything else you remember. Do you remember this place? Do you remember a mother or father? Did you have anything with you when you were adopted?"

A smile came to Friedrich's face. "I don't remember much, but I did have a bear with me, I mean a bear doll, made of cellulose fiber. I still have him."

"Good. Come tomorrow at the same time and bring your bear. It may help your memory." She stood up quickly, reached out and hugged him. It caught him off guard, and he awkwardly hugged her back. "You know, Friedrich, this is going to be a great adventure, and I think we will become good friends."

"Thank you for helping me."

She smiled and started to walk away, then stopped and turned back. "I know I talk a lot, but I listen too. Twice today, I asked if you remembered more, and twice, you did not say *no* completely. I think there is something you are not telling me. Maybe you will trust me soon so we can learn all that we can about your parents." She turned and disappeared into the doors at the end of the grand entryway.

Friedrich sat on the wall for several minutes after Sigrid went inside. He replayed the conversation, processing the information and assessing the strange, intriguing girl he had met.

CHAPTER 10
DIE ADRESSE: THE ADDRESS
1957

At the end of the next school day, Friedrich ran all the way to the orphanage. He huffed and puffed as he reached the front door. He was fifteen minutes early but could not wait, so he went inside. Sigrid sat at the desk, an older woman at her side, appearing to give her instructions. Friedrich approached the desk, but as Sigrid saw him, she widened her eyes as if giving him a message and shook her head slightly.

"Ah, you are here early to take me for a walk as you promised," she blurted out before Friedrich could speak. "Wait outside, you impatient boy." She flashed a smile at the older woman, adding, "He likes me a bit too much, I think." Friedrich was confused but turned to walk outside.

Sigrid emerged at four o'clock and joined Friedrich on the wall where they had sat the prior day. "Hello, Friedrich. I have some information."

"Wait. First, tell me what that was about?"

"I just don't want everyone to know our business, that's all."

It all became clear. "You aren't allowed to look at the records for me, are you?"

"Do you know how long you would wait if you went through official channels? I'm trying to help you. You know, even if they eventually told you something, which they may not, you would not get everything. I am your best hope."

Friedrich needed to learn more about this girl. He was unsure if this was the best way for him to find his birth parents. "How long have you worked here—and I mean worked as a job?"

"It's hard to say. I have been here since I was a day old. I used to help with cleaning even before I was ten years old." She gave a thoughtful look and placed a hand on his shoulder. "I suppose you mean working at the desk and having access to resident records. Two years on the desk and one year for records."

"And they let you release information?"

"I have a key to the records room." She paused and smiled. "Well, I know where the key is, anyway, so I guess so. But I still say it's best we keep this to ourselves. The government has a heavy hand in this place, and you know how the government is."

Friedrich thought of his rigid father and his government job. Someone like Dieter would likely run him in circles for years, he thought. He nodded to Sigrid.

"So, do you want my information, or don't you?" Sigrid said with crossed arms and an exaggerated look of knowing.

Friedrich had to get whatever information he could, and he suspected that, for whatever reason, this girl was going to help him more than anyone else would. He nodded again.

"The date of adoption you gave me was very helpful. First, the most remarkable fact is that you were here only for a day when you were adopted. This is something I have never seen. I can only think it was because you came in right when the war ended. In fact, the day you came in, the Allied army took over Munich. Perhaps the administration here was just happy to place any child in the chaos. Unfortunately, they only had a first name for you, though. It would have been ideal to have the surname, of course."

"I suppose that is why I have no memory of this place. I was here so briefly." The information intoxicated him. He leaned forward and looked into Sigrid's dark brown eyes. "Tell me more."

"Well," she shuffled her position on the wall excitedly, clearly enjoying how he appreciated her information. "The second part you know. Your adoptive parents were Dieter and Minna Becker. The added part you may not know is that two couples tried to adopt you. I did not take down the second couple's information, as it seemed unimportant. They were not successful, so they would not have been told anything about you."

"OK. Was there anything else?"

"There was, but it is so hard to remember when I am hungry. I had a long shift, and my memory gets very fuzzy until I eat something." She stared at Friedrich, tilting her head down to look at him from the top of her eyes.

It took Friedrich a second to comprehend, but he was starting to understand Sigrid's humor and decided to play along. "So, this is extortion, then?" he asked with a smile.

"I see we understand each other perfectly." Sigrid hopped

off the wall and began to walk toward the bakery on the next block. As they arrived, she walked in ahead of Friedrich and ordered two pieces of Bienenstich, then looked at Friedrich to pay. Fortunately, he had a small amount of money left from school lunch. They sat at a small table near the window to continue their conversation.

"Just so I know how much money to bring in the future, is a piece of cake worth the rest of the story, or will there be installments?"

Sigrid smiled, clearly delighted that Friedrich was playing along with her humor. "You act as if there is one price for any piece of information. The information today may be a piece of cake. Next time it may be the whole cake." Sigrid took a bite of the honey-drenched, moist cake and smiled.

"Actually," she continued with her mouth full. "This information may be worth a whole cake already. The staff took notes on what you had with you and what you told them when you arrived. It was fascinating. First, you were correct that apparently you have known your date of birth since a young age, assuming it is correct. You told them you were born March 9. They added that it must have been 1941 since you appeared to be about four years of age."

"Next, you had two important objects with you, I think. First, a handmade cellulose bear, wearing a knit outfit, such as the one you already told me about. Second, was a hand-knit scarf with a lion on it. It is possible your mother made these." She looked at him expectantly.

"Bärli," Friedrich said out loud but almost to himself. Then he looked up at Sigrid and added, "I have the bear here. He retrieved it from his coat pocket. Sigrid took the small bear and began to examine it.

"I see no names or markings on it. The needlework on his outfit is exquisite. Do you still have the scarf?" Friedrich shook his head. Sigrid added, "Well, this is a good clue though. It may not help us today, but perhaps someday."

"This is wonderful, Sigrid. I appreciate all you found, but I don't know how it will help find my parents. I don't know where this leaves me."

"You mean where it leaves *us*, right? I am your partner in this, Friedrich." She reached across the table and grasped his hand. Friedrich felt his face flush and his heartbeat quicken. He had not held a girl's hand before, except his mother's. He was sixteen, but for the past two years, while his mother was ill, he spent all of his time attending to her at home and then, later, visiting her in the hospital. Even before that, his mother was the center of his world. As his father would remind him, he did not make other *associations*.

"First, Friedrich, you have a birth date, which is more than most have, and we will go to the city office and look at birth records. Hopefully, we will find your parents on a document there. Second, I have not told you the best part yet."

"You like to play games, don't you, Sigrid?"

"I do, but you know what else I like?" She paused. "Tea with my Bienenstich."

Friedrich laughed aloud and reached into his pocket. He did not have enough money. "Do you give information on credit?"

"Hmm. I'll buy the tea this time because I like you."

Sigrid went to the counter to fetch two teas, tossing a playful glance back at Friedrich. He watched her and wondered if she meant that she liked him in the way boys and girls he knew in the neighborhood liked each other. He was starting to realize he already liked her in that way. She was unlike anyone he had ever known. She always said exactly what she thought and seemed so confident in herself. This small girl stood taller than her stature. She appeared to own every space she was in.

She returned with the tea and sat, taking a slow sip. "The best part, Friedrich, is that you must have been quite a smart child. You told them the street, square, and city you came from! It was like finding a piece of gold, I almost screamed when I saw, which would have given me away."

"Given you away?"

"I told you that I am not exactly waiting for the process there. I went late at night, and no one saw me," she crinkled her nose with a mischievous grin. "Kaiserstrasse (Emperor Street), Schiller Platz (Schiller Square) in Mönchengladbach." Then she looked puzzled and added, "Except they spelled it *München Gladbach*."

Friedrich thought for a moment. "They changed the spelling at some point, I think. I learned that at Gymnasium. Was there anything else?"

"Of course. I always save the best for last. You told them you were waiting for Frau Amalie. I wonder if that is your mother's first name."

CHAPTER 11
AUSSCHALTUNG: ELIMINATION
1938

Dora Biermann died in 1935, a little more than two years after her husband. She wasted away for months, losing half her body weight with no diagnosis ever given by doctors who gave little attention to Jews. Max would tell friends that she simply gave up wanting to live after her husband passed.

In the years that followed, Max and Gerda continued to work long hours and sell goods for barely above their cost, so they could keep the store going, in hopes there would be a turn in the fortunes of Jews in Germany.

It was Monday, November 14, 1938. Max stood behind the counter as Gerda sat in a chair by him knitting a sweater for a doll. His shoulders were slumped, his head down. He no longer wore a yarmulke, as it was forbidden by German law. The store was empty, but more pressing news than lagging sales weighed on their minds.

The bell on the front door jingled and Max looked up, more fearful than hopeful. A slim, neatly dressed man walked in, wearing a hat, a pressed suit with a yellow tie and a trench coat. His tie pin bore a swastika. "Hello, Herr Biermann," he said, tipping his cap. As he approached, he added, "Apologies, Frau Biermann. I did not see you from the door. I hope you are both well."

"Herr Adler. It is always good to see you," Max replied. Gerda smiled and waved. Manfred Adler was the sales representative for Steiff, the leading maker of stuffed animals in Germany, and many felt the highest quality manufacturer in the world. Manfred Adler would always say: *These are Soft Sculptures, not mere stuffed animals,* while giving his sales pitch.

Glancing at the display of Steiff animals, which included a special stuffed lion with moveable legs that could be positioned so it could stand or lie down, he commented, "Not much change from the last time I visited, I see."

"No, my friend." Max shook his head. "Perhaps you will have better luck with the new owner."

"You are selling?"

"We should be so lucky. Did you not hear about the law passed this weekend?" Max picked up a newspaper and showed the headline to Manfred. It read: *On Saturday, November 12, 1938, the German government issued Verordnung zur Ausschaltung der Juden aus dem deutschen Wirtschaftsleben* (the Decree on the Elimination of the Jews from Economic Life).

"I heard that, but I didn't think ... I mean ... they can just take it from you? That's outrageous."

"You had best keep that opinion to yourself, my friend. It's bad enough where we stand. I would hate to see you caught up in this mess." Max looked at Gerda and his lower lip began to tremble. "My parents built this ..." His voice trailed off and he turned away, hiding his tears. "Maybe it's a blessing they are not here to see this."

Gerda stood and put a hand on his back. "We will find a way, my love." She then turned to Adler and said, "The new owners, apparently people with connections in the government, will be here in two days. All of it, including the inventory, will be theirs then." She shook her head slowly. "I'm sure sales will pick up and they will order more from you when they rename the store something less *Jewish*." She emphasized the last word.

"I don't want that, you must know ..."

Gerda raised a hand of apology. "I did not mean that. I'm sorry. You have always been so kind to us."

"I only wish there were a way I could help you." Adler stood for an awkward moment, added, "I am so sorry," then tipped his hat and left the store.

On Wednesday at eight sharp, the new owner entered the front door and the bell jingled. He was holding the sign that read Biermann Toy Shop in his hands. He was a tall, slender man with round, gold wire-framed glasses. He wore a black suit with a crisp white shirt but no tie. A pin on his lapel bore a swastika. His pale skin accentuated hollow, gaunt cheeks.

Max and Gerda walked from behind the counter. "Your keys to the store, sir," Max said, holding them out, dangling from his right hand. His shoulders slumped, but he held his chin up in his best attempt at pride.

"You may place them on the counter," the man said, wearing a look of disgust as if to say, *I will not touch you.*

Max shrugged off the insult and straightened his back.

"You will find the books in the back. I have written a list of recurring orders ..."

"I am sure I will figure it out. You may go," the man interrupted. "Oh, and you may take this." He placed the sign on a shelf and proceeded to walk past the Biermanns into the back of the shop.

Max looked around the store. He could almost hear the echo of his father negotiating a purchase or feel his mother's presence as she poured over the books behind the counter. He smiled sadly, thinking about the overflowing shelves with mismatched items placed side by side: a set of tools next to a lamp, next to lace kerchiefs. A tear fell down his cheek. Gerda took Max's hand and guided him toward the door. They took one last look around and left their store, hearing the bell jingle behind them.

CHAPTER 12
GRAFENWOEHR: EARLDOM
1941

The Grafenwoehr facility was abuzz with activity when the bus rolled up and the eighteen new recruits stepped off into the ordered chaos. A perfect rectangle of young men jogged in formation, wearing full military dress and packs on their backs, rifles slung over their right shoulders. A large, rectangular, two-story brick building stood before them with four sets of double doors set symmetrically and evenly spaced across the front of the first level and eight widely spaced windows along the second floor.

The sounds of war surrounded them with steady gunfire coming from behind the building. Josef assumed it was from a practice range. The jogging recruits called out their steps, *left, right, left, right*. To their left, in a field, they saw a ropes course, and the sound of whistles and officers shouting orders completed the symphony of sound. To his surprise, the scene and the sounds were exactly as Josef had imagined. It felt like a larger, wider version of physical education at school, a place he always felt out of place. He knew he was what his mother feared he was: soft. He glanced around the group and met Günter's eye. They exchanged comforting smiles.

A uniformed man approached and barked, "Get in line." Josef immediately recognized him. It was the man who questioned him at school the previous day. His heart sank as he thought, *This man knows I am soft.* The group scurried to form a line as if marching, with each boy lining up behind the boy who was farthest forward at that moment. "No! You imbeciles. You form a line side-to-side. Shoulder-to-shoulder. Do it now!" As he yelled with venom in his voice, a bit of spittle flew from his mouth and hung on his thin mustache.

The boys quickly reassembled shoulder-to-shoulder in a straight line parallel to the building before them. Josef stood with five recruits to his left and twelve to his right. There was a whimpering sound coming from his right, and he immediately felt a sense of fear for whichever boy it was, as well as a small sense of pride and relief that it was not coming from him. Then his mind turned to his friend, and he feared it was Günter.

The man with the thin mustache walked slowly to face the boy who made the whimpering sounds. Josef peered out of the corner of his eye, too afraid to turn his head and be noticed. The boy was three places down from him. He was thankful it was not Günter. The officer spoke now in a softer tone. "I am Major Müller. I will be your instructor for the next three weeks." He was speaking to the group, but he stood directly across from the whimpering boy, just centimeters from his face, crouched slightly, as he was half a head taller than the boy.

The spittle still sat on his mustache. "I am here to help you. Help you be men. Help you be soldiers. Help you survive in war. Help you bring victory for the fatherland. What is your name, recruit?"

"Johann Bay, sir."

Major Müller turned to his right and raised his voice. "But I do not help you by holding your hand." He then turned to his left and yelled, "Or by coddling you or making you comfortable. I help you by making you men. Fighting men!" His final words were his loudest, and with that he wheeled around with a closed left fist and struck Johann on the right side of his head with a powerful blow that landed with a sickening thud. Johann dropped to the ground and cried out in pain.

"Get up, now!"

Johann struggled to his knees, clearly dazed, and then stood with a wobble. He stepped back into formation, his face twisted with pain and a trickle of blood coming from a cut by his right eye. He did not make a sound.

"Do you want to cry, Johann?"

"No, sir." The reply came like a whisper.

"Then I have already taught you an important lesson on your very first day."

Josef noticed his heart was beating loudly, like the prior day at school, and his hands had balled into fists. He relaxed them and tried to appear calm. He felt ashamed for wishing that the whimper had come from someone other than himself and Günter. He did not know Johann, but he was someone's friend; someone's son or brother. Why was this better?

Major Müller then barked to the full group, "Line up from largest to smallest."

The group scurried to reorder. Josef looked to his left and right and saw he was bigger than everyone except perhaps one other large boy who walked from the right and moved to the end of the line. Josef took his place next to that boy, so he had one to his left and sixteen to his right. He could see that the line to his right descended and plateaued smoothly, and the order seemed correct. He could make out Günter's wavy dark hair, two places in from the far end.

Major Müller walked to the far end of the line and looked over each boy. "You recruits at this end, don't worry. A gun knows not who holds it. Your weapon will be your equalizer." He continued down the line, occasionally feeling a boy's arms or chest for muscle tone. When he reached Johann, he paused and wiped the blood from the right side of his face and patted his shoulder. He reached Josef and stopped in from of him, then looked at him and the boy to Josef's left. "What is your name?" he addressed the boy to the left.

"Hans Bringmann, sir."

"Ah, yes. I met you a week ago. An eager lad." He turned to Josef, "And this is Josef Zohren, whom I met just yesterday." He shook his head. "Josef does not know who he is."

Josef was confused but said nothing.

"Josef, look to your left at Hans. Do you see my problem?"

Josef looked. Hans was tall, with broad shoulders and a narrow waste. His hair was light blond, and his blue eyes stood out under his blond eyebrows. His nose had a bump and slight bend to it, like one that had been broken before. Light freckles speckled his cheeks. He wore a confident look on his face and met Josef's eye readily. Josef did not know what he was looking for and shook his head slightly.

"You see, Josef, everyone here was able to follow a simple order. Get in line based on your size. But you and Hans failed that order. So, what do I do?" Major Müller put his hand to his chin in an exaggerated expression of confusion. "Do I punish the one who thinks too much of himself?" He glanced at Hans, whose confident expression faltered, "Or the one who thinks too little of himself?" He leaned in closely by Josef's ear and said softly, "You see, Josef, you don't know what you are, or what you can be. But it's OK. It is my job to show you." At that final word—*you*—the major thrust a powerful punch into Josef's stomach that took his breath away. He doubled over but did not fall.

As Josef was bent, struggling for a breath, he instantly knew that his only respite would be to stand straight and did so, looking straight ahead at Major Müller, who gave him a slight tip of is head, nodding toward Hans. Josef moved to the end of the line.

The first night at Grafenwoehr was almost as sleepless as the last night at home. The eighteen recruits who made up their class were housed in a gymnasium with four other recruiting classes, all in neatly aligned cots, one meter apart at each side and each end. The space was laid out like a checkerboard of fifteen and sixteen-year-old boys in burlap cots and green wool blankets.

Josef lay on his cot, acutely aware of the silence. Just a low hum of collective breathing. How could almost eighty boys between fifteen and seventeen years of age be this silent? Fear. The answer rang in his head before the question finished being asked of himself. The ceiling above him was a symmetrical sea of square, white tiles. It reminded him of the cots that lay directly below that ceiling, indistinguishable rectangles. Off to his right and down past the foot of his cot, something dropped to the floor and clanged. It broke the silence with a jarring *ping* of metal hitting the concrete floor, perhaps a rifle munition that one of the recruits was looking at and fumbled. The breathing in the room stopped as they all seemed to wait for some scolding or some harm that never came.

Morning came all too soon as whistles blared at five a.m. Orders barked by officers sent the sea of boys into a frenetic but orderly exercise of folding their blankets, dressing, and heading outside.

The mid-April morning was misty with light rain. Major Müller started by lining them up largest to smallest—there were no mistakes this time. Then they set out on a run that circled the training camp while he rode a bicycle by their side and watched. The boys were in two lines of nine long, forming a perfect rectangle. When someone slowed, breaking the uniformity of the formation, a whistle blew, and Major Müller struck the recruit on the behind with a wooden paddle that he now carried in his left hand. Hans and Josef were in front, as the two largest boys, but they did not set the pace, that was Major Müller, who expected the group to stay at his exact speed as he peddled over the uneven ground.

After the run, they ate breakfast, eggs and potatoes, then headed to the firing range. Each boy was issued a rifle, a Karabiner 98k, which they abbreviated as the K98. The weapon was a bolt-action rifle with a 0.6-meter barrel and a dark chestnut-colored stock. Looking about, Josef could immediately see who in the group had handled guns before. Hans was someone who had. He immediately tested the bolt action and stared down the sight on the barrel. At four kilograms and 1.1 meters in length, it was a large weapon for the smaller boys. Günter lifted his rifle and slung it over his shoulder. The butt struck the ground, as he stood only half a meter taller than the weapon. He shortened the strap to accommodate being able to carry it without it dragging and looked around, embarrassed and hoping no one had seen. Hans was looking at him and scoffed, "Do you need a baby rifle?"

"Well, at least I'll make a small target for the enemy," Günter deflected. A few of the boys laughed but not Hans.

"We will practice shooting now," bellowed Müller. After a demonstration of how to load the bolt-action rifle, which he allowed Hans to show, they took turns lining up at the range to fire. The range was a field, about fifty yards across, with wood planks set up as targets on the other side. The planks had figures painted on them to shoot at. They were caricature-looking figures with exaggeratedly large noses to portray them as Jews. The planks were riddled with holes and splinters from prior training sessions. They moved in by order of their line, with the four largest boys taking the first turn. Josef fired and neither saw nor heard any impact. Hans fired and a splinter flew from the head of one of the painted figures. One of the other boys struck a plank between the figures, and the other missed completely.

Through the first round there were four direct hits out of eighteen shots. Two were to the heads of the painted figures. Those were fired by Hans and Günter. Müller gave instructions to the group on aiming down the sight and shooting for the heads. In round two the group improved, with ten direct hits and four headshots. Josef was among the eight misses. They continued shooting for an hour with each boy taking ten shots. Josef struck the wood planking only twice. One of them only narrowly missed one of the figures. He did not admit that it was not the figure he was aiming at. Through the ten rounds, Günter had never missed the planks and missed hitting a painted figure only once. He had recorded seven headshots. Hans recorded six.

Major Müller decided to end the session with a shoot-off between the four best shooters he had observed in the group. They lined up in each of the four shooting stations and loaded their rifles. "Headshots only. Winner gets extra bread with dinner." They all knew the real prize was Müller's admiration. "Fire."

Hans and Günter struck the heads of their targets. The other boys left their stations. They reloaded and readied to fire again. Two headshots. Hans turned to Günter and sneered, "I hope that doesn't get too heavy for you, little boy."

Günter wanted to retort but came up with nothing as he looked into Hans's hateful eyes. In that moment, Josef saw something in Günter's eye he had never seen before. Was it anger, pride? Günter reloaded and stared at the target—they fired a third time. Hans missed by a centimeter to the right of his target's head. Günter's bullet struck the dead center, sending a shard of wood spinning into the air. Hans turned red and glared at Günter through narrowed eyes. Realizing he had perhaps made a mistake, Günter tried to lighten the moment. "I'm glad it's over. It was actually getting quite heavy for me." Hans said nothing and walked away.

"Where did you learn to shoot?" Müller asked with a pat to Günter's shoulder.

"Well, I guess you taught me, sir." He smiled and shrugged. Seeing confusion on Müller's face, he added, "I have never held a gun until today, sir."

* * *

After a week at Grafenwoehr, a pecking order had been established. Hans was the clear leader in the class of recruits, though Günter was the best shot. Day by day, Günter grew even more deadly accurate. It was clear he was in high favor with Müller, even though he struggled at many of the other physical activities.

Today, following the morning run and breakfast, they had assembled in the gym, which was in reality more of a warehouse or hangar behind the main building. The ceiling was high and large windows near the top let in adequate light. They had seen some officers playing Fussball in here at times. The ground was hard-packed dirt with bits of small gravel.

Major Müller strode to the front of the group and barked an order to assemble in formation, which they did quickly. "Today we test physical strength and hand-to-hand fighting skill." He paused to assess the group; see who looked nervous. "There may be times where you don't have a weapon and must make an enemy submit." He paused for effect and then added, "Or kill them with your bare hands." At that he smiled.

"We won't have you kill each other today, but you will fight until one submits. We will go in twos starting at the small end."

The first two boys stepped forward and looked at each other and then at Müller. He said nothing. They waited and looked again. Then one boy asked, "What are the rules?"

"I already told you. Make the other submit." Then he raised his voice, yelling, "There will be no *rules* when you fight the enemy."

They started at each other, and almost immediately the smaller boy, who was only smaller by a fraction, had gotten behind the other and wrapped an arm around his neck so that the inside of his elbow was at the front of the throat. He pulled hard and spun, causing his opponent to fall face-first. He clamped his arm with the other arm behind the neck and began to choke the other recruit, who pounded the ground with an open hand, signifying submission.

"Good!" Müller patted the victor and lifted the other boy to look at his face, scratched and raw from the dirt and gravel ground he landed on. "You'll fight harder next time, won't you?"

Günter submitted when his opponent knelt on his back and pulled his arms upward. Müller made no comment.

When it came time for Hans and Josef to fight, Josef felt a pit in his stomach and his heart pounded. They stepped forward and Hans immediately struck him in the face with a closed fist and then kicked his leg, causing him to fall backward. Hans leapt on top of him and Josef crossed his forearms over his face to keep from being hit. He felt blows glancing off his arms and head. He reached down and patted the ground.

"No!" Müller roared. "I will not let you surrender that easily. You will keep fighting."

Hans obliged, raining blows as hard and fast as he could. Josef knew he had to move to get out of harm's way. He sat up quickly and pushed with all his might to stop the beating. Hans flew off him and landed with his back to the ground. Stunned, Hans scrambled to his feet. Josef did the same. Hans lunged at Josef and ducked his head to wrap his arms around Josef's waist. He was attempting to lift his opponent but could not, so he tried to turn him to the side. Josef felt the pressure and adjusted his weight so he would not fall.

"Why do you just stand there like a tree?" Müller yelled.

Josef looked at Müller who had circled behind him and felt a stinging blow to his back. As Josef turned, Hans moved behind him and put a choke hold around his neck. He spun to try to shake his opponent off, but he was getting no air. He tapped his neck, and Müller finally called an end to the fight.

"Since you obviously can't or won't compete at your size, we will find someone you can fight." At that, Müller grabbed Johann Bay, the boy who had whimpered on the first day and had become a favorite selection every time Müller wanted to make an example. He thrust both boys out and said, "Now fight."

Josef looked across at Johann, a boy half his size, shaking in front of him, and then he looked at Müller. The major took his paddle out, held it up in his left hand, and started thumping it on his right hand. Josef reached out and grabbed Johann's shoulders. The boy swung at him but could not reach. He then pushed downward, buckling his opponent's knees. When he had him on the ground, he turned him face down and knelt on his back. Johann tapped the ground to submit.

"No! Not so easy. You must learn to fight."

Josef looked up, confused. He had won, what else could he do? Then he felt the sting of the paddle. "I have won."

"No. You must crush your enemy. Keep fighting." Another blow of the paddle landed.

Josef could hear Johann whimper beneath him. He felt his own weight crushing his smaller opponent. He did not know what to do. Another paddle blow landed, stinging him so badly it felt like it broke through his skin. His eyes darted and his mind raced like a caged animal seeking a way out. *Whack*, the stinging singed his nerves. He rose to his feet, looked at Müller with a hateful sneer, then bent to pick up Johann and slammed him to the ground so hard he heard a bone crack. Johann lay motionless on the ground.

"Good. I see you woke up," Müller said.

At dinner that evening there were seventeen recruits.

* * *

On the last day of April, the recruits were settling in for the night. Josef reached into his pack to remove a T-shirt to sleep in. It caught on something in his pack as he pulled it out, and onto the floor dropped Bärli. He was slightly worn now, his head starting to collapse, having been pressed inside the bag for weeks. Hans was two cots to Josef's left and always seemed to be watching him. There had developed a level of competition on his side of the relationship, though Josef did not really understand it. He jumped to his feet.

"Do you have a doll? Haha, the big baby has a doll, do you see this?" Hans was grinning ear-to-ear and holding his hands wide. "Our big Josef plays with dolls. I'm sure the enemy will have an easy time with him." Several recruits laughed along.

A whistle pierced the air. Four officers rushed in. This was the first disruption in fifteen days with the four recruiting units. Seeing where the commotion was, three officers looked at Major Müller and smiled as they turned to leave the room. Even at a distance, the boys could see he was boiling over. He carried his paddle.

"What is the meaning of this?" he roared. "Who is responsible?"

All the boys had instinctively lain down in their cots, with the exception of Josef and Hans. Hans spoke first, seeing an advantage to be won. "I saw that Josef brought a doll to Grafenwoehr, sir. We were to bring our personal underclothes only, sir, so I was reprimanding him. I should have retrieved you, sir, I am sorry."

Josef looked at Hans. He was smarter than expected. It was a good speech and gave proper deference to the major. He knew this was a critical moment. The truth would not help him here. He brought a bear doll, made by a Jewish woman no less. He brought it because he promised this bear he would always protect him.

Müller strode in front of Josef and picked up the bear. He studied it, then looked back into Josef's eyes, standing close in front of his face. "Josef Zohren. Explain yourself."

Josef was steely-eyed, looking almost through the major. "Sir. My mother is a true patriot. She worships the Fuhrer. It has been her great shame that her husband could not serve due to his physical problems." Müller studied Josef's face, clearly intrigued by where this was going. "In her joy that I may now serve, she gave me this bear that she had made for me, awaiting the day I would be fortunate enough to serve. She prayed and begged for me to take it with me. She said it would bring me good fortune and ensure victory for the fatherland. I did not wish to refuse her, sir."

The major stared into Josef's unflinching eyes for a full minute, searching for any sign of faltering, even attempting to force him to falter. Josef stared ahead. "Very well. You should always listen to your mother. She is a patriot." He looked at the bear in his hands and added, "And she is skilled with needle-work." He tossed the bear on the bed and left the room.

* * *

The recruits woke on the first Sunday of May, their twentieth day at Grafenwoehr. Fifteen of the original eighteen remained, injuries having removed the other three. No reports were given to the recruits about the boys who were taken away. They were just gone. Josef thought each night about Johann, about the sickening cracking sound when he slammed the poor small boy to the ground. *Perhaps he is recovering. Perhaps he does not need to go to war*, he would think, comforting himself and pushing back his guilt.

The fifteen recruits in Major Müller's unit marched outside and lined up for orders prior to their morning run. "Today we will have guests. It is a glorious day for you all. You will be assigned to your units. Our guests will watch what you have learned and make selections for your service to the fatherland." Major Müller lifted his paddle high above his head and then tossed it aside. "We will have no need of encouragement today. Your honor and service will be encouragement enough."

Three officers walked out of the building and stood to the side. One was a tall, blond-haired, blue-eyed man with broad shoulders and a square jaw. He looked like the men they showed on war posters. He looked to be in his late twenties. His muscles puckered his military-issued dress uniform at the chest. The second officer was a trim man with a thin mustache and narrow face. He looked like a shorter, younger version of Major Müller. The final officer had a round face, short, sandy hair and a scar that ran from his left eye down to the jawline in front of his left ear. He stood to the left of the trio and seemed eager for the recruits to see the scar.

It was a sunny morning with light wind. In any other place, Josef would have thought it beautiful.

The run came first and felt uneventful as there was no paddle and they stayed in good formation. The three visiting officers took notes. Shooting was next, and to no one's surprise, Günter and Hans were the final two battling for the top shooter of the day. All the recruits had improved significantly throughout the three weeks of training. Even Josef hit the planks almost every time and landed three headshots, though that still put him in the bottom group.

It took ten shots before Hans missed. Günter did not miss a single headshot.

Finally, the recruits battled head-to-head and hand-to-hand on the hard-packed, gravel-filled dirt of the gym. Since there was an odd number, they started with three boys fighting at once. Josef felt ashamed that he found it entertaining and he was starting to enjoy the fights. He still, though, had a pit in his stomach when it came time for him and Hans to battle.

"I think you will enjoy seeing our last two recruits square off," Müller said, grinning at the visiting officers.

In three weeks, Josef had not beaten Hans, but the past three battles were close. Hans was quicker on his feet than Josef, but Josef had realized that he was bigger and stronger. The key would be to get hold of him and get to the top position. He had an idea. Müller's voice rang in his ears from the first battles. *There are no rules in war.* As they stepped out to battle, Josef held a hand up and bent to tie his shoe. It was a gamble. Would Hans remember that *there are no rules* and attack him while he did this?

The gamble paid off. Hans hesitated while Josef scooped up some gravel from the surface of the ground and flung it in Hans's face. It stunned him just long enough for Josef to lunge forward and wrap his big arms around Hans's waste. He lifted his opponent off the ground and threw his body forward, coming down on Hans with all his weight. He felt the air go out of Hans's chest. He let go, sat atop him, and started punching, hard. He had landed three blows when he felt himself being grabbed from behind.

"Enough! Enough!" Müller panted as they rolled off of Hans, who had blood trickling out of his cheek and nose. Müller leaned in and whispered, "You finally realize who you are."

* * *

Müller and the three visiting officers emerged after meeting in private and called the recruits to order. "You have learned well and will serve the fatherland and lead us to victory." Müller's voice rose in intensity with each word. "Now, we will give you your assignments. Each is an equal honor because each is what the Fuhrer demands of you."

The major stepped back and extended his left hand to signal that the visiting officers would now speak. The first to step forward was the slim man with the thin mustache and narrow face. "I am Colonel Klein, leader of the Scharfschützen." The recruits knew that this was an elite sharpshooter unit, and all stood a little straighter when hearing his rank and role. "Günter DrieMüller. You will join my unit." He stepped back.

None of the recruits spoke, but the air carried the weight of a silent, collective gasp. Josef peered down the row to the far end where Günter stood and saw his friend staring straight forward, looking stunned.

Next, the large, muscular, blond officer stepped forward. He wasted no time. "I am Captain Schmidt. Josef Zohren, Hans Bringmann, you will join me in the Einsatzgruppen.

Hans nudged Josef with his left elbow and flashed a smile to his left. The Einsatzgruppen was an elite task force used to keep order at home. They managed the Jew problem in particular. Josef was not sure if this was good or bad news yet.

Lastly, the round-faced officer with a scar on the left side of his face stepped forward. "I am Major Rademacher. The remaining recruits will join me in the 109th Infantry." All the recruits knew this meant the twelve remaining boys were going to the front. Josef heard at least one quiet groan of regret.

"You leave in the morning. Today you may collect your things and rest. We will have no more drills." Major Müller smiled at the group and then retreated with his fellow officers.

Josef walked toward Günter, who had a crowd around him, but Hans stepped into his path. For the first time, Josef noticed the damage he had done. Hans's face was already swollen, and dried blood marred his left cheek. It was hard to tell if the previously broken nose was fractured again.

"Good fight, Josef, but I'll get you next time." Hans smiled. It was the first friendly gesture from Hans that Josef could recall. Josef thought to himself, *Is this what it takes?* "We are the lucky ones," Hans continued. "The Einsatzgruppen cleanses our homeland. We won't go to the front and may even see our families sometimes. Only the best get chosen, and we are the best here."

Assessing Hans now, he seemed smaller, younger, as he looked eagerly back at Josef, talking about being the best. Josef thought back to three weeks earlier and wondered how he could have thought to line up to the right of this small boy. "OK, Hans. I need to talk with Günter now." He patted Hans's shoulder and walked past.

Günter was in a crowd of boys, being congratulated and having his hair tussled by the larger boys, which was most of them. Even a few recruits from other groups had come over to see the sharpshooter, the *Scharfsch*ützen. Apparently, word had spread that he was the only one selected amongst all four classes there. He looked up and saw Josef on the outer edge of a circle of enthusiastic boys.

"OK. Thank you. I need to go now." He pushed his way through the throng and stood by Josef. Josef motioned with his head to have him follow and the two walked toward the corner of the building. The throng moved on to Hans.

As they reached the back of the building, they were alone. Günter looked up with moist eyes. "I can't let them see me now." His voice shook as he spoke. "What am I going to do?"

Josef was puzzled. "I'm sorry, Günter, I don't know what you mean. You will go and learn more. Your unit will be farther from the fighting, shooting at a distance. You will be safer than the infantry. Isn't that a good thing?"

Günter shook his head. "No. No. No. It's all wrong."

"What is all wrong? I'm sorry, I don't understand."

"You will say I am stupid."

"Never."

"I can't …" Günter's voice broke, and he dropped to his knees, sobbing.

Josef looked around to ensure they were unseen. There was no one. "Get up, Günter. What if they come looking?"

He stood and wiped his face. "I'm sorry. Forget about this."

"No, Günter. You are my best friend. You can tell me."

"I can't shoot a person." He blurted it out quickly and then turned his head to not look at Josef.

"But Günter, you had to know that eventually …"

Günter nodded his head. "I told you it was stupid. How could I think all that shooting was just for practice? Just for fun?" He paused. "Of course I knew, but I just ignored it. I hoped the war would end, or maybe I would get hurt like some of the other boys. But when I looked at those targets, I started to imagine them as real people, and I knew … I knew I could never do it."

"I don't think you will have a choice, Günter." Josef put a hand on his friend's shoulder. "I mean, you can say your gun jammed once or twice, but at some point, you will have to shoot. And even if you try to miss, they will eventually know."

"I know. I have thought about every way around it. There is no other way, right?" He grabbed both of Josef's arms and stared up at him with searching eyes. "You are the smartest person I know, Josef, if you tell me there is no other way, I'll know it's true."

The look on Günter's face was the saddest thing Josef had ever seen: a mix of hope, desperation, and resignation. "I'm sorry, Günter. There is no other way."

On the morning of May 5, 1941, the recruits awoke for the last morning they would spend at Grafenwoehr. Josef had spent a fitful night of sleep, thinking about his friend, his desperate face as he searched for any solution to his problem. As he gradually came to consciousness, he noticed the hum of the lights above him. They buzzed like a beehive and the sound of the recruits stirring was like the hive coming to life. Springs of cots whined as boys swung their legs over the edge and struck the floor. A soft murmur of conversation and groans began. A recruit next to Josef unlatched his sack, pulling out fresh clothes for the day.

Their time here was ending, and Josef listened and watched to remember this place. His memories weren't fond, but they were important. He knew this place had played a meaningful role in his life, for better or for worse. Müller's words echoed in his mind. Had they unlocked something in him? Could he ever lock it up again? Then his mind went back to his friend. What could he say to Günter now that might help him? Could he be there for his friend in a way he had failed to the night before?

As he swung his legs over the side of his cot, he looked over to Günter's cot. Empty. His wool blanket was neatly folded, and his bag was packed. Josef scanned the room and did not see his friend. He walked to the neatly made cot and saw a piece of paper folded on top of his bag, which was neatly placed on a folded blanket. The only thing missing from Günter's perfectly kept quarters was his K98. As Josef unfolded the paper to read the note, he heard a loud bang from outside. His head jerked around to look for the source of the blast. It sounded like the firing of a K98 rifle. He felt a pull on his chest as the air rushed from his lungs. His hands felt cold and numb. His mind raced, trying to solve the puzzle in any way other than what he immediately knew in his heart. He could picture Günter's sad eyes from the night before searching, pleading for an answer.

Josef could feel every breath he took but nothing else. He lost the sense of whether he was standing or sitting, whether it was day or night. He could not feel his own hands. He looked down to find them and saw the note, still pinched between his fingers. It read:

Es gab keinen anderen Weg: There was no other way.

CHAPTER 13
DIE ELITE: THE ELITE
1941

The Schutzstaffel were the primary paramilitary police force under Hitler, better known by their abbreviated name, the SS. Josef and Hans joined the Einsatzgruppen, a task force under the SS charged with keeping order inside Germany and cleansing the country of its "Jew problem," as it was often referred to. As a first step, they attended the Adolph Hitler School (AHS). Not to be confused with the many primary schools that had been renamed for the Fuhrer between 1933 and 1941, the AHS was a twelve-day program teaching Nazi ideology.

They were told that they were elite and selected for their exceptional qualities, but early on, Josef noticed that real education was lacking. Most of the students had not been selected to attend the top-level academic schools, Gymnasium. In fact, teachers at AHS scoffed at the Gymnasium system, calling it

outdated and unnecessary. They mocked education and edu-
cated people. Selections for AHS were obviously made based
more on physical ability and appearance.

Back in his Gymnasium school, Josef was the largest student
by a good margin, and the vast majority of the boys were closer
to Günter's size. Here, Josef was still above average but at least
half of the boys were close to his size. He also noticed that
almost half had blond hair and close to that percentage had
blue eyes. The few smaller boys in the school were either exceptional athletes or boasted that their fathers were in the SS.

Schooling consisted of pledges to the Fuhrer, films about
the evils of Jews and other impure races, and the need to cleanse
the fatherland. Chants would break out frequently with the
students fervently saluting and proclaiming their patriotism in
coordinated yells of "Sieg Heil" or "Heil Hitler."

Throughout the twelve-day program, they would recite
their core slogans:

- *"Ein Volk, Ein Reich, Ein Führer": One People, One
  Realm, One Leader – To emphasize the unity of the people
  under Adolf Hitler.*
- *"Juden sind unser Unglück": The Jews are our Misfortune –
  To name the cause of Germany's problems.*
- *"Blut und Boden": Blood and Soil – To show that pure
  German blood was connected to the German land.*
- *"Gemeinnutz geht vor Eigennutz": The common good
  before the self good – To promote self-sacrifice for the
  fatherland.*
- *"Unsere letzte Hoffnung: Hitler": Our last hope: Hitler
  – To pledge allegiance to Adolf Hitler as the savior
  of Germany.*

All of these messages were shouted enthusiastically at graduation. The fervor with which the boys yelled these slogans was confusing for Josef. There was nothing he felt this strongly about. He knew that his country was at war; he knew that his country had economic problems before the war; and he accepted that the Jews must have caused these if his leaders were convinced of that fact. He did not understand, though, the level of enthusiasm around him.

Josef joined the calls with as much energy as he could muster. The loss of Günter weighed on him. Günter was smart, creative, and caring. He was certainly smarter than almost anyone at AHS. Why would Günter have taken such a final action as to shoot himself?

Josef's mind went back to that moment two weeks prior. He played it in his head over and over, running out the door at Grafenwoehr, seeing his friend on the ground next to his rifle, a bullet hole under his chin and the top of his skull missing. He imagined Günter propping the butt of the rifle against the ground and then pressing his chin on it. His friend then reaching down to press the trigger. Why?

The final words they had spoken outside were recounted in the note to his parents. Had Josef himself caused this? *Why could I not have told him there was another way?*

He felt a slap on his shoulder, it was Hans who had been standing next to him at the AHS graduation ceremony. "What's wrong with you?" Hans still had some bruising on his face from the last fight with Josef.

Josef realized he had stopped chanting and even may have missed a Heil Hitler salute or two. "Oh, sorry. Just thinking," he said, still partially in a fog.

"Well, stop it. We are supposed to have fun today—and soon we will get to move some dirty Jews to the trains. Aren't you sick of all this training? I'm ready to serve the Fuhrer." Hans smiled broadly in a way that asked for a response in kind.

"Of course," Josef said, forcing a smile. "I hear we are in the same unit, under Captain Schmidt."

CHAPTER 14
ANNAHME: ADOPTION
1945

Evenings in the Becker home had a quiet, almost hypnotic feel. Dieter would sit in his blue fabric chair, his back to the window, a newspaper unfurled before him. Minna sat at the piano, playing notes softly and slowly. She loved to play pieces that were composed specifically for piano. She usually played them at half tempo to create a magical sound. She would say that it made her feel like she was in a dream.

The pace of her music ran so opposite her personality. The lively, effervescent woman used these moments to meditate on life and simply be in the moment with her husband. Dieter sometimes did not turn a page of the newspaper for thirty minutes as he listened to her play. This was their time together when Dieter had returned from work, usually refusing to talk about his day. He used to share his work with her before the war. Now, he would shake his head and ask her to play her piano.

The headlines in the paper, still controlled by the falling German government, put forth the pretense of German resistance, while citizens saw Allied forces in the streets and read foreign reports of Hitler's death days earlier.

The phone rang, breaking the trance that had enveloped the room. Dieter rose and strode to the small table that held their phone and put the receiver to his ear. He did not speak, he just listened. After a few moments, he said, "We will be there in the morning."

Dieter looked across the room at Minna. She was trembling, still seated on her piano pedestal, but now facing away from the instrument and toward her husband. Her hands were over her mouth as she stared at him with anticipation. He nodded and she let out a joyous scream.

* * *

As Dieter and Minna walked up to the high-arched entry of the Munich Municipal Orphanage on Waisenhausstrasse, a woman in a neatly pressed white, nurse-like uniform approached them. Her hair was pinned up in a tight bun and she wore glasses. "Herr Becker, I assume?"

"Yes. My wife, Minna." Dieter nodded to his right.

"You must be an important man. I was given strict instructions to call you as soon as a new child under the age of five arrived. You were to be given priority for immediate adoption. With the state of the war, we don't know what will happen in the coming days, so if you are agreeable, we will finalize everything today."

"We look forward to meeting the boy," Minna said without trying to conceal her excitement.

They began walking to the entry and the woman stopped

and faced the Beckers. "Understand, we know little of the boy's background, or …" She paused and raised an eyebrow. "His heritage."

It was clear she was alluding to the potential that the boy they were about to meet may be a Jew.

Dieter met her gaze and gave her a serious look. "I have not asked, nor will I ask you what his heritage is. What I do want to know is whether all efforts were made to locate his parents. I think you would agree that they would have a right to know that their son is here if they are alive."

The woman cleared her throat and looked down. "Of course, Herr Becker. My apologies. The boy was brought in by an Allied soldier who suggested that the boy was alone and did not have surviving parents. It is all we know, sir."

* * *

Inside the doorway, a boy sat on a bench, clutching a small bear. He looked up at Dieter and Minna approaching, and his dark eyes and lush lashes took Minna's breath away. She rushed ahead and dropped to her knees in front of the boy. "What is your name?"

"Friedrich."

"And what is this Bear's name? He looks like a very good friend."

"Bärli. I am protecting him."

"That is an important job. Did someone make that for you?" Friedrich shook his head.

"Would you like to come with me? We have a room for you, and I think Bärli will find the bed quite comfortable."

Friedrich shrugged.

Minna's eyes welled with tears as she turned to Dieter.

"After all these years, I can't believe we will have a child to care for."

He nodded and put an arm around his wife.

There were only a few signatures required before walking out the door as a new family of three. It seemed surreal. Minna turned back to the looming building behind them, almost expecting someone to rush out and tell her there had been a mistake. Instead, she saw the round face of a girl, perhaps a year or two older than Friedrich pressed against the glass of a third-floor window. Their eyes met and the girl gave a wave of her pudgy hand. Minna smiled and waved back.

CHAPTER 15
VATER: FATHER
1957

"You have been absent at dinnertime these past days," Dieter said, without putting down his newspaper, as Friedrich entered the apartment.

"I've been working on the research we discussed, Father."

Dieter folded the newspaper and placed it on the side table. "You know this will only lead to pain. It is best to leave the past behind. It serves no purpose to you now. Nothing can be done about what happened."

Friedrich looked quizzically at his father. "What do you mean, *about what happened*? Do you know something you aren't telling me?"

"I just mean your birth parents are dead. What happened is tragic, but there is nothing to be done."

There were those words again—*what happened.* "If you know what happened to them, you must tell me."

Dieter leaned back and folded his hands. It was hard for him to imagine how his boy had no knowledge of the war, given how it had dominated and shaped his own life, but he also knew that the German schools taught nothing of the atrocities that took place under Adolf Hitler and the German people rarely spoke of it. It was their hidden shame.

"Sit down, Son," Dieter said while motioning with his left hand and rubbing his chin with the right. "Terrible things happened in the war," he began.

"I know. So many died in battle," Friedrich injected.

Holding his hands up, Dieter urged his son to wait for the full story. "That is the tragedy of all wars, but I am referring to something more sinister. They won't teach you this in school, but Hitler ordered the deaths of so many Jews, countless, really. They exterminated them by the thousands like insects." He shook his head and clenched his strong jaw. "It will be a shame on our country forever."

Friedrich could not believe what he was hearing. "They just killed them? Not even in battle? That can't be. No one would carry out such an order."

"It was not just an order. It was years of propaganda, teaching all of us that Jews were the cause of our problems, that they were subhuman. It started long before you were born. When you came along, Germany was at the height of its power and pride, but it was the lowest of moments for the Jews. By the end, most of them had been killed."

His father's face was set in a painful grimace of sadness and anger. Friedrich could not comprehend such a thing. He did not personally know any Jews but believed it was just another religion. He had never given them much thought. "That is awful, Father, but why are you telling me that? What does it have to do with finding my birth parents?"

Again, Dieter looked at his son and marveled at his youth and ignorance. "Because they were Jews, Friedrich. They were murdered for the crime of being Jewish. Ultimately, I suppose your mother and I were the beneficiaries, because we got you."

Friedrich rocked back in his chair, his breath still. His parents were Jews? They had been murdered? How could he have lived so blindly all these years? "What were their names? Where did they die?"

"We didn't know any of that."

"Then how do you know they were Jews and that they were killed?"

"Son, you don't know any Jews because so few remain here. Do you know what they look like?" Without waiting for a response, he added, "Many look like you, Son. Dark skin and eyes; dark, curly hair. You were brought to the orphanage by a soldier from the Allied army. It was believed that your parents hid you successfully when they were taken to the camps." Dieter saw the question on his son's face and answered it without being asked. "The camps are where they killed most of them."

"*Hid me*," Friedrich said softly to himself, the hint of a memory swirling in his brain. "Why did you never tell me any of this?"

Dieter swallowed and cleared his throat. "I suppose it was shame."

"Shame? For what reason?"

"Do you know what my job was during the war?" Dieter's voice rose slightly and quivered. "As an engineer for the government, I was put to work at a munitions factory. We made mortars and bullets." He looked directly at Friedrich and added, "My bullets killed many people, perhaps even your parents."

The pain was raw. Friedrich had rarely had a conversation with his father that went deeper than the day's school assignments. Now, in the wake of losing his wife and watching his son seek out his birth parents, this guarded man was telling him his darkest secrets. It was unnerving.

"You can't possibly feel responsible. You were simply doing a job. You didn't kill anyone."

"Simply doing a job," Dieter repeated softly. "Just as the guards at the camps might have said."

Friedrich desperately wanted to talk about anything else. He had gone from marveling at his father's newfound openness to wishing he had never resurfaced this painful memory. "I'm sorry about all of this, Father. No matter what you think, I know you would never intend to hurt anyone. And it seems we don't even know if my birth parents are dead. You said they killed most of the Jews but not all of them. Either way, I hope you understand that I must try to find out what happened."

Dieter nodded but said no more.

Friedrich walked to his room in a daze. *I'm a Jew?* he asked himself quietly. He did not know what it meant. He looked down at his bed and could see himself as a young boy, kneeling for nightly prayers on one side of his bed with his mother facing him, kneeling on the other side. They would say the same prayer each night before sleep.

Jesus Kindchen klein (Little baby Jesus)
Mach mein Herzchen rein (Make my heart pure)
Soll niemand drin wohnen (So no one may live there)
Als Jesus Kindchen allein (But little baby Jesus alone)

He could picture his mother's face, with her eyes closed and hands clasped together, repeating this prayer. He was supposed to keep his eyes closed as they prayed, but he would peek through squinted eyes to watch her. She would sometimes look up and catch him peeking but would just smile. On the wall at the head of his bed, this prayer hung, stitched by Minna with blue thread on a sheet of linen that had turned a tea-stained color over the years. How had his parents never told him he was a Jew? Was his entire life a lie?

CHAPTER 16
MÄRCHEN: FAIRY TALE
1957

The town hall was about halfway between the orphanage and the Gymnasium school. Sigrid arranged to leave an hour early from her shift and was waiting when Friedrich arrived in front of the building at three thirty. She ran to him and gave him a hug.

"I have a good feeling about today," she said as she hopped up and down like a child. Friedrich just nodded, still reeling from the conversation with his father. "It's OK to be nervous," she added. "This could be a big day."

As they walked up the steps to the front door of the building, she took his hand and interlaced her fingers with his. The building was a spectacular sight. They had each seen it many times, but it still demanded that they stop and stare up at the numerous spires, the clock tower and the ornate designs that blanketed the exterior. At the center of the building was the primary attraction in all of Munich, the Glockenspiel. Standing four stories above them on the front facade of the old building, the Glockenspiel was a spinning carnival of sight and sound. Each hour, characters would spin on the carousel, playing music to the delight of onlookers in Marienplatz below.

They made their way through the throngs of people in the Platz to the main entry of the town hall. In the lobby, there was a sign with government departments listed by floor and room number. Records were on the second level, up a stone staircase. The steps were narrow, and the sound of their feet echoed as they climbed, creating an air of gravity. The high ceiling and ancient stonework made Friedrich feel small and insignificant. Perhaps, he thought, that was the purpose of a building like this.

The woman at the records desk had gray hair pulled up into a bun. She was heavyset and wore glasses with a chain to hang them around her neck when not in use. Her name tag read *Magda*. She looked up, appearing to assess the two young people before her. "What do you need?" she asked curtly.

Before Friedrich could start to speak, Sigrid began, "Hello, Magda. I'm Sigrid and this is Friedrich, though to be honest we don't know if that is his original birth name. We also don't know his surname, but would you believe we know his exact birth date, or at least we think we do."

Exasperated, Magda interjected, repeating her question. "What do you need?"

"Well, his birth certificate. That's what I was saying." Sigrid tossed an eye roll to Friedrich.

"Fill out the form over there," Magda said, pointing to a long table against the far wall. There is one for birth certificates specifically. Bring it back here, and we will put it in the queue."

"How long is the queue?" Friedrich asked, obviously feeling let down.

She looked at him and removed her glasses. "Are you searching for parents, young man?" Friedrich nodded. She gave a slight smile and nodded understanding. "Fill it out quickly and return five minutes before five o'clock. I will tell you if I have found anything. Be here at exactly that time. We close at five o'clock sharp."

As they exited the building at three forty-five, they looked for a spot to wait. Halfway down the block, they found a café to sit in. The air had turned colder overnight, and there was a slight wind. Sigrid went to get tea, but Friedrich stopped her. "I haven't paid your bribe yet today, so I'll get the tea." He smiled at her and patted her shoulder. It was the first time he had initiated contact with her, and it seemed as if they both noticed.

They sat with their tea for a moment, and then Sigrid reached across the table with her left hand and held his right. "You know, I think that woman at the records department, Magda, thought you were quite handsome. She didn't really care for me, but one look into your eyes with those long lashes, and she was ready to run and find your birth certificate."

"I don't think she thought that."

"Of course she did. I mean … you are quite handsome." She smiled at him.

Friedrich felt himself blush. He didn't know what to say or do.

Sigrid let go of his hand. "Well, it seems you don't think I am pretty, or you would have said so. Oh well. I suppose I'm not." She picked up her tea and sipped it.

They sat silently for a minute or two, but it seemed longer

to Friedrich. He finally leaned forward and said softly, so no one in the café would hear, "I don't know what to say because I've never had a girlfriend." He stared at her. He loved the round shape of her cheeks, the brightness of her eyes, her constant motion, her confidence. He hoped that he had said the right thing.

"So, you think I am your girlfriend?"

"I don't know. I, I thought."

"And were you going to ask me to be, or just assume that I am?"

"I want you to be," he said, then paused, adding, "and I do think you are very pretty."

She stood up, leaned over the table, and kissed his lips softly. "You finally said the right thing. I hope it doesn't take my prompting in the future."

He laughed and held her hand. This was an entirely new experience for him. He had never had a girlfriend and, in truth, had never had any close friends. He spent most of his time either with his mother, reading, or playing the piano. Now, he only had his father. His mind went back to the conversation the prior evening. His face became serious. "There is something I have to tell you though." He met her eye and then looked down. "Apparently, my parents were Jews, which means I am a Jew. I only just found out."

"Aah," Sigrid said, nodding as if she was putting something together in her mind. "This is what was troubling you earlier."

Friedrich nodded.

"So that I understand, are you troubled that you are a Jew or that you just found out?"

Friedrich was stunned by the question. He had not thought about it in this way. Was he bothered to be a Jew? He didn't think so. He did not really know what it meant, and he felt no different than before. Was he bothered to just learn about it? He understood his father's pain and reluctance to share this with him, so—no.

"Let me ask you another way," added Sigrid. "What would you have done differently in your life up to now, if you had known your parents were Jews?"

The corners of his mouth curled up and he shook his head slightly at how clever and perceptive her question was. He leaned forward and kissed her.

* * *

Arriving back at city hall, they rushed through the crowd gathering outside to watch the Glockenspiel at five o'clock. It was ten minutes before five as they rushed up the stairs to the records department. Magda was already waiting for them and waved them over. "This is what I have found for you. Seventy-nine babies were born in Bavaria on March 9, 1941. That's a bit low, but fewer people had babies during the war, which helps narrow down who you might be. Forty-three of the babies were girls. I think we can exclude those." She smiled at Friedrich, seeming proud of her attempt at humor. "There were no mothers named Amalie. There was one boy named Friedrich, but I was able to find his school records. Also, he had blue eyes. I also found school records for all but three of the other boys; two of them have died. One just a few days after birth, the other in an accident as a toddler."

"So, what of the last boy?"

"This is what is strange. We have no record of school and no record of his death. It is as if he disappeared after birth."

Sigrid and Friedrich looked at each other with wide eyes. Turning to the woman, Friedrich smiled and said, "I can't tell you how much I appreciate you doing this for me. I never imagined someone would do so much. Thank you."

Magda cleared her throat and straightened her blouse. "I think helping you after all that happened back then is only right." She looked over her shoulder, where two other government workers spoke to each other. "You must understand that I cannot give out a copy of a birth certificate to anyone but the individual it belongs to."

"But without the name of the parents, we ..."

She held her hands up. "Excuse me. I have to check on something. I'll be back in two minutes." She stood up and walked to where the other government employees were talking. She left a single birth certificate on the table. The parents were Julius and Henriette Amberg. They named their boy David.

Friedrich and Sigrid read the document and nodded to one another. As they began to walk to the stairs, Friedrich turned to Sigrid and asked, "Will you wait for me a moment?" He walked back to the desk and waved to Magda, who came to him. Sigrid watched as the two spoke, and then Friedrich shook her hand and returned.

"I am not David Amberg, I'm afraid. He was probably just another Jew that went into hiding."

Sigrid was stunned. "How could you know that? The boy had brown eyes and was born the same day."

"I just know."

"But ..."

"Please." Friedrich stopped and held Sigrid's hands. "Just trust me. I am not that boy. Besides, I was probably born in the north, closer to the address I gave the orphanage in 1945."

The two walked back to the Munich Orphanage in silence.

* * *

"I have my own room here," Sigrid offered as they came to the cavernous entryway to the Munich Orphanage. "I'd like to show it to you."

Friedrich swallowed, his face flushing red, then nodded. He followed her through the entry and up two flights of stairs to a long hallway. Pendant lights hung every five meters from the high ceiling. It was quiet, clearly a place where the staff stayed and none of the resident children. Sigrid stopped at a wooden door with "17" nailed to the center. The room was decorated in bright, primary colors. Handmade drawings covered the walls. Streamers of colored paper were strung from the ceiling. A poster of Elvis Presley adorned the inside of the door.

"I moved into this room from the dorms two years ago. I like it better here, having my own space." She looked at him expectantly.

Friedrich knew he was supposed to say something and searched for the correct words. "It's a nice room. I like your decorations." Her look confirmed that he had given the right answer.

"Come sit on the bed with me." She took his hand, and they sat. "You still won't share things with me. You won't tell me what you said to the woman at city hall or why you know you are not that boy on the certificate." She leaned forward and kissed him, then added, "And you won't tell me what else you remember."

Friedrich lowered his head and shook it slightly.

"If you take off your shirt, I will take off mine," she said, trying to sound casual.

Friedrich looked at her bright eyes and round cheeks. Her smile was so beautiful. Then he glanced down at the cream-colored sweater she wore, at the curves of her breasts. He started to take off his brown sweater and then paused.

"Before I take this off, I will tell you what I said to Magda, because you will see anyway."

Sigrid gave him a perplexed look.

"Do you know what a Nebenwarze is?" Not waiting for an answer, he added, "It's an extra nipple. I have one. I asked that woman if such a thing would be noted on a birth record, and she said it would. The Amberg's baby did not have a Nebenwarze." He slid his sweater up slowly and then pulled it over his head.

Sigrid reached over and placed a hand on his chest, sliding it down to feel the extra nipple. She smiled and let out a small laugh. "Well, this is a problem, Friedrich."

He searched her face, trying to read her thoughts.

"It's a problem, you see, because I only have two and now I fear you will be disappointed." She pulled her sweater over her head, then undid her bra, exposing her breasts.

Friedrich wanted to laugh at her humor, but his eyes were fixed on her figure. He leaned forward, wrapped his arms around her, pulling her body against his.

They kissed and touched each other for what seemed like hours. It was the most exhilarating experience of Friedrich's life.

As they lay on the bed with bare chests, Sigrid was turned toward Friedrich with half of her body on top of his and her left arm extended across him, holding his right hand. She said, "I think you should tell me all you remember now. I mean, I know about your birthmark, so really, there can be no bigger secrets." She laughed.

He kissed the top of her head and said, "If there are no secrets, tell me about how you came to be here, then I will tell you my story."

"There is not much to tell, I am afraid. There are no records of me at all. Believe me, I have looked. I was dropped here and I have lived here for more than seventeen years. I have had many friends through the years but most of them pass through. I was never adopted, as you may have guessed. Most people want boys, I find, and the ones who want girls take the skinny ones." She showed a slight quiver in the corner of her mouth. I know that even now I am not slim like girls in posters but as a younger child, I was quite round." She forced a laugh. "I supposed people did not want that. They come to this place and it's like shopping in the store window. No one buys the ugly sweater."

Friedrich could feel her pain, the rejection she tried to shake off with a joke and a smile. "I think you are the prettiest girl I've ever seen. I guess it's my luck no one adopted you, as we would not have met here."

She tilted her head up in and kissed him long, holding both sides of his face. Then she smiled and said, "I was worried about you at first, but you are really learning the right things to say. Now, tell me your story. I hope it is more entertaining and less sad than mine."

"Oh, I think it is entertaining, but I fear you won't believe me. I'm not even sure what I believe, but the memories are so vivid when I see them. They are like a fairy tale, and I'm afraid none of it is real, but it's all I remember from before."

Sigrid pulled her sweater on, sat on the bed with her back against the wall and looked intently at Friedrich. "Go ahead. I promise not to laugh, but you must tell me everything."

"There are flashes of memories, and they don't make sense. I recall being in a box for many days. I could not open the lid; I was trapped and starving. When I finally emerged, I saw a giant as tall as two men standing atop one another and the width of two or three men standing shoulder to shoulder. I know it sounds crazy, but I remember him as a demon from fairy tales. His eyes were blue fire. He was good to me though, I think. We went to a castle, larger than the Munich City Hall, that sat at the side of a roaring sea."

Friedrich looked up and realized he had told his story with his eyes closed. Sigrid looked thoughtful and kept her word not to laugh.

"We are going to find out about your birth parents and your demon and castle too, Friedrich. I promise you."

CHAPTER 17
BLUT UND BODEN: BLOOD AND SOIL
1941

"*Blut und Boden*," Captain Schmidt yelled out, his right arm thrust into the sky, hand balled into a tight, massive fist. "*Blut und Boden*," he repeated, staring out at the eager faces of his charges.

They picked up his cue the second time and repeated the phrase in unison. "*Blut und Boden! Blut und Boden!*"

"Why do we say this? What does it mean?" He paced in front of the eight young men in his charge, staring at each of them in turn, as they stood at attention. Captain Schmidt commanded attention with his size and strength but he also demanded it with his intense stare. He was not waiting for the response. He simply wanted his words to land with maximum effect. "We say this to remind us that pure German blood, like ours, is the blood that feeds our land. It means that we must rid this land of those less pure, those who have corrupted our land, stolen our successes, impeded our glory."

He paused and stared again at each young man in turn. "You will restore our purity by driving out the impure. And if that means you must spill their blood, then you will." He yelled again, "*Blut und Boden!*" He raised his gaze above their heads, as if speaking to God, and added, "And if your blood should be spilled on our sacred land, it will be to purify it. Are you here to serve the fatherland?"

"Yes, sir!" They yelled in unison.

"Then you begin today. We will start clearing Jews from the settlement and lead them to the trains. These Jews are like vermin, they multiply. They are overflowing and we must make room. We will be one of ten units on site, but we will be the strongest, the fiercest, the most efficient."

"Yes, sir!"

* * *

Josef and Hans were two of the eight members of the Einsatzgruppen task force assigned to Captain Schmidt. Most were some version of Schmidt himself, large boys with blond hair and blue eyes. When they aligned outside of the settlement with the other units, it was clear that their unit was different. Josef thought that perhaps Schmidt had hand-selected his group in his image, but Hans had another theory.

"You see, Josef, we are the best of the best. Not only are we in the Einsatzgruppen but we are in the top unit." He beamed with pride.

Josef didn't understand being proud of his height or hair color, as he had not contributed to these things, but he shrugged and responded, "I guess so." It was the closest he could come to a response that wouldn't dampen Hans's spirits.

The Einsatzgruppen soldiers had all been issued red

armbands to identify them as a division of the SS. Each member had also been given a sidearm, as a K98 was too cumbersome for the work they would undertake today. The sidearm was a Luger P08 pistol with a brown handle and a black metal barrel. According to Captain Schmidt, its eight-round capacity made it the ideal weapon.

The settlement was a series of drab, gray four-story buildings that had made up the poorest section of Munich. Many of the people who had previously lived here were in the military now and those who were not had been moved into the least desirable of the confiscated Jewish homes. The more desirable of the confiscated homes went to government officials or allies to the government, including those who built weapons or munitions.

A two-meter chain-link fence with razor wire surrounded the settlement. Through the fence, Josef saw a smattering of people out in front of the buildings. A few children played in the dirt, where there likely had been grass at one time but had been trampled in the overcrowded slum. He suspected that most people were indoors because it was an overcast day with a light, misty drizzle.

"Now we begin," shouted Captain Schmidt. "Our unit is vacating the first building this morning." He pointed to the leftmost building. "There are four apartments on each floor and four floors. We must begin on the first floor and will ascend the stairs only after the first floor is clear and we know that none of the Jews are in hiding or pose a threat."

Josef thought the idea of these people, living in the poorest of conditions, with almost no possessions, being a threat to them seemed ridiculous. He realized he wore a skeptical expression just before Schmidt looked his way. He relaxed his face and stared straight ahead.

"Each apartment should take no more than one quarter hour, and so we will complete the building in four hours." He paused, looking at each of them in turn. "Remember, these Jews were given these accommodations by the Fuhrer as an act of kindness. They are owed nothing, as these are not their homes."

Josef knew that this was true but also knew that their original homes had been seized. He wondered if any of his counterparts understood this. The AHS selections were not based on intelligence, and he had come to understand that most of his fellow soldiers blindly followed their leaders. He reminded himself each day of his father's words. *Not everything they tell me is true and I must decide for myself.*

The train station was about a one-mile walk. No mention was made of where the train was headed, but Josef assumed it would be the Dachau work camp, which was the nearest camp to Munich.

"Now march. Stay vigilant. The Jews are cunning."

The unit of nine, including their captain, marched to the gate, where an armed guard stood. He opened the gate, saluted Captain Schmidt, with a Sieg Heil and his arm extended at forty-five degrees up from his shoulder. They filed through the gate in twos, Hans was to Josef's right. They marched to the front of the first building and opened the door leading to a narrow hallway. Inside, it was dark; only the light from the open front door illuminated the dank hall. There were four doors, two on each side of the hall.

Schmidt ordered Hans and Josef to join him inside and the other six in the unit to wait at the door to give armed escort to the Jews out of the camp. The process would be that Josef and Hans would clear the apartments; the other six would surround and escort the Jews from each apartment out of the camp; then soldiers from another unit would take the Jews in larger groups to the train. "Draw your weapons," Schmidt ordered.

Josef's heart pounded. Was he being naive? Was his life at risk right now, with Jews waiting to pounce as they stormed through the door? He and Hans would be the first ones in the door and he did not know what to expect. Schmidt nodded to him, and he banged on the door.

"Hello?" A shaky man's voice responded.

"Open the door, please," Josef responded, immediately seeing Schmidt's displeasure with his courtesy. The door handle turned slowly, and the door opened a crack. Schmidt then kicked it with a loud thud, followed by a second thud when the door struck the wall. There was a chorus of startled yells from inside, followed by children crying.

Josef stepped through with Hans by his side. They had rehearsed their lines. "You are being taken to a train that will bring you to your next home." They did not mention the camp in an attempt to maintain calm. "You are to exit the premises now and will be directed when you pass through the gate." He looked around the room at the stunned and frightened faces. There were so many. How could they all be living in this one apartment? He saw what appeared to be three couples, in all three cases the men stood in front of the women, appearing to shield them. Two of the women were holding small children and a few older children stood behind the adults.

"Yes. We are going." It was the same voice he had heard through the door. A man in his thirties, short, with round glasses. "We want no trouble." He turned to the group. "Line up now and walk out. Move slowly but steadily. Listen to the officers and we will be OK." He clearly had command of this group, and they did exactly as he instructed.

Once the apartment was emptied, they were ordered to search everywhere for hidden Jews. They found none. Josef started to relax, feeling his initial instinct was correct, there was no threat, and Schmidt was just overly eager. These poor wretches would follow orders, allowing the squad to complete their tasks quickly.

The other three apartments on the first floor were cleared as easily as the first. There were between seven and twelve people in each. The apartment with twelve had a wretched smell. The plumbing had clogged and left a nauseating stench of excrement.

"You see how these animals live?" Schmidt asked rhetorically. "This is the filth they bring to our land."

At the first apartment on the second floor, there was no answer at first knock, so Josef knocked again. Schmidt gave him a look of disgust and then stepped in from of the door and banged on it with three furious blows that shook the entire door frame.

A yell came from inside. "What do you want?"

Schmidt nodded to Josef, as an order to speak. "You are to exit the premises …"

"You took our home already. We are not leaving again!" It was a young man's voice that rose in volume as the words came out. Then there was a chorus of voices inside arguing. They could make out little other than a woman saying, "You will get us all killed."

Schmidt nodded again and Josef kicked the door with the bottom of his boot. The first kick cracked the frame next to the door handle and the second kick sent the door swinging in and shards of wood flying. Schmidt stepped aside and waved his soldiers into the room. Six people were in the room: an older woman, perhaps in her seventies; a man and woman of about fifty years; a young man and woman in their late teens; and a girl of seven or eight years. The boy in his late teens was large and muscular. The girl, whom he shielded with his body, was of a similar age. She was slender and striking. Her dark eyes shone, as did her wavy dark hair. Josef was reminded of Liesel. He could picture her at the dinner table with Günter and Frau Kimmich. He could recall her embrace outside the front door of the Kimmich home.

The middle-aged woman was staring at the teen boy and holding up a hand. It was clear to Josef that the boy was the one yelling when they were outside the door. They locked eyes, and he saw the hatred and anger reflected back at him. He felt suddenly self-conscious about ordering this boy, older than he was, to leave his home. Josef looked away and saw Schmidt glaring at him. He collected himself and recited the words he had practiced.

"Of course. We will leave right away," the middle-aged woman responded, keeping her head tilted slightly down and looking at the floor.

Josef was relieved. They would avoid confrontation. But he had not anticipated Captain Schmidt's anger at being ignored in the hall.

"Names!" Schmidt shouted.

After a pause, the middle-aged woman took the lead

again. "We are all named Hirsch. My mother-in-law, Lotte; my husband, Felix; my daughter, Lilli; my son, Albert; and my youngest daughter, Henriette." She attempted a smile, then added, "And I am Rosa."

"What was the meaning of your insolent answer, forcing us to break the door?"

"We apologize. It has been a difficult time. We will cause no more trouble."

At that, Albert shook his head and let out a small grunt of dissatisfaction. His fists were balled tightly at his sides.

Schmidt glared at him. "Do you have something to add, Jew?" he added emphasis to *Jew*, to make his disdain obvious.

Albert turned red but said nothing. Rosa spoke for him, "He does not. I assure you we will be no more trouble."

"Oh, I am quite sure you won't," Schmidt said as he strode toward Albert and stopped directly in front of him. He then looked at Lilli. "What a lovely girl." He turned to Josef and Hans and added, "It is amazing how sometimes even a Jew can look quite beautiful on the outside."

Hans let out a laugh and then stared. "Yes, sir. She looks very good."

Josef started to perspire. He would not look at Schmidt. He feared what would happen next. He prayed silently. *Please just let them go to the train.* He felt his head shaking slightly and caught himself. When he looked up, Schmidt was staring at him.

"You know, I think Josef should interrogate Lilli. It seems she could help uncover what happened here."

Josef felt confused by the suggestion, until Hans responded, "I would be happy to do the interrogation, sir." He elbowed Josef playfully.

"Yes. I think Josef must do this. Josef, take Lilli into the bedroom."

"Sir, I'm not sure ..."

"Now!" Schmidt shouted.

Josef walked toward Lilli, who was positioned directly behind Albert. He took her wrist gently. Albert was breathing so hard Josef could feel his hot breath. Suddenly, Josef felt a powerful blow to his chest. Albert had pushed him, and he staggered back several steps before catching his balance. He heard Rosa cry out, "No, Albert."

"Stay away from her, or I'll ..." He stopped himself as he registered his mother's plea.

"I—I just need to interrogate her. I won't harm her, I promise."

"Nooo!" Schmidt bellowed in rage. "This is not how we deal with a violent Jew. We make no promises to them." He grabbed Josef by the ear; stood him directly in front of Albert, face-to-face, then drew his sidearm and shot Albert in the right eye. Josef was so close that blood from the right eye spattered across his face while the left eye registered his surprise and then went blank almost instantly. He watched Albert's lifeless body crumple to the floor, as if he were a tossed towel, folding haphazardly as it landed. He heard Rosa scream again as she lunged at Schmidt. Everything seemed to move in slow motion as Josef watched, stunned, frozen.

There was another gunshot. Rosa dropped to the floor and lay face down, motionless. Josef turned to see Hans standing over her with a wisp of smoke curling out of the barrel of his Luger. Hans wore a blank expression, staring down at the woman on the floor.

Josef could feel his heart beating so hard it seemed it would explode, and yet he did not move. Fear and confusion gripped him as he tried to understand what had happened in the few brief seconds that had just passed. His eyes darted around the room as if taking photographs of this place, this scene, but he did not move. A family photo hung on the wall. In it, Albert stood behind his sister, Lilli, resting his chin on top of her head, both of them smiling broadly. He thought to himself, *I wouldn't know they were Jews from that photo.*

Josef's trance was broken by Schmidt glaring at him, nose-to-nose. He then walked to Felix, who stood silently weeping, frozen with fear. He placed the barrel of his Luger against Felix's forehead. "You will vacate now with your mother and younger daughter, yes?"

Felix nodded.

"Hans, you may stay and interrogate the older daughter."

Hans walked to Lilli and motioned to the bedroom door. She was silent but tears streamed down her face. As she looked back toward Josef, all he could see was Liesel.

* * *

Lying in bed that night at the barracks, Hans and Josef stared at the ceiling. They had not spoken since the events in the second-floor apartment. Fortunately, the third and fourth floors had gone smoothly and no one else was shot. Schmidt made clear his appreciation for Hans and disgust with Josef for the rest of the day.

Josef thought about Albert, replaying the look on his face as his right eye exploded; the way he crumpled and folded as he fell. Most of all, he thought about Lilli, seeing her face when she glanced back, in tears, as Hans led her to the bedroom.

Günter had killed himself because he could not imagine shooting another person. He had concluded that *there was no other way.* Josef had not shot anyone yet, but he knew that day would come, perhaps even tomorrow. Was there truly no other way?

His thoughts were interrupted by a whisper in the dark from Hans. "Josef. Did you see that Jew woman fall? I shot her in the back of the head as she went for the captain."

Josef was not sure if Hans was proud or just trying to sound that way. Was there a tinge of regret in his voice? He had known Hans as a bully; a boy full of bombast and pride, but he was less than a year older than Josef himself. Killing someone, a woman no less, must have weighed on him. "I saw, Hans." He decided to take a chance at learning more about his colleague. "That must have been difficult. I'm sorry."

There was a long pause, as if Hans were processing the comment. "No more difficult than shooting a dog." After another pause, he added, "You will see. I know you can do it too."

The comment was intended to be supportive, but Josef hated the sound of it because he feared it was true. Perhaps he could do it.

* * *

The next morning, they went back to the same settlement to clear building two. The process was the same. Captain Schmidt addressed the team with the same fervor as the prior day. This time, though, rather than scanning to meet every young soldier's eye, he stared at Josef each time he hit a key point.

Unlike the prior day, the sun shone in the early morning hour. The beautiful blue sky with wispy clouds and a light breeze felt at odds with the dark task that lay ahead. Captain

Schmidt called for the group to march, and they passed the sentry who once again saluted with an enthusiastic Sieg Heil. Schmidt positioned himself next to Josef and spoke softly, attempting to address him only. "It was your first day. I understand from Major Müller that you took some time in training to find your true self, so I will exercise patience." He paused. "For yesterday only." He put his large hand on Josef's shoulder. "You must never let a Jew disrespect you again. If the Jew does not face a consequence, then you will face it for them. Do I make myself clear, Josef?"

"Yes, sir."

As they entered the building lobby and approached the first door, Schmidt nodded to Josef. Yesterday, Josef's heart pounded, wondering what risks could be behind the door. Today it pounded not for fear of any danger to himself but in fear of the danger he might be to those inside. He thought to himself, *perhaps there really is no other way.*

The first two floors went smoothly, as did the first two apartments on the third floor. Josef thought that all the inhabitants here would likely know about the two dead from the prior day. They would surely comply. They entered the third apartment on the third floor and the smell was awful. Ten people were assembled there, and Josef read out their instructions. Several members of the group looked nervously at one another. Before even looking for Schmidt's glare, Josef raised his voice and pulled his sidearm out. "Walk to the door, now!"

The oldest man in the group, a short, gray-bearded man with a potbelly, raised his hands over his head and asked, "May I tell you something, sir?" He was looking directly at Josef, who had been the one addressing them.

"Speak," Josef ordered, trying to sound more sure and authoritative than he truly felt.

"My mother is quite ill. She is in the bedroom, unable to walk on her own. May we carry her?"

Josef looked to his captain who pointed to the bedroom. Turning back to the man, he said, "We will take a look first." Hans drew his weapon and stood watch as Schmidt and Josef went to the bedroom. As they opened the door, a stench met them that smelled of sickness and human waste. It hung in the air with a thickness they could almost taste. Josef gagged and put a hand to his mouth. A used bedpan sat on the floor and an old woman, appearing to be in her eighties, lay in the bed breathing through heavy congestion. Her rattling chest labored up and down under a thin sheet, sounding like a bag of marbles being gently stirred.

"Animals," Schmidt muttered through a look of disgust. "She is not fit for the trains. You will take care of this," he ordered and then left the room, not waiting for a reply.

Josef could hear Schmidt in the other room. "All of you, go. We will take care of the old woman. You will head to the train."

"No. Please. I beg you," the man who had first spoken pleaded.

A pistol cocked, and Josef braced for the sound of gunfire. It didn't come. Instead, he heard shuffling feet and then the apartment door closed. The threat had apparently had the intended effect.

There was no doubt in Josef's mind what was being asked of him. He looked down at the woman in the bed, her hair matted, her breath labored. A wet cloth lay next to the bed that someone had likely used to mop her brow. She let out a cough that rattled the bag of marbles in her chest. She turned her head toward him and asked, "Could you get me some water, please?" She gave a small wave with her hand.

Josef stood, staring, realizing that this room had become an important place, marking a key moment in his life. He paid attention to the old, tattered curtains moving slightly in the breeze. He noticed the lone picture on the wall, which looked like a wedding photo, perhaps the old woman's. He saw the swirled pattern of a water stain on the wall behind the bed.

There was no sound in the apartment. Hans and Captain Schmidt had not returned from bringing the family down to the ground level, sending them with another unit to be escorted to the train. He entered the other room and found a small pitcher with water and a ceramic cup. He filled the cup and brought it to the old woman, lifting her head so she could drink. She sipped lightly and laid her head back down. "Thank you, dear." She closed her eyes and turned her head, still breathing loudly.

"This is Günter's moment," Josef said softly to himself. "It is one way or the other." He removed his pistol from its holster and looked at it closely. "Such a small thing this is to have such power to change a life." He slowly placed the barrel under his chin and pointed it up. He imagined the angle of Günter's rifle. Would his hole be in the same spot? There was a sound in the hallway, then the outer door to the apartment opened. The bedroom door was closed. He had seconds to decide. Josef picked up the moist cloth from the side of the bed and dabbed the old woman's brow. She smiled. He draped the cloth over her face, pointed his pistol at the center of the cloth, and fired.

CHAPTER 18
VERSTECKEN UND SUCHEN: HIDE AND SEEK
1941

The Einsatzgruppen spent weeks clearing Jewish slums and moving people to the trains. The German soldiers referred to the destination as *work camps*, but Josef heard several Jews call them *death camps*. Captain Schmidt would repeat the slogan used by all of the SS: *Arbeit macht frei*, or "work sets you free." Josef did not believe that these people whom he pulled from their encampments were ever going to be free. In a way, it comforted him to know they were not likely to survive anyway. It made his task easier. He had shot three more people, all men, since the old woman in her bed. He told himself that he had spared her a painful end and that the three men may have been spared a painful death at the camps.

Josef had cried himself to sleep the night he shot the old woman. He even retrieved Bärli in the dark of night, pulled him under the covers, and spoke to him quietly. The first man he shot had pushed past him and tried to run. He had no choice. The second had tried to tackle Hans, and the third screamed and cursed until they could not take it any longer. He never enjoyed it, as some others in the ranks seemed to, but it was getting easier to sleep. After the last shooting, he actually forgot about it by bedtime, then recalled it again the next morning after a good sleep.

Having cleared the Jewish housing zones, their unit had been assigned a new task: finding and arresting Jews in hiding, as well as those who harbored them. They would receive leads from the SS in the morning and spend their days following those leads.

It was early June, 1941. The unit was on their way to the town of Olching, outside of Munich. They rode in a military transport that had bench seats along each side. Hans sat next to Josef, as he always did, and talked most of the way.

"I have killed six Jews. I think that is most in the unit," he boasted. "If they would just learn to comply, I wouldn't have to do it, but I won't hesitate—bam—I will put a bullet in their head." He mocked a gun with his finger to pantomime the act.

Josef did not respond. He noticed that the less he talked, the more Hans seemed to seek his approval.

"How many is it for you?"

"I don't count." He did, in fact, know it was four, but felt uneasy turning this into a game.

"I think it's four for you." Hans paused. "But who knows, you may have killed more when I wasn't looking." Then he laughed.

Josef gave no response. The truck came to a rumbling stop and Captain Schmidt, who had been riding in the cab, stepped out of the passenger side door. He told the driver to stay there and await further instructions.

"Men. Today, you get to be real Einsatzgruppen. You will be sent in pairs to four different locations where we have received information about Jews in hiding. This town has too many liberal Germans. Too many who don't love the fatherland and break the law, harboring Jews. Today, we send a message." He paced back and forth like a lion in a cage. "This town is only three miles by four, easy to hike. You will use your skills learned in training as well as what you have learned while clearing the slums."

Josef's heart pounded. He knew he would be paired with Hans, as Schmidt believed in keeping pairs together to build teamwork and brotherhood. Would the two of them, teenagers, be sent to round up and arrest Jews alone?

"These traitors who harbor Jews will be arrested. And these Jews that think they are so smart and avoid work must not realize that Olching is halfway to Dachau from Munich. They made the trip shorter." Schmidt let out a hearty laugh, which the unit echoed. "I will travel with Horst and Walter. You will each have a radio, allowing you to confirm when you are ready for pick up." Come collect your assignments.

That was it then; they really were going to be on their own today. Hans and Josef were assigned a farmhouse near a lake. The SS had been alerted that Jews may be hidden in the barn. The farm owners were known sympathizers who had perhaps been too outspoken in their contempt for the treatment of the Jews.

Captain Schmidt handed the papers to Josef and addressed both soldiers. "I'm proud of you both. Josef, you have come a long way. I knew what you could be, and now you have become the best version of yourself. A true German."

Josef felt a strange mix of pride and revulsion at the words. He realized that he did truly crave the captain's approval, but he knew his father would not want him to be the version of himself that Schmidt described. He simply responded, "Thank you, sir."

It was a warm day with a light breeze. Josef and Hans walked along a dirt path toward Olchinger See (Lake Olching). Beech trees surrounded the path, and the light breeze swayed the lush green leaves, creating a kaleidoscope of light and shapes on the ground. Another day, Josef thought, where the beauty of the moment felt so at odds with the ugliness of the work at hand.

Hans was talking about the people he had killed or roughed up and planning how he would do the same today when Josef stopped walking and faced him. "What's wrong? Did you see something?" Hans asked as he swung his head around to look.

"What did you do with Lilli?"

"What?" Hans looked confused.

"What did you do with the Jewish girl in the apartment that first day, the one Schmidt let you *interrogate?*"

Hans laughed, "Are you jealous?"

"No." Josef looked deadly serious.

"Are you serious?" Hans paused. "Whatever I did, she loved it. I can tell you that." He attempted a confident look, but it failed as he stared back and could not hold Josef's gaze.

Josef stepped forward and grabbed Hans by the front of his uniform and lifted him, so his toes were barely touching the ground and Josef was supporting most of his weight. He stared into Hans's eyes but said nothing. Hans's face twisted into an expression of outrage. He opened his mouth to speak but said nothing. After a moment, Josef released his grip and walked on.

They walked in silence for the next half hour and then reached the water. The lake was calm. The trees on the far side cast a clear reflection in the water with the slight movement of the water appearing to make the trees sway gently. Josef pulled out the map and confirmed that the farmhouse would be a quarter mile up the right side from where they stood. He started to walk on, but Hans grabbed his arm. "Is this going to be a problem?"

"No. We have a job to do. But we won't be interrogating any girls today."

"OK, but we have to cover each other there. We could be up against ten people. I won't hesitate to …"

"I know. You will shoot."

"If there is no other way."

At those words, Josef had a pang of pain in his heart. He just nodded.

As they reached the edge of the farm property, they crawled behind a cart at the edge of the field from where they could see the farmhouse and barn in the distance. It provided enough cover not to be easily spotted but allowed them to look at the farmhouse and barn from under the wooden cart, which had a clearance of about one meter. The barn stood about three hundred meters ahead and to the left, while the farmhouse was about the same distance ahead and to the right. The two structures were about one hundred meters apart. Both structures were sided with unpainted, vertical wood planks. The farmhouse was a single-story, rectangular home that appeared to be only large enough for a bedroom and living area. It took only minutes until they saw activity at the house. A woman walked outside with clothes or towels and began hanging them on a line.

"We must go to the house first," Josef reasoned. "We must be sure the owners have no guns to come after us in the barn. We can also question them about the Jews."

"Yes. That makes sense." Hans nodded in agreement.

"We also can't be seen approaching the house from the vantage point of the barn. If the Jews see us, they will run. There are only two of us, so we would not be able to chase in all directions." Josef rubbed his chin, thinking through the logistics. "And we must not separate from each other, no matter what happens."

Hans again nodded his agreement. "How shall we approach without being seen? The fields are cut low."

"We will back out the way we approached and then circle far to that side." Josef waved to the right of the farmhouse. When we are far enough away, we will approach the house so that the barn is behind it and the house hides us from the barn."

"That's what I was thinking also." Both boys knew Josef was the smarter of the two, but it was not something Hans would admit freely, and Josef never pointed it out either.

They carefully backtracked, keeping the cart between them and the barn as long as they could. When they were far enough back, they started to circle around. As they approached the farmhouse, a man emerged with a rifle. As soon as he saw the uniforms and armbands, he leaned the rifle against the house, put his hands up, and smiled.

"Good morning, sirs."

"Heil Hitler," Hans responded, throwing his right hand up at a forty-five-degree angle.

"Oh yes, of course, Heil Hitler," the man responded with a quick and ineffective salute. He looked to be in his fifties with shaggy white hair. He wore a bathrobe and house shoes.

Josef stepped forward. "Is there anyone else in the house?"

"My wife."

"And no one else?"

"No. What is this about?"

"Please lead us inside, so we may look. Leave the rifle where it stands."

They walked in and the man called out, "Hildi, we have guests." A woman emerged from the bedroom. She had short-cut salt-and-pepper hair and wore a light brown frock.

"You are Karl and Hilda Weber, yes?"

Karl nodded as he reached for Hilda's hand.

"Are there any more guns in the house?"

They both shook their heads to indicate there were none.

"And the Jews are in the barn?" Josef stared at Karl as he asked.

Karl gripped Hilda's hand more firmly, which Josef noticed, and shook his head again.

"So, when we go to your barn and search right now, there will be no Jews. Or will we need to add *lying to the Einsatzgruppen* to your charges?" Josef paused and softened his voice. "You want to keep them safe, yes? The best way to do that is to lead us to the barn so they are not startled, causing us to shoot them."

Karl looked at Hilda. They leaned together, their foreheads touching, and she began to cry. Karl said, "I will take you."

"Your wife comes as well so we know no one is unaccounted for."

The four of them walked to the barn with Hans and Josef behind Karl and Hilda, pistols drawn. Karl approached a small side door to the barn. It was deadly quiet inside. He looked back at Josef with a pleading expression, but Josef just nodded toward the door. Karl knocked twice quickly, paused, and then knocked twice again quickly. There was scurrying inside, the sound of panic. They listened for a moment longer and then heard a door open on the opposite side of the barn.

Josef looked at Hans, who wore a confused expression. "The knock was a warning, Hans." Josef turned and struck Karl on his head with the butt of his pistol and began to run around the far side. He saw six people running across the field. Two adults with two children were about fifty meters away. Another two adults were much closer. The woman was running slowly and awkwardly with the man pulling at her and urging her along. Hans aimed and shot. The woman dropped and the man yelled in agony. At the sound of gunfire and the man's scream, the four Jews who were farther across the field stopped and then started back toward the woman, now lying face down, away from where Hans and Josef stood.

As they approached the woman on the ground, the two adults and two children approached from the other direction. The man who was urging the woman to run faster was on top of her, yelling, "No, no, no, no." He convulsed and sobbed loudly.

They could now see the reason she ran slowly. This woman was pregnant and fairly far along. The man rolled her over, still sobbing loudly. She was a petite woman and no older than her late teens. Blood oozed from the front of her neck, where the bullet had exited. The man repeated, "No, no, no," but these were no longer sobs. They were angry retorts, getting louder with each repeated word as if pressure were building. Then it erupted. He lunged at Hans. Caught off guard, Hans fell over backward with the man on top of him, a hail of fists coming at him. Josef pointed his gun and fired; the man's body went limp on top of Hans. The man who had run back from the field ran forward, toward Hans and the man on the ground and said, "My so ..." His words were cut short by a bullet to his head.

Behind Josef there were cries of anguish, and he spun around to see Karl and Hilda charging in his direction. He fired four shots. He was unsure which, or how many struck them, but both fell to the ground. He spun back around and pointed his gun at the woman who returned from the field. She had fallen to her knees and held both children under her arms, shielding them. Josef's hand shook. The woman sobbed and cried out words of pain. Most could not be understood through her tortured cries, but Josef heard her say, "You are a demon."

* * *

They radioed the truck for pick up. Their three surviving Jews sat ten meters away in the open field. There was no risk of an escape now. Josef and Hans sat on the ground. Hans said, "I guess you passed me now." Josef glared at him, and Hans immediately knew it was the wrong thing to say.

"What could I do? He came at you, and I had to ... then the other man, his father ran to you, or to him, I don't know ... but it happened fast, and I had to. Then the damned farmers running up behind me like that? There was no other way." As he said those last words, they stung. But he repeated them anyway. *There was no other way.*

* * *

In the days that followed, they found more Jews, more traitors harboring them. They were fortunate that no shooting had been required in more than a week. Josef had not slept more than a few hours any night since the Olching farm. He replayed the events in his head, each time hoping to reach the conclusion that he did what he had to do; each time failing. He pulled his bear under his covers each night, no longer even worrying if he would be seen. The coarse cellulose fibers left a rash on his skin by morning, but it gave him comfort. He would tell Bärli what had happened that day and the bear never judged him.

With the *success* they had achieved, according to Captain Schmidt, Josef and Hans were always given the strongest leads and left to work independently as the captain supervised other teams. The result at the farm in Olching had solidified them as a top-tier team.

It was a sweltering day in July. Team assignments were passed out. Josef and Hans would be transported to Waldstrasse (Forrest Street) on the east side of Munich. The SS received a tip from a neighbor that five Jews were being hidden in a cellar; several adults and a teenage girl. As soon as he read the papers, Josef turned to Hans, but he did not get a word out.

"I know, we won't *interrogate* the girl," Hans said, preemptively.

Josef nodded. He thought about the lines he drew, where and when he took a stand. He was not sure any of it made sense. He had killed so many people. He shot the two farmers in Olching because he was startled when they came from behind. He shot the older man there, who lunged at Hans, but he knew now that he was just moving to embrace his fallen son. He shot an old woman in her bed because she could not make the trip on the train. But if he could protect a girl, keep her from being forced into sex, perhaps he could hold onto some piece of himself. Perhaps his father would be proud of at least this small thing.

They arrived at Waldstrasse and located the house. It was ten in the morning and already the hot sun cut through their uniforms. "The neighbor said the Jews are in the cellar. There is an entrance at the back of the house. They have rarely seen anyone go in or out, but they have seen people there a few times and have heard sounds from the cellar." Josef paused. "We will approach the traitors first. Hans nodded.

Josef knocked softly on the front door. He did not want to alert anyone in the basement to a problem. A man came to the door. He was dressed in a loose-fitting shirt with large sweat stains on the chest and under the arms. A woman stood several paces behind him wearing a frock of thin material that clung to her in the heat. Both were in their fifties.

"Hubert and Maria Schiffers?" Josef stated, with just a hint of a question in his tone.

"Yes, I am Hubert. This is my wife, Ria."

"Please step outside and make no noise on the floor as you do so," Hans said while drawing his pistol and pointing it at Hubert to emphasize the consequence of not heeding the order.

"Of course. What is the problem, sir?"

After they were all outside, Josef spoke softly. "I know you have Jews in your cellar. I am not even going to ask you." He paused and observed the flinch on Hubert's face and the glance that his wife threw toward him. If he did not know before, he did now. "You will lead us to the back door now, quietly."

The four walked to the back. Hans and Josef behind Hubert

and Maria. They walked slowly, cautiously. Maria kept glancing at her husband, appearing worried about what he might do.

"Stop here," Josef ordered when they were three meters from the door. He nodded to Hans. "My associate has a gun to your wife's head. You are going to walk to the door with me and give the knock that you have prearranged with the Jews inside, so that they know it is safe."

Hubert turned and nodded. His perspiration had doubled from the combined effects of the oppressive heat and the tension of the moment. "Please don't harm them, they simply sought safety here."

"You have all broken the law. Whether we hurt anyone is up to you now." Josef leveled his stare at Hubert. "You will do them one last kindness by providing the correct knock. It will help keep them safe. If they run or attack, they will be shot, as will your wife."

Hubert broke down crying. Through sobs he pleaded, "They are just people, like you and me."

Hans broke in with a raised voice, "They are not like me. I am a pure German. These vermin are not like me, and you are not like me. You are a traitor to your race."

Josef held a hand up to Hans. "We must not alarm them." He then nodded to Hubert, "Now—the correct knock."

Hubert walked to the door, his shoulders slumped, perspiration running from his neck down his back. He knocked three times, paused, then once more. After a moment, the door opened, and he said, "I'm sorry."

Josef pushed past Hubert and pressed the barrel of his pistol to the forehead of the man who had answered the door. He was a head shorter than Josef and had a thick, black beard. He pushed forward, forcing the man to back into the room. The cellar was about seven meters square, side-to-side and back-to-front. Three other people were present, a tall man and woman with a shorter teen girl in front of them. The man and woman had wrapped their arms around the girl and stood frozen. Josef asked, "Is there anyone else here?"

"No," said the bearded man. "There is no need for the gun. We will cause you no trouble."

Josef kept the gun out but backed away. The barrel left a circular impression on the bearded man's forehead. "Names."

"I am Max Biermann." Motioning with his hand, he added, "This is Otto Eisen; his wife, Ursula; and their daughter, Karin."

"Biermann," Josef said softly as if trying to recall a memory. "Is there no one else here? Do you have a wife?"

"Sadly, no."

Max then looked past Josef, out the door at Hubert and Ria and began to address them. "Are you the owners of this house?" The Schiffers nodded, showing confusion on their faces. "We apologize for breaking in here and staying in your cellar. We were desperate, with nowhere to go, but it does not excuse what we have done." Max bowed his head with a look of contrition.

Josef looked at Hans, who seemed bewildered. He then looked back at Max, who met his eye readily. It was a look of pleading. He stared into Josef's eyes and nodded his head almost imperceptibly. "Hans, I need to interrogate this Jew. Watch the group, including the Schiffers." Hans nodded. Josef grabbed Max by the collar and led him outside with a gun to his back.

Once outside, he spun Max around to face him. "Do you think I am stupid? The Schiffers knew the secret knock for the door. When I confronted them about Jews in their basement, I could tell immediately they knew. Why are you lying?" Josef's voice rose as the words came out and his hand shook with the gun pointed at Max's chest.

Max held his hands up and shook his head. "I don't think you are stupid. It's quite clear you are not. And because you are not stupid, you know what will become of me and of the Eisens." He looked straight into Josef's eyes. "I don't think that has to be the Schiffers' fate. There is enough suffering." He nodded his head slightly. "I don't think you are stupid, young man—I think you are kind." He paused. "And I think you are smart enough to find another way."

The words rocked Josef, and he took a step back. It was as if this man was inside his head—as if he knew of Günter—knew the words that have haunted Josef since his first days in the military. He couldn't know, of course, but those words. Could there be *another way*?

Josef stared at Max for a long time before leading him back into the cellar. He turned to the Schiffers and ordered, "Get back in your house." He then called Hans outside and declared, "We are taking in the Jews."

"What of the traitors? Don't tell me you believed that Jew."

"We will take in the Jews. That is our primary objective. We will tell Schmidt that they broke in. Look, the lock is broken." Josef closed the door and then kicked the handle with his heavy boot. The door broke open, sending splinters flying. Turning back to Hans, he put a hand on his shoulder and added, "Are you with me, Brother?" It was a gambit. Would Hans's desire for Josef's approval outweigh his need to be seen as an elite member of the Einsatzgruppen?

Hans stared at Josef, swallowed hard, then replied, "Yes, Brother."

CHAPTER 19
SYMPATHISANT: SYMPATHIZER
1940

The home on Dachauerstrasse was mostly empty now, in June of 1940. Max and Gerda had sold most of their possessions in order to survive. With no income from the store that had been stolen from them, Max earned money as a day laborer, when he could find work.

Gerda sold her handmade goods on the street. She had repurposed a bread crate and one of Max's old belts to form a makeshift basket that she slung with the belt around her shoulders and the crate resting against her belly. She made fine knit and crocheted goods that she sold for a fraction of their worth. German customers knew she had no bargaining power. At times, people would simply take what they wanted and walk away without paying, knowing she had no recourse. But there were those who looked at her with sadness and kindness in their eyes, sometimes paying more than she asked. She felt she had learned more about the good and evil in humanity in the past years than in all her life before.

Gerda returned home in the dying light of an evening in early June. The sun set near nine p.m., so she assessed it was perhaps nine thirty. She had a long, successful day selling her goods. The booties, sweaters, and doll clothes she had sold that day took most of the week to make. But she had earned enough today to feed herself and Max for the next two weeks, so she figured she came out ahead.

She rounded the corner of their building and looked up at the looming outline of the four-story building against the navy-colored sky. Crows sat perched along the rooftop, cutting sharp silhouettes against the sky. A group of children played hopscotch on the walkway as she passed. The sound of children's voices still made her smile, even now. She reflected. *Today was a good day.*

Gerda scurried up the single flight of stairs that led to her home and swung the door open. Max sat on a crate he had salvaged from the alley behind their building. It was dark in the room, lit only by fading light from outside coming in through their two windows. Electricity was a luxury they could not afford. While it was now bare, this had been a beautiful home at one time. On the walls there was a single picture: the two of them, young, smiling, on their wedding day.

"No work today, my love. I'm sorry." He shook his head, not looking up.

"Well, I almost sold out, so it's OK. We will go to the market tomorrow and get what we need for the week. I'll pick up more yarn too."

"You are a marvel. What could I have ever done to be this lucky ..." He smiled half-heartedly.

"We are both very lucky."

Max pressed his hands to his head. "Lucky," he repeated. "They take everything." His voice cracked.

Gerda saw his pain. Over the past two years, they had taken it in turn, alternately losing hope or being the one to lift the other's spirits. But lately, Max was slipping deeper into darkness. The man she loved was in a pain she understood but could not heal.

She walked to him, put her hands on his cheeks, and kissed his forehead. Then she walked toward the bed, pulled her frock over her head, and stood naked before him. In the dim light, she was just an outline of curves. "They cannot take everything, my love."

* * *

The morning light streamed into the room. Max and Gerda lay naked on top of the sheets to keep cool. They heard a commotion outside the building and ran to the window. There were German soldiers outside, dozens of them, armed. They might have been SS or the Einsatzgruppen. Some of their neighbors were outside as well. The air was filled with the sounds of chaos, soldiers yelling, mothers screaming for their children, running feet. They tried to understand what was being said, but it was difficult to distill any one voice in the confusion.

Max caught sight of his downstairs neighbor, Herbert Zimmerman, engaged in a heated argument with one of the soldiers. Herbert's wife, Elisabeth, was holding their two young daughters, both under four years of age. He could not make out the words. Elisabeth turned and started to walk briskly back toward the building. A soldier cut off her path and grabbed her arm. Max and Gerda could hear her yell distinctly amongst all the clamor. Herbert rushed at the soldier and pushed him to the ground. Then he held his hands up, looking as if he were trying to explain something.

The whole scene seemed surreal. Max and Gerda were frozen. They felt as if they were watching a drama unfold on a movie screen. Then they caught site of a large German soldier, he looked like an officer, as he wore a different uniform than the other men. He had a square jaw, and his muscles puckered the uniform shirt he wore. He strode with purpose, quickly closing the thirty meters' distance between himself, Herbert, and the soldier that Herbert was arguing with. As he came behind Herbert, he drew a pistol and shot him in the back of the head. His body fell awkwardly to the ground and folded forward in a way that no living body would fall. He was dead before he even hit the ground. It was a sickening scene. One that Max and Gerda immediately knew would be burned into their memories forever. Elisabeth shrieked and fell to her knees. Both girls were screaming.

The officer calmly holstered his weapon, stood to the side, and extended his right arm, showing Elisabeth where she was expected to go. She rose, shaking, and walked as instructed.

Max looked about the room frantically, trying to think of what they would take with them. He saw nothing he cared about until his eyes landed on their only photo hanging on the wall. He walked in front of it to look closer. It hung slightly askew, so he straightened it and stared. It was their wedding day. The happy couple standing in the center of the frame, blurry figures in the background that would be unknown to anyone but them.

Still shaking from what he had seen out the window, he said. "It seems like another life. Such joy."

Gerda hugged him from behind. They each felt the tremor in each other's bodies. With a slight quake in her voice, she said, "If that was like another life, then someday this will feel like another life too."

Max took a deep breath, straightened his shoulder then removed the photo from the wall. He put it under his right arm, taking Gerda's right hand in his left, and walked to the door. A German soldier was about to knock when they opened the door.

It was a young boy, under eighteen. He pulled a paper from his pocket and began to read aloud. His voice broke slightly as he read the words: "You are instructed to leave these premises. They are required by your government. You must leave all of your possessions behind. As a kindness, your government has provided housing at the address on this card." He then handed Max a card with an address.

"Thank you, sir. May I take this photo with me, please?" Max smiled and nodded his head in respect.

The boy looked surprised, likely expecting more confrontation. "Um ... Yes ... I think that's OK."

"Thank you." Max and Gerda walked out of the building and did not look back as they turned left and kept walking down Dachauerstrasse.

* * *

When they had reached a safe distance, Max turned to Gerda. "You know we can't go to the housing they offered."

"I know."

"As they fill up, they send people by train to work camps." He shook his head. "I doubt many return." He took Gerda's hands. "I have a way for us to hide while we work through what to do next. Do you remember Hubert Schiffers?"

"I don't think so."

"He is the man who replaced our glass at the store." He paused. "Many times."

"OK."

"Well, I spoke with him during those times. He sympathized with the Jews. He confided that he hated Hitler almost as much as we do. A dangerous thing for him to tell me. Well, I saw him last week."

"How? Where?" Gerda was growing anxious. She knew her husband built friendships with many different people but worried that he would trust the wrong person and put himself in danger.

"I was looking for work. He needed a day laborer and hired me for a window installation. He told me that he knew Jews who were driven out of their homes and that he was not willing to stand by and let good people suffer. He gave me his address and told me to call on him if we were in need."

"We hear of spies. Are you sure he is not ..."

"Yes," Max interrupted. "I know this man. He is good."

* * *

The homes on Waldstrasse looked like many others near Munich center: close together, narrow, two-story structures. Beech trees with bright green leaves lined the thin strip of grass in front of the homes that stood just five meters from the road. Gerda paced nervously on the opposite side of the street from the Schiffers' home as Max approached the front door at 217 Waldstrasse and gave a light rap. A few moments later, Gerda saw a woman in her fifties answer the door. She only poked her head out slightly and then closed the door. Gerda's heart sank.

Max stayed by the door. About a minute later, a man,

also in his fifties, poked his head out and said a few words to Max. Max walked away from the door and started to make his way back across the street when the man emerged again and shouted, "And don't come back here, you dirty Jew!" He slammed the front door.

"What happened? I thought this man was your friend."

"Shhh, my dear. Just keep walking. Everything is arranged."

Gerda gave him a confused look but just walked on. When they reached the next block, Max smiled at her and asked, "Did you enjoy the show?"

"Aah, I see." She smiled. "So, what do we do next?"

"We go to the back of the house when it's dark."

* * *

At eleven that evening, it seemed sufficiently dark, and the road was quiet. Gerda and Max slipped to the rear of the house where there was a small stone stairway, just five steps, down to the cellar. Max smiled at Gerda, "I have the secret code." He rubbed his hands together and tried to behave like a secret agent. He knocked three times, then paused, followed by a single knock. The door opened and they slipped inside.

To Max's surprise, neither Hubert Schiffers nor his wife greeted them. Instead, it looked to be a family of three. Looking around the dirt-floor basement, it became clear that this family had been living here. They were also Jewish refugees.

"Hello. My name is Otto Eisen." A gray-haired man with a bushy gray beard greeted them at the door, speaking in a low voice. A light hung over the door on the outside, but the interior was dark, making it difficult to make out his features. "Please step inside." As they entered, they saw two more figures. "This is my wife, Ursula. You can call her Ullie; and our daughter, Karin."

Ullie was a tall woman in her late forties. She stood straight with impeccable posture, giving her an even taller appearance. She wore her hair pinned up and looked like a serious woman, with a steely gaze, but when she spoke her voice was kind. "Welcome to you both," she said, leaning forward and extending both hands. "To your new home, such as it is."

Karin was fifteen and had a warm, inviting smile. She was shorter than both of her parents and wore shoulder-length brown hair and a simple gray dress. She surprised Gerda by hugging her in greeting, then did the same with Max.

"Why don't you show them around, Karin?" Ullie suggested.

Karin smiled. "Of course." She bowed and joked, "Welcome to the Waldstrasse Inn. It is our great pleasure to receive you." Then she giggled. The room had a dirt floor and a ceiling less than two meters high. Otto and Ullie stood only slightly clear of the beams, but the rest of them had more room above their heads. In total, the room was a square, about seven meters each way. "You know the code-knock already. This is the only way we can open the door. In the back corner we have two barrels of water. The left is to drink, and the right is to bathe."

Gerda glanced at Max when she heard bathing mentioned. How could they bathe in this small room with so many people there?

Sensing the unspoken question, Karin added, "We turn away for each other to bathe. Mostly, we use a rag to wipe ourselves down. You will appreciate that we have that barrel, as my father can smell quite bad if he skips even a day." She glanced at her father with a playful smile, and he shook his head and held his arms apart in feigned insult.

"Next is the sleeping quarters. Well, we have been using these." Karin pointed to two single cot mattresses lying on the floor. "You may take one of these, and I will sleep on the floor."

"No. We couldn't," Gerda argued.

"It's OK. I have some extra clothes that I will make some padding from." She shifted the subject quickly. "Let's talk food. The Schiffers rarely come down but look above you now." They looked up. They were near the center of the room. They could make out a square cutout in the floorboards between two beams. "This is where they pass us bread, fruit, sometimes some meat, and buckets of fresh water. As you already know, they are very kind people, but they do not like to take unnecessary risks."

Otto added in, "They told us this afternoon of your impending arrival. They called down through the hatch in the floor. They also said you would be the last. I think Hubert would take in all the Jews." He let out a small laugh. "But Ria, his wife, is scared. I don't blame her. They have taken an incredible risk for us all."

* * *

The group sat on crates in a circle and talked softly until well past midnight. Max talked of the store and bragged about Gerda's skills with a needle. Gerda shared the story of their neighbor, Herbert. She wept as she told the story and when she looked up, with a tear-streaked face, she saw that all four people with her in the basement were weeping as well.

"I'm sorry. I should speak of something more fitting for meeting new friends."

Ullie reached her hand across the circle and squeezed Gerda's hand. "I don't think we can avoid these stories now."

Gerda wiped her tears. "Ullie, tell me about your life before all this."

"Well, the first thing is to say we are a family of five, not three." She gave a sad smile to Otto, who patted her leg in reply. "We have two boys; Jacob is twenty-four; Heinrick is twenty-two. They left Germany more than a year ago. They were headed to England. It's been six months since we have had any correspondence, because we are here." She shrugged and gave a small laugh. "I mean if the mail could find us, we are not very well hidden."

Otto joined in. "It is our greatest lament that we did not let them take Karin. We thought she was too young, better off with us." He looked at his daughter. "I'm sorry, my dear."

"This is where I want to be, Papi. It is OK." She smiled at her parents and then looked at Max and Gerda. "Besides, I would have missed all of this."

When they settled for bed on their thin, single mattress on the floor, Gerda whispered into Max's ear. "You did this. You kept us safe because you are so wonderful at judging people and making friends. I know you are disappointed. We will both miss our home, but that place is not all we are, just as the store was not. We met fine people today. I'm happy to be here with you."

Max squeezed his wife tightly. "You know, I think it's my turn to lift your spirits, so I would appreciate you being a little more depressed." He smiled.

"Perhaps tomorrow."

CHAPTER 20
HEIMWÄRTS: HOMEWARD
1957

Dieter sat in his blue upholstered chair, stone-faced as Friedrich recounted what he and Sigrid had learned so far. Sigrid was uncharacteristically quiet, sitting in a chair in the Becker living room, watching Friedrich's father.

"So, the only real lead we have is what Sigrid found on my intake form, a woman's name, Amalie, and a location in Mönchengladbach. She even found that there were two applications for my adoption back in 1945. She has been so helpful." Friedrich smiled and nodded toward his girlfriend.

Dieter thought for a moment, then turned to face the girl. "So, Sigrid, you work at the Munich Orphanage."

"Yes, Herr Becker. I have been a resident there all my life. Now I work there."

"And you are authorized to share all of this information?"

She hesitated to answer and then replied, "I am granted access to the records for my job, sir. I do like helping people."

"Would you be going on this trip to Mönchengladbach that my son is proposing?"

"Yes, sir."

"Is that part of your job?"

"No, sir." She paused and stuck a hand out to her left, reaching for Friedrich, who looked at her with surprise but slowly put his hand out and took hers. "I like Friedrich. He is my friend, and I want to help him."

Leaning forward in his chair, Dieter held Sigrid's gaze. She did not look away. After an awkwardly long pause, he broke the silence. "Very well. You will have to leave bright and early in order to make it there and back in one day. I'll help with the train schedule and provide a street map of the location so you can walk from the train efficiently."

Friedrich and Sigrid exchanged surprised glances, then nodded agreement.

* * *

It was a Saturday in mid-October. The plans had been drawn up, and Dieter waited with Friedrich and Sigrid at the Munich train station. As boarding was called, Friedrich hugged his father and thanked him. He knew this was difficult for him, but he also knew that his father was proud of him for following through with his plans. Sigrid then hugged Dieter, which caught him off guard. He held his arms out, surprised, seeming not to know what to do, then lightly patted her back.

Sigrid had never been outside of Munich, and Friedrich had not ventured outside of the metro area in all the time he could remember. The train ride was an adventure for them both and they stayed glued to the windows, pointing out every hilltop, bird, or brown hare they saw.

After a change of trains in Köln, Sigrid drifted to sleep. Friedrich watched her face and smiled at how it rested awkwardly against the window. He had only known this girl for a few weeks but already realized what he had missed in not having close friends. His father had been right that he needed to make more *associations*. He already couldn't imagine not knowing her.

The train rattled to a stop in Mönchengladbach. The two travelers walked out into the station wide-eyed. It was a new city, a new place to explore. The station looked similar but smaller than the one they left in Munich. Leaving the station, they saw drab streets that appeared to have recovered less from the war than Munich. It was clear that this was a working-class town with old buildings in need of repair. There were no elaborately carved statues in the squares and few buildings with architecture worth noting. The buildings looked like salt boxes stacked in a row.

They read the map on which Dieter had carefully drawn a walking path for them. The document, with its perfectly drawn lines and marked distances, reflected his engineer's approach. Following his instructions, they reached Schiller Platz in five minutes.

Friedrich stopped at the corner of the Platz and stared ahead, then looked back instinctively at the third floor of the building behind them. A feeling of familiarity washed over him. "I played here," he said slowly, pointing to the grassy square with its ragged bushes on the corners. "I think my mother watched me from there." He turned and pointed to the third floor. "That must be Kaiserstrasse."

They looked for a sign and studied the map and it was, indeed, Kaiserstrasse.

"You remember your mother, then?"

"I don't know if I would say that. It's more like I remember being here and feeling her watch me. I cannot picture her. And I have no memory of a father."

"Do you know which was your door on the third floor? There are several."

"No. I'm afraid I don't."

"There, on the first floor, a piano store. Let's ask there; see if someone remembers you."

As they walked toward the store, everything around Friedrich felt like a living memory, as if the moments he spent here echoed all around him. He walked slowly, as if pushing through the remnants of the past he felt all around him. His steps felt awkward and forced. He reached the store and pushed open the door, on which was emblazoned the name Van Doren, in gold lettering. Seeing the array of handsome pianos with beautiful, stained wood, Friedrich felt Minna's presence like a blending of his different lives into one. No one came to the front of the store immediately, so he sat down at a dark wood studio upright piano with an ornate design on the panel above the keyboard. He always felt at peace with his fingers resting on the keys. He could feel Minna's hands atop his own as he struck the C-sharp that began "Moonlight Sonata", another song by her favorite composer, Beethoven.

As he played the notes in half-time, the way his mother liked it, Sigrid held her breath. The notes poured out of the instrument, filling the small store with the beautiful, haunting sound of Beethoven. As he finished, Sigrid stared silently. A voice came from behind them, "Surprising skill from such a young man. Who taught you to play so beautifully?"

"My mother," Friedrich replied, not yet turning to see whom the voice belonged to. "Well, my adoptive mother," he added, remembering what they came to ask the shopkeeper. He turned on the small bench seat to see a short man, about equal to Sigrid's height, with salt-and-pepper gray hair and a matching thin mustache. He wore a charcoal-colored suit and white shirt with no tie. "We have actually come to find my birth mother."

"I was rather hoping you came for a piano," the man said through a smile. "I don't think I can help you find your mother."

Sigrid joined in. "Was your store here during the war? Were you working here?"

"My dear, my name is Herbert Van Doren. I am the owner and only employee here. I have been here for more than twenty years."

"Wonderful, then you may know a woman who lived on the third floor during the war. She would have had a small child, perhaps three years old in 1944 or the start of 1945?"

Van Doren's face turned as white as his shirt as he looked back and forth at the two young people before him. Then his face twisted into a snarl, as he barked, "Who sent you here? Get out of my store."

The reaction startled Friedrich, causing him to stand quickly. It was the wrong impulse, as Van Doren looked threatened and pointed to the door, repeating his demand that they leave.

As they reached the door, Friedrich turned. He had to make one more plea. "I beg your pardon, sir. I was the boy who lived here. I just want to find my mother."

Van Doren's mouth dropped open, his expression changing

from anger and fear to wonder. He took a step forward, looking more closely at Friedrich. His face began to tremble, tears forming in his eyes. "It's, it's not possible," he stammered. "I saw them take you after they killed her. I knew for sure you had been killed too." He staggered backward, sat on a piano bench, and whispered, "I am so sorry."

"Can you tell me which apartment, please? And who did they kill? What was her name? Was she married?"

He pointed listlessly upward. "It's on the end there. Renate Brunst. No husband." Then he looked up and added, "You are really Friedrich?"

A wave of emotion hit Friedrich. He knew his name now—Friedrich Brunst. "Yes. I am Friedrich."

He took Sigrid's hand and walked from the store. They ascended the stairs in bounds. When they reached the door at the end of the third floor, Friedrich knocked. A young woman in her twenties answered the door. A baby cried from inside the apartment. "Hello. My name is Friedrich Brunst." A powerful feeling of belonging and purpose flowed over him as he said those words. "I used to live here, during the war. I have some memories I am trying to sort out. May I look inside, please?"

She looked suspiciously at him and then at Sigrid. "No. I don't know you. You cannot just knock on my door and expect to come into my home." She stepped back to close the door, but Sigrid put her foot in the opening.

"We are so sorry to intrude. It's just that Herbert, I mean Herr Van Doren, downstairs, told us you would be helpful. It will just take a moment." She pushed the door open as the woman watched, slack-jawed. Sigrid put an arm around her as she pulled Friedrich into the apartment. "You are so kind as to allow us in. Thank you."

There was a familiarity to the room, like a place from a dream that you could not fully remember. Friedrich was drawn to the back wall and stared at the paneled surface. "I think she hid me here," he said, sounding far away as he spoke slowly and softly, almost to himself.

The woman was holding her baby now, who had quieted. She stood behind Friedrich and Sigrid. "What do you mean? There is nothing there. I have lived here three years now, and ..."

Friedrich put his hands against the wall and felt the panel give slightly. He attempted to slide it to the right with no movement, then to the left. It shifted, and the weight of the panel leaned forward onto his arms. He lowered it and placed it on the floor.

"I swear, I never ..." The woman said, without finishing her thought as she stared at the small compartment behind the wall.

"I stayed in here a long time. Hiding. This is the box from my fairy tale dream. They shot my mother here." He heard the woman gasp. Friedrich peered into the small compartment and shuddered to think of being closed in there. "I think this is why I am afraid of closed spaces." He turned to Sigrid. "We know that at least part of my memory was real."

They left the apartment and walked slowly down the exterior stairway. Sigrid stopped on the landing between levels. "I'm so happy for you. So, now that you solved your mystery, I suppose you won't need me anymore."

"Thank you for coming here with me and for everything you have done. You know that you are my best friend." He smiled. "Don't get too full of yourself, though, because I don't really have any other friends. But the point is, I better keep the best one I have."

They returned to the piano store, hoping to get more information about Renate Brunst. They found Herbert Van Doren still sitting in the same place, his head in his hands. "Herr Van Doren, I hoped you could tell me more about my mother."

"I'm sorry, Friedrich. I did not know your mother," he replied softly, without looking up.

"But you told me her name and the apartment she lived in. You have been here twenty years. I don't understand."

"No, my boy, you do not." He looked up, his face streaked with tears. "Renate Brunst was not your mother."

Friedrich felt a bubble of confusion and anger rising in his chest. He had found his mother within the past hour and shed years of wondering. He learned his name at long last. Now this man was saying she was not his mother; this was not his name? "What are you saying?" he replied, his voice rising. "You told me she was killed, for being a Jew. I was hidden and taken by the same men who murdered her. Now what is it?" he yelled.

"Renate was not killed for being a Jew because she wasn't a Jew. She was killed for harboring you; for treason, or so they called it then. I'm sorry."

Friedrich put his hands to his head and was about to respond again when Sigrid stepped in front of him with her hands up. She rubbed his chest and nodded, signaling she would take over.

"Herr Van Doren, when did all of this take place?

"They came in November 1944. I will never forget it all my life."

"And how did Friedrich come to be here?"

"I don't know exactly. She was never with child though; I knew that much. One day I saw her cousin here. I think he was from Munich, but I don't know his name. Then, I started to hear a baby cry sometimes. That was back in the Spring of 1941. It wasn't until 1943 that she started letting the boy, you, I mean, outside. I suppose she thought by then that everyone believed it was her own son."

Sigrid stood up and motioned Friedrich toward the door. Van Doren still sat, weeping on the bench. "One more thing, Herr Van Doren," she said, turning back to him in the doorway. "Renate figured wrong, didn't she?"

"What?" He looked up at her with pleading eyes.

"Someone did know that Friedrich was not her son." She held his gaze as his lips trembled, then she walked out the door with Friedrich.

* * *

The walk to the train station in Mönchengladbach was quiet. As Friedrich processed the day's emotional swings, he became more discouraged. Sigrid watched him closely, holding back her urge to speak. Waiting on the train at the station, her resistance broke. "At least we have our next clue," she said, pausing for a response. "How many male cousins might Renate Brunst have in Munich?" Still no response from Friedrich. "What's more, we now know that you left here in November 1944 but did not arrive in Munich until the start of May 1945. We must learn where you were for all that time." She seemed excited by the mystery.

Friedrich turned away. She put a hand on his back, but he shook it off and barked, "You don't understand," his voice rising. "This is just a game to you. I've lost two mothers in just weeks; the one who cared for me here for more than three years and the one who raised me from a child."

Sigrid turned red and pushed Friedrich with all her strength. It rocked him back a step. "I don't understand?" she screamed. "I don't understand?" she shrieked louder. People at the station stopped what they were doing and watched. Friedrich felt their eyes on him, but she continued. "You have lost two mothers, yet there is still a third we have not found out about. That first mother may have died trying to protect you. She got you into hiding before the soldiers came, wherever she was. Then Renate loved you enough to die for you. Last, there was the mother you have known all these years, who loved and raised you with care."

Friedrich stood in stunned silence, waiting for the inevitable and obvious end of Sigrid's point. His heart sank, already knowing how wrong he was.

"Then there is me. The girl who was never adopted. The girl whose mother didn't care enough to find out if I was even taken into the orphanage. I am Sigrid Yorck. Do you know how I got my surname?"

Friedrich silently shook his head.

"The orphanage is on Waisenhausstrasse but right across the road from the side entrance is Yorckstrasse. That's where I was found. Left outside in a box. So, they named me Sigrid Yorck. Sigrid means *beautiful victory* and Yorck is the street I was found on. They saw it as a miracle that I was found and survived—a beautiful victory." As she stopped, her chest was heaving as if she had been running hard. Tears pooled in her eyes that looked more angry than sad.

There were no words worthy of a response, but Friedrich had to try to find them. After a long silence, he placed his hands on each of her shoulders and shook his head. "Oh, Sigrid ..."

"Stop," she interrupted, holding a hand up. "I don't need to hear it. I gave an excellent speech and now we both know that you are stupid. That's enough for me, so let's go get tea before the train comes. You are obviously paying, and you will also explain to me how I never knew that you were a piano virtuoso until today."

CHAPTER 21
HEIMKEHR: HOMECOMING
1943

The journey ahead was more frightening to Josef than going out on another assignment. He was going home. He would see his parents for the first time in nearly two years. He'd had many opportunities to go home but avoided them all. Schmidt demanded that he and Hans take this time off. Josef had refused it every time prior. He feared facing his father, not because he expected any scolding or punishment but because he expected kindness and caring. That would hurt more than any rebuke he could imagine. His mother would be bursting with pride. His father would see him as the same boy who left home, but Josef knew that he was not.

The military transport dropped him in the center of Freising where he began to walk. The town looked far too unchanged. It made him angry. There were the familiar signs of war: posters and banners with pro-war and pro-Hitler sentiments, but those were there even when he was at Gymnasium school. It was the unchanged look of things that felt at odds with the world he now understood. How could people be going to the market? How could the market itself look unchanged? Even the trees and the grass, their unvarying appearance felt like an insult to all of those who had died, or even to the pain that he felt.

As he passed his former Gymnasium school, he thought, *I would be graduating in May and headed to university in the fall.* That life felt like an old book he had read and now could only recall part of. He walked mindlessly on his path from school and soon found himself in front of Günter's home. He had walked this way so often with Günter that his subconscious path from school took him here, rather than directly to his own home.

Josef stood, staring across the narrow road at the Kimmich's front door. What was happening inside that home now, more than a year after Günter died at Grafenwoehr? What would Frau Kimmich think of him now, the woman who had adored him so much as a friend to her son? What would Liesel think? She had hugged him and thanked him for always protecting her brother. But he had failed to protect him when he needed it most. Would they hate him? Would they forgive him? He was not sure which would be more painful.

He stood in that spot for an hour, thinking about his friend, when the front door opened. Günter's mother stepped out and gave a sad smile to Josef. "You should come inside."

Josef walked down the hall toward Günter's room without asking. He opened the door and saw that the tower was still in place, stretching from floor to ceiling. Günter's bed was made up and clothes were put neatly away. It must have been how he left it when leaving for Grafenwoehr. It looked nothing like the chaos of his room when he lived in it. But perhaps it was the way they liked to remember him.

The family sat at the kitchen table, and Josef joined them where he had eaten so many meals. Frau Kimmich sat across from him. She had put out biscuits and four cups of water. Herr Kimmich sat at the head of the table to Josef's right. It was Saturday, so he had a rare day off. He was a medium-height man with wide shoulders and a potbelly. He had dark hair on the side of his head and was bald on top, in the fashion of a monk. His thick-fingered hands, with dirt under his nails, were on the table and he gazed down at them. Liesel sat at the other end of the table to Josef's left. She looked even more beautiful than he remembered. Her long hair was in a braid pulled to one side, hanging in front of her right shoulder.

"How have you been, Josef?" Frau Kimmich asked.

Josef thought of the ways he could answer that question. He could speak of the pain of losing his best friend, the aching knowledge of all he had done, the faces he saw every night when he tried to sleep. He just shrugged his shoulders.

There was a long silence before Liesel spoke up, looking alternately at her parents. "If you aren't going to ask, I will." Then she turned to Josef. "What happened with Günter?"

"We know what happened!" Herr Kimmich slammed a hand on the table, making Josef jump. "They told us what he did. He took the coward's way."

"We don't know what was happening. We don't know why?" Liesel protested. She leaned in toward her father, clearly not intimidated, matching the fire in his words. Turning to Josef, she lowered her voice. "Tell us, please." She was pleading. She was in pain and needed to know.

Josef swallowed hard and gripped his two large hands together. "It's like his note said."

"Note? He wrote a note?" Liesel was animated and both parents sat up straight, clearly hearing new information.

"They didn't give it to you? It was written to you."

"What did it say, Josef?" Liesel leaned in and put a hand on his arm. There was a time that this gesture would have caused Josef to blush and set his heart racing, but today he just felt sorrow for Günter's sister.

Josef thought about his conversation with Günter the night before he died. How Günter pleaded for any way to avoid shooting and killing people. How he had failed his friend. He could not confess all of that. He could not face them. "He wrote, *I'm sorry, there was no other way.*"

Liesel shook her head. "I don't understand."

Herr Kimmich gritted his teeth and said, "What's to understand? It's what they said. He was a coward."

"No!" Josef smashed both of his hands down on the table creating a thunderous thud. The biscuits bounded off the plate and two cups of water toppled over. He clenched his fists and stared down at the table, trying not to directly challenge the man of the house. He spoke quickly and forcefully. "Günter was the best sharpshooter in the entire facility. He won every competition. He was awarded the highest position as a result. But Günter was kind. He could not imagine killing people from a great distance. He understood what it would take." Josef gripped the sides of his head and began to cry, his face turning bright red. "He understood what he would take from others; what it would take from him. Günter was the bravest one of us all."

He stood up and pushed his chair back. "I'm sorry for the mess I've made. I'm sorry if I've upset you." He walked out of the room and left the house.

Liesel ran after Josef and called his name as she burst out the front door. He stood ten meters away but did not turn around. "I am sorry for what you have had to live through, Josef. No one can change what has happened, but you don't have to lose who you are. I know who you are."

Josef did not respond. He resumed walking toward home.

* * *

Ingrid was in the garden, and Karl was eating bread in the kitchen when Josef walked in. They both rushed to greet him, and he was wrapped in a long embrace before he even took five steps inside the house.

"Hello, Mutti, Papi."

"My goodness, let's have a look at you. You are even bigger." His mother always felt proud of his size.

Josef looked at his father and wondered if he had shrunk. They had been close to the same height seventeen months ago when he left for training. Now, he was at least five or six centimeters taller than his father.

"So, we have our very own member of the Einsatzgruppen here." His mother beamed with pride. "Tell us about the work you do. You know all of my friends know you are a hero. I told them I knew from early on that you were exceptional. You know, the other day ..."

"Let's let Josef sit down, dear." Karl smiled and put a hand on his wife's shoulder. They walked into the house. Josef sat on the small sofa while his mother and father each scooted chairs across from him but within reach to pat his knee.

"So, tell us," his mother implored, still wearing a smile and a look of pride that felt unfamiliar to Josef.

"What shall I tell you?" he answered with a shrug. "We find Jews and give them to the unit that transports them."

"Ach." Ingrid made a guttural sound, dismissing his simple response. "You make it sound so easy. I know you have to ferret them out, and you put yourself in danger. My son, the hero, is too modest."

Josef searched for the words that would satisfy his mother but stop the questions. "The work is secret, Mutti. I cannot say more." He saw the furrow in her brow relax and the beam of pride return. He looked at his father, who looked worried.

"Very well," Ingrid said, rising up from her seat with a proud, suppressed smile on her lips. "I don't want to make you reveal state secrets. But I must feed you. My goodness, how you have grown. I may need to make more food." With that, she departed to the kitchen.

Karl looked appraisingly at Josef and leaned back in his chair. Josef could feel his eyes probing for his secrets.

"How are you, Son?"

It was the question Josef feared most, and he knew his father would be the one to ask it. If he told his father about the pain he felt, he would have to reveal the evils he had done. His father would never look at him the same, perhaps never love him again. "I'm OK, Papi."

"You know, I don't expect you to be OK. I can't imagine the difficulty you have faced or what you have seen. I'm sorry for what you have had to see."

"It's OK, Papi. There is no other way." Josef stood and placed a hand on his father's shoulder, then walked to the garden. It was March and the ground was bare of any flowers. His mother had been preparing the ground, which was neatly raked with fresh lines in the loose soil.

I'm sorry for what you have had to see. Josef thought about those words. His father did not say ... *for what you have had to* do. Perhaps he thinks I have only seen terrible things and not done terrible things. Or perhaps he knows better than to say it. Looking back through the door at his father, he saw the kindness he had always known, now mixed with sadness.

The evening was mostly quiet, with Ingrid occasionally attempting to lead Josef into bragging about some accomplishment. Karl said little but watched his son closely. In the morning, Josef stuffed his clothes in his pack, along with some snacks his mother had prepared, and headed to the door. He hugged both of his parents and gave his mother a kiss on the top of her head.

"Make us proud, Son," she said, with a slight catch in her voice. She turned and went inside quickly.

Karl put his hands on each of Josef's shoulders, gripping his large son. He then slid his hands to Josef's cheeks, his eyes glassy. "We love you. No matter what, Josef."

Tears formed in Josef's eyes. His father knew.

CHAPTER 22
NEUE AUFTRÄGE: NEW ORDERS
1944

In 1944, the German war effort was failing. All of the signs were there. It did not take Josef's sharp mind to see them, everyone knew. Allied bombings intensified; supplies ran short; orders were often frenetic and changed daily. The typically organized and orderly German war machine was spinning out of control. In addition, the German economy was collapsing due to the effectiveness of the Allied naval blockade and rising fuel costs. Ground troops were advancing, taking back German positions, from all directions.

By November of that year, the only capability the German military still excelled at was propaganda. The talk of imminent victory only intensified as the war slipped through their hands. It was as if they believed they could manifest victory through posters, films, and speeches.

Captain Schmidt was one such true believer, or at least

he played that role convincingly. He still spoke to the Einsatzgruppen with fiery determination. "Our enemies spread lies and deceit. The Jews destroyed our economic well-being. But you stand in the way of our enemies and will assure a German victory." The veins in his neck pulsed as his pale skin turned beet red.

Several of the men glanced at each other but looked away quickly, seeking the doubt in others that they felt themselves, but also fearing to show it. Josef looked at Schmidt and saw him in a new way, this man who was larger than life. He looked weak and pathetic. His denial and protest so glaringly obvious that he seemed laughable. But the order instilled over three and a half years would not crumble so quickly. No one spoke out.

"I have good news for you." Schmidt smiled and scanned the group of young men in his charge, meeting their eyes in turn. "You no longer need to call for extraction and arrest. We are entering a new phase in which you will have more authority to execute your work." He smiled grimly. "Each team will receive a group of assignments. You are to fulfill each of them and return to camp after they are complete. We will expect you here in two weeks."

The unit had relocated three months prior to Düsseldorf, housing themselves at a military installation adjacent to a Nazi prison. Having cleared most of the Jews in hiding near Munich, they had begun moving north in 1942. By mid-1944 most of the work was in outlying towns.

Schmidt's words—*more authority to execute your work*—still rang in Josef's ears when Hans approached. "What does this mean, Josef?"

Josef looked down at Hans's face, which wore a quizzical

look. He thought back to lining up to Hans's right, thinking himself smaller and now looked down at his partner who seemed small physically and in his capacity to grasp what they were being asked to do. "It means we are to kill Jews, Hans." Even saying the words out loud caused Josef's heart to sink and he shook his head.

"He didn't say that."

"No more extractions. No more arrests. Yet they are giving us a list of Jews to find. What do you think it means?" Josef said it more harshly than he intended, and he saw the hurt on Hans's face.

Hans tried to straighten his shoulders and appear confident. "Well, it makes no difference. We know they die in the camps. This may be better for them."

"Tell yourself what you must, Hans. There is no other way, right?"

"Well, there isn't, is there?" Hans held his hands up at his side. "You can brood about it, but it's true and you know it."

The words stung because Josef knew them to be true. "Let's just get our assignments and go." Josef retrieved an envelope. It was thick. He opened the top flap and removed a single piece of paper with a suspected location, then another, and another. "So many," he said softly.

"We have two weeks. They are giving us a Kübelwagen to travel in." Hans tried to look excited.

* * *

The assignments were scattered across towns West of Düsseldorf. They mapped them out so they would work west and then loop back around over two weeks. There were twelve assignments, each could lead to multiple Jews. Josef worked the math and thought it may be fifty or more people. He shook his head, trying to get that thought to disappear. He didn't know what he might do when they got to the first one. The thought of executing people who complied with orders was yet another step beyond what he believed he was capable of, but he also knew that he had crossed many lines he did not expect to cross over the past years.

They set out on November 28, 1944. It was a Tuesday. Josef reflected back on his first day of service, a Tuesday, when he entered the Grafenwoehr training facility with Günter, just a day after meeting Major Müller in the nurse's station at school. The things he could tell those two naive boys now.

The Kübelwagen was a manifestation of the German military in the form of a vehicle. Every element of its design was for function over form. The flat metal fenders and angular corners made for easy replacement of panels. The drab beige exterior designed not to be seen. The rigid suspension made to endure many years of use while passing every bump and vibration from the road to its occupants. It was a model for efficient transport with minimum comfort. Hans drove as they left for the first of their missions. They could feel a steady breeze even with the top up and the windows raised. Gaps between the windows and the burlap roof created a whistling sound as the vehicle rattled down the roadway. A small red flag with a black swastika fluttered in the wind on the front right side of the hood, indicating that this was an official vehicle of the SS. Each door bore the standard *Balkenkreuz* (black cross) that marked all official Nazi vehicles.

The two did not speak during the journey. Josef was thinking about what to do when they arrived at the first assignment location. There would have to be another way. He hoped Hans was thinking the same thing but did not dare to broach the subject until they were far from Düsseldorf, far from Captain Schmidt.

Düsseldorf was pockmarked with the signs of a war being lost: ghostly, hollowed-out buildings, gutted by Allied bombs, standing side by side with active businesses. As they left the city, the signs were less frequent. The countryside looked mostly unblemished, other than seeing the occasional tank left by the side of the road due to a lack of fuel or needing to steer around a hole in the road left by a bomb dropped prematurely, likely intended for the city.

The first location was just twenty-five kilometers to the west, in the town of Korschenbroich. The SS intelligence had given them the address of a building on Brauereistrasse (Brewery Street). There were alleged to be Jews hiding in an empty building that was partially destroyed by an Allied bomb.

As they drove into town, most of the buildings were intact. The evidence of war was less obvious here in the outskirts. There was a larger town just five kilometers away, München Gladbach, which was a more regular target. Still, the occasional hollowed-out corpse of a building would send a reminder of the force that was overcoming Germany.

When they arrived at Brauereistrasse, their target building was obvious. It was the only shell of a building on the street. It was previously a four-story building with a white-painted concrete facade. Rubble was piled close to the base in front, as the locals had cleared the roadway. The damage was predominantly to the top two floors, and the lower levels looked to be intact, though windows and doors had been blown out.

Josef said to himself, *living there seems punishment enough.* As Hans went to exit the driver's side of the Kübelwagen, Josef reached over and grabbed his shoulder. "Let's just assess the situation when we get in there. I have not worked out what to do." Hans nodded.

They approached the opening that had once been a front door. Shards of concrete struck out around the opening as if they were walking into the jaws of a beast with ragged teeth. The interior was a ruin. It seemed as if the building had been lifted, turned over, and shaken. Broken furniture littered the floor. They stepped over torn clothing, pieces of children's toys, and shards of wood that may have previously been molding or parts of doors.

Josef and Hans communicated with head nods and hand motions. They scoured the first floor and found no one. Josef began to feel relieved that they may not have to encounter Jews in hiding here. He still had not decided how to handle the situation if they did find them.

The staircase to the second floor was missing several treads. The remaining treads were splintered and twisted. They could see footprints in the concrete dust covering almost everything in the building. The prints served as a map of where to step and which treads would support them. Hans went first. The remaining full and partial treads creaked under his weight. At one point the whole stair listed to the right slightly and he held still. Josef followed and the creaks were louder under his large feet and massive size. Halfway up he placed his right foot in the exact outline of prior steps in the dust, but the step gave way. He reached up and caught the stair above with his forearms to avoid falling through to the first level. He then clambered up the remaining steps, using both feet and hands, distributing his weight more evenly, a strategy he realized he should have employed from the start.

As he scrambled, he heard scurrying on the second floor and his heart sank. There were people there. Reaching the second floor, they followed the sounds and came to a family of three huddled in the far corner. They had cleared one of the former apartments of rubble and piled old dusty clothes into makeshift mattresses.

The man looked to be in his early thirties, with dark hair and a beard. He was skinny and frail looking. The woman was older, perhaps forty, and she clung to a younger boy in his early teens. "Please," said the man. "Leave us here. We will bother no one. This is my sister and her son. Her husband was already sent to the camps." He paused and looked at his sister. "If you must take someone, take me."

"Just wait here a moment. I need to talk to my partner." Josef motioned to Hans to follow him and started to walk away. Seconds later, there were three loud bangs. The gunfire echoed loudly in the hollow building, making it seem like more shots were fired. Josef wheeled around to see all three Jews on the ground. Blood poured from the heads of both adults. The teen boy was shaking on the ground, holding his chest. Hans stepped toward him and fired again. There was no more movement.

"What have you done?" Josef roared.

"Our job."

"We agreed to talk about this. Look for another way," he cried out.

"And what other way would that be?" Hans yelled and then paused in an exaggerated expression of waiting for an answer, his hands up and eyes wide. "I am listening. What other way? There is no other way. We have orders. I did it because I feared you wouldn't. What are we to do? Go back in two weeks having not completed any of our assignments? Do you think the SS will not hear? Do you think they will not shoot us?" He rattled off questions in machine-gun fashion, then stopped. He lowered his voice. "Do you think I like this?"

"I don't know," Josef answered reflexively.

"I don't. I don't. I don't!" Hans yelled with increased volume at each repetition, then broke down crying. "You think I am a monster, but you have done the same things as I have. We have had no choice. The only difference is that I accept that fact."

Josef stared at Hans and felt the weight of his words. He was right. There was no difference between them. They had both done these things. Hans just had more clarity about the situation.

Hans sat down against the outer wall, put his gun on the ground, and covered his face with both hands. Josef dropped to the ground in the middle of the room, rolled onto his back, and stared up at the ceiling.

"Do you ever think of Günter, Hans? I mean, I know he was my friend, not yours, but do you think of what he did— why he did it?"

"Not really. Because I would never do that. I did not want to shoot those people." He motioned to the three bodies on the floor. "But I will choose my life over theirs every time. They will die either way."

There it was again. Clarity. He hated the pure calculation that Hans laid out, but Josef had to admit to himself that he had made the same calculation. Günter had made a different one.

The two stayed there for an hour and then returned to the Kübelwagen. They would head to München Gladbach and start their next assignment in the morning.

CHAPTER 23
DAS GESCHENK: THE GIFT
1944

They awoke as the first light streamed into the window of the small inn where they stayed the night in München Gladbach. German businesses were required to provide services to the military, so accommodations, food, and fuel were typically not an issue. But last night they had a meager dinner and breakfast would be the same. The inn had no meat or eggs due to the supply shortages that ravaged the country. They were given a room, some bread, and boiled potatoes. The owner had a few bottles of beer stored away and handed them over somewhat begrudgingly while commenting that they were his last with little prospect of more.

In 1941, they had eaten well, and supplies were abundant. The German citizens they met were enthusiastic and supportive. They were treated as heroes. Now, both goods and goodwill were in shorter supply, further evidence of the imminent fall.

Josef had slept little, thinking of the events of the prior day. They had killed many people before, but there had always been some thread of justification; a Jew had lunged at them or tried to run. The only justification for the three they killed yesterday came down to orders, nothing more. In the dark of that night, while he lay awake, listening to Hans's heavy, steady breathing in the bed to his right, Josef held Bärli, squeezing the small bear to his chest. He resolved that there was no other way, and he would finish the assignments they were given. He whispered to the bear, "Today marks the day I first got you, twelve years ago. At least I have protected you, my little one. It is one promise I have kept."

They grabbed the last crusts of bread and headed to the Kübelwagen for the short drive to the next assignment. The paper had an address and two names: that of a woman who harbored a Jewish child and that of the man who had reported her. They were to interrogate the man first to ascertain the child's current location.

They arrived at Schiller Platz, a small square on the outskirts of town. Four roads surrounded the small patch of grass and the one they sought was Kaiserstrasse (Emperor Street). Herbert Van Doren, owner of the piano store at the base of a three-story residential building, was the first name on their assignment sheet. As they looked about the square, they saw two bombed buildings, still smoldering. There was no activity, not a single person on the streets.

Josef strode up to the piano store and opened the door. A small man wearing a white shirt with black pants stood up. He had a thin mustache and black hair. Hans came in a moment after Josef. The man looked nervous. "How may I help you?"

"You made a report. We are here to look into that."

"What report?" The man looked appraisingly at them.

"Are you Herbert Van Doren?"

"Yes."

"Did you not tell the SS that Renate Brunst, a woman living in this building, was harboring a Jew?"

"Not exactly, no. I said ..." He stuttered and shook his head. "This is all wrong." Van Doren sat back on his piano stool and put his head in his hands.

Hans took over the questioning. "Are you saying you made a false report? We can take you in now so you can explain to the SS."

"No," he said, without looking up or removing his face from his hands. "I'm saying I did not say the child was a Jew. I just told them he showed up as a baby three years ago and that she had never been pregnant." He shook his head and stood up with a pleading expression on his face. "They told me the bank would extend my loan if I gave good information. No one buys a piano in wartime. She is a good woman. I think she just wanted to help a child."

"Slow down, Herr Van Doren." Josef held his hands up. "What you are saying is the woman upstairs took in a baby during the war without telling people where the baby came from. Correct?"

"Yes," he said, looking defeated.

"We will investigate. Now, this is important: When did you last see Frau Brunst and the child?"

"She ran up the stairs with him when she saw your car with the flag on the front. The boy had been playing in the square. She took him and ran to the apartment." He looked at Josef and then Hans. "Please don't harm her."

Josef looked with disgust at the small man as he shook. People like him were why he had all of these assignments. Now, he dared to plead for mercy on behalf of the woman that he had placed in their path. He stepped toward Van Doren, whose head rose only to the midpoint of Josef's chest and looked down at the shaking man. "We will do the job that *you* have set us on, Herr Van Doren."

They walked up the exterior stairway to the address on their sheet. Josef banged on the door. There was no response. "Renate Brunst, open the door." Again, there was no response. Hans yelled, "Open it now!"

"No," Renate yelled from inside.

Josef lifted his boot and kicked the door with a thunderous blow that broke the latch easily, swinging the door open. He looked at the woman standing in the center of the room. She was not cowering in the corner, as he had seen so many times, as he had expected to see her. She stood still, only two meters back from the door he had just kicked open. She was tall, slender, and had a strong jawline.

"Where is the child?" Josef asked.

She just shook her head and stared back at them.

Hans yelled, "You are harboring the enemy. We have witnesses."

Renate lowered her head, shook it slightly, and then raised her eyes to meet Hans's. "He's gone. Yesterday. You will never find him, you devil." As she shrieked the word devil, she charged at Hans. He fired two shots, and she fell forward. Her head slid down Hans's leg, leaving a smear of blood on his trousers.

"No. No. No," Josef yelled. "It's bad enough what the assignment is for the Jews, but we can't do this."

"What would you have me do? She came at me?"

"She is a skinny woman, and there are two of us."

Hans stormed out. Josef looked around the apartment and saw no sign of a child, so he followed Hans down the steps into the square.

Hans turned. "You blame me for what we have to do."

"I don't blame you." Josef spoke softly. "But maybe I do take it out on you. I'm sorry."

"You know something else, Josef?" Hans shook his head, his eyes glassy. "I did not do anything with that girl, Lilli, on our first day moving the Jews. I told you I did because I was ashamed. Schmidt gave me a beautiful girl and I went into the room and did nothing. I wanted to at first, but then I saw her shaking and crying and I couldn't do it. So, I held my pistol to her head and told her I would shoot her if anyone ever found out I did nothing."

Hans wore an expression Josef had not seen before. One that begged for forgiveness for all he had done. Josef put a hand on Hans's shoulder. "I'm glad you told me that. It makes a difference."

"We still have to finish our assignments," Hans said, nodding up toward the apartment.

"I know. I think the boy is in the apartment, hidden somehow. We will search."

They walked back up the steps and through the door. At first, they searched lightly, looking behind chairs, under the bed, in a pantry. When it was clear he was not in plain view, they began to toss clothes out of drawers and tip furniture over.

"Could Van Doren have been wrong?" Hans threw his hands up, indicating the child was obviously not there.

"I don't think so. He is very well hidden but look at the little wool jacket on the floor," Josef whispered, putting a finger over his lips to urge quiet. "Let's put a blanket over the woman, in case he comes out. We will talk outside." As they covered Renate, her face still bore the look of determination she showed in denying the child was there.

They stepped outside and Josef said, "He is in there. We will just wait. Let's take it in turns, two hours each. Whoever is there when he comes out will complete the assignment. That way one of us does not have to see it."

Hans nodded. "It's a good plan. I will take the first shift."

Josef appreciated the gesture. He hoped he would not be the one there to have to deal with this. He had not killed a child yet and the thought of it horrified him. But there was no other way.

Josef sat in the square, waiting as Hans took the first shift. He did not have a brother, but he wondered if this was what it would feel like. Brothers fight and sometimes don't even like each other. But they know they are bound together. You don't choose your brothers, and he certainly had not chosen Hans, but they had been together through the most difficult time in either of their lives. They were bound.

Two hours passed and Josef walked slowly up the stairs. He looked in the opening of the broken front door and saw Hans sitting in the green fabric chair near the door. Josef raised an eyebrow, asking a question without words. Hans shook his head. Josef's heart sank. The task would almost surely fall to him in these next two hours.

Time moved slowly in the dead silence of that apartment. Renate's body lay just a few steps away, covered in a light blue blanket with a red stain of blood by her shrouded head. Josef checked the wall clock and realized only four minutes had passed since he last checked it. He sat in fear of hearing a sound and finding a child emerging from hiding. He thought about his father. The last words he heard from him were, *We love you no matter what.* He knew his father meant the words but also knew that his father did not understand them. He could not know the depth of *what.* He could not promise love unconditionally without knowing *what.*

Josef heard something and was startled from deep thought. His heart sunk, thinking it would be the child. Instead, it was Hans. Two hours had passed, finally. The two shook their heads in disbelief that this game of hide and seek continued. They exchanged places again.

Out in the square, Josef felt sure the child would emerge during Hans's shift. The back and forth felt like a twisted game of Russian Roulette, except the gun would be pointed at a child rather than their own heads. Time is a funny thing, Josef thought. When he was inside, minutes took ages to pass. Now, outside, praying he would not have to go back in, two hours passed in the blink of an eye. He trudged up the stairs and relieved Hans.

"You really think a young child could hide this long?" Hans shook his head. "That woman was telling the truth. He's gone. I'll bet you a week's wages."

"He's here. It is impressive. Now I just want to meet this boy." Josef slung his pack on the ground and took a seat in the old green fabric chair that faced the window. He imagined that Renate watched the boy in the Platz from this spot sometimes. Looking out over the Platz in the fading light, he remembered playing outside as a boy, his father teaching him to fish, to ride a bike. Those things seemed so far away now, so foolish to indulge in, now that he understood what the world was. He thought about building the tower with Günter's erector set. He wondered where that tower was now, probably dismantled for scrap metal. Metal supplies were short and the government held frequent metal drives. Perhaps it had been recycled to make munitions. Yes. That's it, he thought, the metal found its true form, its true purpose—a bullet. Perhaps even the bullet that killed Renate, who lay under a blanket just steps away.

A sound roused Josef from his circular thoughts. He reached for his sidearm. It was dark now. Some rattle from the back of the apartment had woken him. He stood quietly and walked to the back, trying to make no sound, his pistol pointed ahead of him. The rattle came again, and he located it as being from the back wall. He lit his flashlight and pointed it to the back. The third time the sound came, he saw the wall panel shift slightly. The child was in there and trying to get out.

Josef felt the wall for seams and pushed against it. He heard a whimper from inside. He pushed right and then left and felt the panel shift and lean forward so he was supporting its weight. He let it down slowly and shined his light inside. The boy squinted his eyes and held a hand up against the blinding light. It was a boy of about four years of age, Josef thought, based on his height. He had dark hair and dark eyes that were surrounded by thick, long lashes. Even after being in a wall all day, he looked angelic.

Josef smelled that the boy had soiled himself. "You've made a mess in your pants."

The boy cried. "I know. I'm sorry. Are you a demon, sent to punish me?"

The words caught Josef off guard. *Was he a demon?* He was certainly sent to punish this child. Did this child see this clearly? "Why did you ask me that?"

"*Struwwelpeter*," Friedrich responded.

Josef let out a small laugh. All German children knew the stories in *Struwwelpeter*. They had given him nightmares as a child. "No. I am not here because you soiled your pants." He put his hand on Friedrich's head. "You stayed in that wall a very long time. You listened very well." He lowered the boy from his perch in the wall and led him to the middle of the room.

"Where is Mutti?"

For just a moment, Josef had forgotten the task he was sent to do. He met this boy who had stayed hidden in a wall, silently, all day; a boy who feared demons from the same fairy tales he himself had as a child. But the question "*Where is Mutti?*" snapped him back to the reality he faced. He was charged with killing this child. It was his duty. He turned away, raising both hands to his head, trying to grip his short hair, as he opened his mouth and mimed a scream of anguish. There was no sound. When he turned back, Friedrich was crying, clearly sensing the danger or at least the pain in Josef.

"So, what do I do with you, huh?" Josef shook his head, still held by both hands. "You are a Jew. I'd know that even if we did not have intelligence that you were being hidden here. Look at you. The color of your skin, your hair. You look as a Jew does."

The boy stared blankly at the man before him, eyes full of tears, mouth curled at each corner, but he did not make a sound.

"You know the Jews caused all of this. You know this is not my fault. If you die, there is one less Jew to grow up. Why should I care?" Josef's voice trailed off as he said those words, then he bellowed them. "Why should I care?" As the scream left him, he quaked with emotion, bent at the waist, and tears streamed down his face.

Hans rushed into the room, having heard the shouting. "You were right. Where was he?"

"In the wall at the back. Clever woman," Josef said, nodding his head toward the body under a blanket on the floor.

Hans saw the tears on Josef's face and hesitated. "Look, Brother, you know our orders. This is not your fault. It is not *our* fault."

"I know. But we are the ones here, aren't we?" Josef responded with a blank, resigned expression.

"We must follow orders. There is no other way," Hans pleaded.

There it was again. His life had been ruled by those words. His best friend had implored him to help find another way. He had killed so many people because there was no other way. The war was collapsing around them. He was exhausted by it all. How could there be no other way?

"Go outside," Hans said softly.

Josef knew what that meant and he knew Hans intended to do a kindness for him, as if walking out of the room would absolve him of responsibility. This child's life or death would be out of his control, out of his reach. It would be so easy. Just walk out. There is no other way.

"Josef, I'll do it," Hans said, giving him an assuring nod.

"I know you will, Hans." Josef looked down, wiped his eyes and repeated, "I know you will." He walked to face Hans and placed his large hands on each of Hans's shoulders and gave a squeeze. "I'm sorry, Brother."

Hans pressed his lips together in a sad smile, then said, "It's OK."

"No, Brother, I don't think it is." Josef slid his hands around Hans's throat and squeezed with all of his strength. Hans's face showed his surprise as he gasped for breath and grabbed at Josef's arms. Unable to move the huge arms, he began flailing, striking Josef's face with powerful fists. The blows felt to Josef as if they were punches thrown underwater, slow, buffered. He felt no pain, although he was aware that damage was being inflicted. He could hear Major Müller's voice like an echo— *There you are, Josef. This is who I always knew you to be.*

Josef knew now that Hans was no match for his strength and size. But it did not give him a feeling of power, just of control. He had decided to defend this child, and Hans would not stop him. He squeezed harder and felt his thumbs collapse his partner's esophagus with a sickening crack. Hans's legs gave way, and Josef gently lowered him to the ground. As Josef released his grip, he saw the confusion frozen on Hans's face. There was no breath.

There was no turning back now. He had made a decision in that moment; for good or ill, this was *another way*. He looked back at the boy, who was backed up against the wall and shaking. Josef composed himself, straightened his body, and wiped his face. He looked at the child, with softer eyes now. "I'm sorry that I scared you. I'm not going to harm you. It is now my job to protect you."

Josef knelt down. "Did you know that today is my birthday?" A trace of a smile ran across his face and disappeared quickly. "Yes, my birthday. I've not had a good birthday in a very long time." He stared at the ceiling and shook his head as tears filled his eyes again. He reached for his pack, swung it around in front of him, and set it down between himself and the boy. The smile returned to his lips, faintly, as he untied the top of the sack and reached slowly inside.

"You know this was the best birthday gift I ever received, and it was made by a Jew woman, wouldn't you know." Josef let a small laugh escape through tears as he pulled Bärli out. The little bear had lost one eye, and its head was slightly concave now, but the neatly stitched clothing had held up well. He stared at the bear and smiled with moist eyes. He rubbed the course cellulose head and muttered, "Bärli."

"I'll tell you what, little boy. If you tell me your name, I'm going to give *you* a present on *my* birthday."

Friedrich stared, studying the man's face, still frowning and holding back tears.

"Come now, what is your name."

The boy looked at the bear with its slightly lopsided head, one missing eye, and finely knit gold and white clothes. He said, "I'm Friedrich."

"Good. And your surname?"

Friedrich shrugged his shoulders and looked down. Josef could see the boy did not know.

"Well, Friedrich, this is Bärli. He has been my good friend for twelve years. I think he will be your friend now. That means you are charged with looking after him. The three of us are going to leave now. Will you come along with me?"

Friedrich took the bear and nodded.

CHAPTER 24
LIEFERBOTE: DELIVERY MAN
1957

Oktoberfest was in full swing in Munich, and Friedrich and Sigrid wove their way through the busy streets toward city hall. Having started in 1810, the same year Beethoven wrote "Für Elise", Minna Becker's favorite song, the festival had run annually. It paused during World War II, and Munich celebrated a smaller Autumn Fest following the war until reestablishing Oktoberfest in 1949. Each year since, the celebration had grown.

People spilled out of bars onto the road, carrying large steins of beer. Music filled the air, coming from every direction in different beats and melodies, yet somehow harmonizing in a way that fit the atmosphere. The urge to join was too great, so they stopped at a beer garden for a pint of strong German beer. Sigrid attempted to get Friedrich to dance but had to settle for parading alone through the throng of people while he watched from a bench and laughed.

It was four o'clock as they walked into the city hall and bounded up the steps to the records department. An older man sat at the table, but they saw Magda by the rows of filing cabinets, so they hung back and waited to make eye contact. There was no sense in hoping to find another helpful soul amongst the government bureaucrats. Eventually, she looked up and Friedrich waved.

Magda met them near the stairway. "Have you had some luck finding your parents?"

"We came across some important information, but I'm afraid it is just a step toward identifying them. We were hoping you might assist us."

She looked over her shoulder at the man at the desk. He was watching them now. "What is it that you have?"

"A woman by the name of Renate Brunst in Mönchengladbach cared for me for several years after I was born. We learned that her cousin, a man, brought me there as an infant. We think he might be the key to locating my parents. He was from Munich, so we were hoping you could help us locate him."

"Were you able to ask Frau Brunst about this?"

Friedrich gave her a solemn look and shook his head. She understood.

"Was Brunst her married name, or ..."

"She was unmarried."

"Good. Then, there is a chance they will share the same last name if they are paternal cousins. I can narrow it down further based on age. My best hope, though, is connecting with someone in records for North Rhine-Westphalia to follow her parentage and connect it to someone here who could be her cousin. Meet me tomorrow at the café across Marienplatz at five fifteen. I will walk over after we close and share what I have learned." As they walked away, she added, "Thank you, and say hello to your parents for me." The man at the desk seemed satisfied by the ruse and went back to his work.

* * *

Magda walked into the café at precisely five fifteen p.m. Friedrich and Sigrid were seated at a table with three cups of tea ready and steaming.

"Well, I have good news for you. I found him."

"That fast?" Friedrich asked, sounding stunned.

Magda gave a sly smile. "The German government may have done evil things, but you can never accuse them of being poor record keepers." Both Sigrid and Friedrich let out involuntary laughs, loud enough to cause the other patrons to look. They covered their mouths after and giggled.

"You are quite funny, you know," Sigrid said, patting Magda on the shoulder. "And you have been a wonderful friend to us. Thank you."

Magda blushed, then reached into her bag to remove some papers. "I suppose the only thing that matters is the information, but I have to tell you how I was able to find it." She lit up with excitement, clearly reveling in her sideline detective work. "I started with the last name Brunst. There are seventy-two people with that last name in Munich. Thirty-one were men. I then eliminated anyone under age thirty-three since our man drove you to Mönchengladbach in 1941 and must have had a license to drive. This left me with eighteen men. I then looked up Renate in the death records, as I have access to those for the entire country." She glanced up from her papers, looking proud. "She died at thirty-nine and would be fifty-two today. I took a chance and looked for men closest to that age. Cousins can be much older or younger, but the best chance would be within five years. There were just five men. This is where it gets interesting," she exclaimed.

Friedrich and Sigrid looked at each other and knew they were having the same thought—this was *already* interesting.

"Since I have just five names, I wanted to look at their parentage and see who had fathers with brothers. Three of them did. Then I looked at the grandparents, and do you know what I found?" Without waiting, she added, "One of the men had a paternal grandmother named Renate." Magda threw her hands in the air and then clasped them together in prayer.

"That has to be him, right?" Sigrid exclaimed. "Close to Renate's age and she must have been named after the grandmother."

Magda nodded. "The chances seem very good. He is five years older than your Renate. I am hopeful for you. Here is his name and address, right here in Munich."

Friedrich stood up, then leaned over the table to hug Magda. "You are an angel. How can I thank you?"

"Just find out about your parents. Maybe let me know when you do."

"You will be among the first, I promise."

* * *

Franz Brunst lived on the first floor of a four-story building in a one-bedroom apartment with his wife, Hildi. It was six thirty p.m. when Friedrich and Sigrid arrived, coming straight from the café with Magda, having walked briskly halfway across the city. There was a light on inside, and the sound of a phonograph playing.

Friedrich could feel his heart pounding as he lifted his hand to knock. He glanced over at Sigrid. Her face showed the same nervous anticipation. They could feel that this would be a pivotal moment, though they each also worried they would face another letdown, as they did in Mönchengladbach. He knocked and stepped back.

An attractive short woman in her fifties answered the door. Her silver hair was braided in a single strand in the back and draped over her right shoulder, spilling halfway down her chest. She smiled. "How may I help you?"

"Is Franz, I mean Herr Brunst, here?" Friedrich asked through a shaky voice.

A man appeared behind the woman. He was tall and lean, bald except for a ring of hair around the edge of his head. "I am Franz."

"Is your cousin Renate Brunst, sir?" Friedrich asked, then held his breath. This was the moment they would know if they had the right man.

His face became grave. "Renate *was* my cousin. She has passed. What is this about?"

Sigrid joined in. "We are sorry to upset you, sir, but we believe you brought a child to her in 1941."

"Who are you and why would you make such a claim?" His face turned red, and he stepped in front of his wife, guiding her behind him in a protective motion.

"I am the child you brought her, sir." Friedrich stepped forward and looked him in the eye.

Franz's face went blank. "But, but, that's impossible. That child ..."

"Was believed to be killed, I know." Friedrich took a risk

and placed a hand on his shoulder. "I survived, sir. Can I ask you if you got a good look at the baby, at me?"

"Yes," Franz answered as if in a daze. He looked back at his wife, who looked equally confused.

"I am Franz's wife, Hildi. Why don't you come in so we can discuss this more." She swung the door wider and guided them inside. Music played in the background. Hildi walked to the phonograph and lifted the needle. Suddenly, the room was still and silent. "Please, sit."

There was a small green fabric couch and two yellow side chairs with a coffee table in the center. Friedrich and Sigrid sat in the chairs. The older couple took the couch, alternately looking at each other and their guests.

"Why did you ask me if I had looked closely at the baby? Do you think I would recognize you today if I saw you at a day old?"

"I wondered, sir, if you noticed any distinguishing marks." Franz's eyes dropped immediately to Friedrich's chest. Friedrich stood up and lifted his sweater, revealing his third nipple.

"My god, it is you," Franz said as tears formed in his eyes. "You have no idea how much Renate loved you. No mother could have loved a child more."

"I know that now. We went to Mönchengladbach and visited the apartment. We know now that she died for me."

Franz nodded, more tears leaking down his cheeks. "She would not regret that. You can't feel guilt for that."

Sigrid put a hand on Franz's knee and asked, "Can you tell us about Friedrich's birth parents?"

He nodded, wiping his cheeks. "I had done electrical work in their store before the war. It was a lovely toy store."

He looked at Friedrich. "Your mother had such a talent for needlework. She made beautiful outfits for the stuffed animals and dolls. Her name was Gerda. And your father, Max; Max Biermann. He could make a friend of anyone. He remembered every man's name, even their wives and children, and he would ask after them. He was kind." He shook his head.

The information was overwhelming for Friedrich. He was hearing for the first time not only his parents' names, his own real surname, but hearing about them as people. He stared and nodded but was unable to speak.

Sigrid saw that Friedrich could not speak for himself and asked, "How did it happen; I mean, you taking Friedrich to Renate."

"His father arranged it with me. He knew I was sympathetic to what was happening to the Jews. He called on me and I didn't hesitate. Your mother resisted the idea, too afraid to lose you, but, in the end, she knew it was the only way to ..." His voice broke as tears formed again in his eyes. "To keep you safe. All these years I thought the plan had failed. If they were alive, they would be so proud that you made it."

"So they are dead then," Friedrich said, finding his voice again, which cracked as he spoke the words.

"I suppose I don't know for sure," Franz added. "It's just that I have never heard or seen them since the night I picked you up. You may find out more from Hubert and Ria Schiffers. That was the home where they hid; the home where I took you from the cellar in 1941."

The group spoke for an hour longer, filling in details and sharing stories. Franz and Hildi seemed to enjoy hearing about school and playing the piano. Friedrich begged for more stories of his parents' kindness. As they parted, they each hugged each other for a long time.

Sigrid kissed Franz's cheek and said, "You are a brave man. You saved Friedrich's life."

Franz looked thoughtful for a moment then replied, "You have reminded me of something important, Sigrid." He turned toward Friedrich and took his hand. "You were given the name Friedrich by Renate. It was important to have a name that sounded less Jewish, to keep you safer. You were named after your father. Your birth name is Max Biermann."

* * *

Munich looked different to Friedrich, walking home at night after leaving Franz and Hildi Brunst. The Oktoberfest celebrations drifted into the background, just part of the canvas on which his life's story was now vividly painted. It was crisp and cold with a steady breeze, but it felt comfortable. The chill only heightened his senses at this moment. He was aware of everything around him and was at peace with all of it.

Weeks ago, he lost his mother and, with her, his sense of who he was. She was the only person who understood him. Now, he held the hand of a girl he would never have met without that tragedy, a girl who seemed to understand him already, even after such a short time. And now he knew his parents' names, his own name.

Ahead of them, people poured out of a beer garden onto the street, locking arms and singing loudly. Friedrich walked through the crowd, patting strangers on the back and laughing. He stopped at the street corner and turned to Sigrid. "I can't believe what we have done—what you have done." He hugged her tightly. "I never could have done this without you, but I am fairly sure you could have done it without me. I know there is more to learn about my parents, but I already know more than I ever imagined. Thank you." He bent down and kissed her lips long and gently.

A tear rolled down Sigrid's cheek. She tried to speak but couldn't.

"I'm sorry if I've upset you. I'm here celebrating something that I know you want for yourself. I'm so sorry."

"No." She shook her head. "I don't know if I have ever been this happy in my entire life." She kissed him again and they held the kiss so long that the crowd outside the beer garden started to cheer for them. They ended the kiss laughing at the commotion they had created.

As they walked on toward the orphanage, Sigrid asked, "Do I have to call you Max now?" They laughed again.

* * *

Dieter was waiting when Friedrich got home. He stood as his son entered the door. "Did you meet this Herr Brunst? Was he the man you sought?"

"I was born Max Biermann. My birth parents were Max and Gerda Biermann. They owned a toy store."

Dieter was silent for a long pause, nodding his head in thought. "It's no small thing what you have accomplished, Son. No small thing at all."

This may have been the most effusive compliment his father had ever given him, Friedrich thought. Perhaps even the most generous compliment he had given anyone. "It was mostly Sigrid, and we had help from a wonderful worker at city hall." Seeing his father stand stiffly a few steps away, absorbing the information about Friedrich's *real* parents, it felt as if he was standing so still to keep the tumult from spilling out of himself.

He had to ease his father's pain, but he didn't know how. He tried to imagine what Sigrid would say if she were in his place, and it came out almost involuntarily. "I love you, Papi. Thank you for supporting me in this." He had not called Dieter Papi since he was seven.

The stoic man trembled slightly. He swallowed and cleared his throat, but his efforts to suppress his emotions failed. Tears welled in his eyes. "You're a good boy, Friedrich. Tell me, what is next in your investigation?" he said, composing himself and wiping his cheeks.

"We will go to the house where sympathizers hid several Jews, including my parents. No one has heard from them as far as Herr Brunst knew, so it is logical to assume they are dead."

"That is a good plan. Perhaps a trip to the Arolsen archive will also be needed."

Friedrich looked at him quizzically.

"It is an archive established by the postwar German and Allied governments. It is in the northern city of Arolsen. They have all the records from the camps and have organized them over the years since the war. It is likely that your parents' names will be there."

"Thank you, Papi," Friedrich said with a soft smile. "Would you like to go with us to the house where they hid?"

Dieter nodded and turned away quickly.

* * *

The houses on Waldstrasse were all two-stories and tightly packed together, like a row of perfectly aligned teeth. It was a cold October day with overcast skies and a chilly breeze. The beech trees that lined the road had lost their leaves, blending into the stark, drab landscape. Dieter stood behind Friedrich and Sigrid as they all looked across the road at 217 Waldstrasse.

"Well, we won't know what we will find until we knock," said Friedrich as he started to walk across the road. The three walked up the front steps and were surprised to see the door open before even reaching it. An older woman emerged and then a man behind her. Her hair was short and almost pure white. She was pear shaped, with a thinner upper body anchored by wide hips. He was taller and slim. His white hair was wispy on top and fluttered in the breeze by the door.

"We saw you watching the house before walking across the road. What is it you want?" the woman asked. Her tone was businesslike but not unfriendly.

Sigrid smiled and responded, "We are looking for this boy's birth parents, and we think you may have known them."

The woman and man looked at her and waited without responding.

"Their names were Max and Gerda Biermann."

The couple looked at each other, obviously recognizing the names, then looked back. "Who are you?" the woman asked, pointing to Dieter. Are you from the government?" Her tone had turned frostier as she folded her arms across her body.

"I do work for the government as a roadway engineer," Dieter responded matter-of-factly. "But that is unrelated to our visit. My late wife and I adopted this boy," he said, placing a hand on Friedrich's shoulder. "He was named Friedrich by that time, but we now know he was born Max Biermann, and the people we are asking after were his parents."

The woman gasped and put her hands over her mouth while her husband grabbed both of her shoulders from behind and pulled her toward him in an embrace. He said, "I am Hubert Schiffers, and this is Ria, my wife. You must come in. There is so much we can share."

CHAPTER 25
GEBURT: BIRTH
1941

The latest contraction bit hard and a yelp of pain escaped her for the first time. She knew she had to remain quiet. Gerda had imagined being a mother all her life. She married Max at the age of nineteen in 1929. Max was two years older and had such wonderful plans for them. They would take over his parents' store and make it more successful. They would raise their children together in Munich.

The first few years they lamented that no children came. It appeared to not be in their destiny. After five years of marriage, amid Hitler's rise and growing anti-Jewish protests, they were relieved to have not brought children into this hate-filled country. Now, on March 9, 1941, at the height of Nazi power, with an expanding German empire, as they hid in a dirt cellar, their child was finally coming—and there was no stopping it.

Five Jews were living in the crowded, dirt-floor cellar. With their homes seized by the Nazi government and countless of their friends and relatives shipped off to work camps, they counted themselves among the lucky to have survived this long. Their hosts, the Schiffers, brought them news when they could get it: mass shootings, riots, the expanding war, massacres of Jews. They had no choice but to stay in place and ride out a regime that they prayed would come to an end.

While Max paced frantically, young Karin mopped Gerda's brow. She looked down with kind eyes at the olive-skinned mother-to-be, seeing beads of sweat on her brow and tears leaking from her dark eyes with lush, thick lashes. "You are doing wonderfully," she soothed.

"I'm more than twice your age and this is my first child. How are you so assuring and calm? You are sent by God, Karin, there is no doubt." Another contraction came, squeezing her midsection, which hardened to look like a mountain peak under her loose-fitting frock. She repressed the urge to yell, gritting her teeth hard instead. "I think the baby is coming now, Karin. Bring my husband." Her voice was a whisper, but Max heard, from just a few steps away. In an instant, he was there kneeling by her side and gripping her hand.

"We should not have brought a baby into this, Max."

"That was God's decision, my love. It will be fine, I promise you. I will keep you both safe." He leaned over and rested his forehead on hers, their sweat mingling, and added, "On my life, I will keep you both safe."

Ullie stepped in. "Max, back up now. The baby is coming." She ordered everyone to give them more space. Her height and posture gave her an air of authority and confidence that made them all feel like she could handle any situation. Gerda lay on the thin cot mattress, which they had propped up on all of the crates they had, which were usually used as stools. This kept her elevated about a half meter above the dirt floor. The Schiffers had boiled water and provided some clean rags to Ullie.

Tying a knot in a clean rag, she handed it to Karin. "Have her bite this when she wants to scream." She pushed Gerda's dress up, and the two men faced the wall, looking away. She took a clean rag and dipped it in the purified water to wipe away the fluid that began to leak out as the baby's head crowned.

Gerda bit down hard and made almost no sound. They didn't fear sound reaching the roadway from this dirt cellar. They feared the neighbors. The German government rewarded those who brought them news of treachery and severely punished, sometimes with death, those who aided the Jews.

The baby's shoulders emerged, then the full body of a baby boy slid out. Ursula tied and cut the umbilical cord and cleaned the boy with fresh rags. Karin was so excited to be near this miracle she could barely contain herself from pulling the child from her mother. Sensing her longing for involvement in this miracle, Ullie handed the baby to Karin and asked, "Would you finish wiping him down, then wrap him in a shirt so Gerda can hold and feed him?"

Ursula cleaned and covered Gerda's lower body then called for Max to join his wife. Gerda held their boy, and he began to nurse immediately. He was olive-skinned like his mother, with dark eyes and thick eyelashes. "He looks like an angel, Max." She then unfolded the shirt he was wrapped in and giggled. "Look, he has a Nebenwarze."

Max looked at his baby, swaddled in an old, clean shirt, his exposed chest showed a small third nipple on the right side, below the full nipple. Then he scanned up to his boy's face, taking in his dark skin and full lashes. Father and son locked eyes, the infant looking curiously at the bearded man above him. Max's eyes welled. "He looks like you," he said, his voice breaking slightly. "I swear to you, on my life, I will keep you both safe. Trust me."

"I know you will, my love. It is why we are here and safe now. You have made so many friends. People love you, so they want to help us. So I always trust you. You always find a way."

Max gripped his beard tightly and shook his head side-to-side. "Yes. I always find a way. But sometimes that way is not what we want, my love. I'm sorry."

CHAPTER 26
ABSCHIED: PARTING
1941

In the morning, there was a knock on the door to the dirt cellar. It was the prearranged knock, letting the Jews know it was safe, that a friend was on the other side of the door. Three knocks, a pause, then one more. A tall, slim man with thinning hair, appearing to be in his forties, stepped into the cellar. He smiled, but no one seemed to know his purpose until his eyes found Max, and the two men nodded to each other. "Hello, Max." He sounded somber and reticent. He looked at Gerda, holding her baby, before quickly looking down at his own feet.

"Max?" Gerda looked at her husband questioningly.

"This man worked on our electricity at the store back in 1936." He took Gerda by the arm and led her into a corner to have a quieter conversation. "He is not a Jew, but he is opposed to what has happened to our people. He spoke to me years ago during the Jewish boycotts. He hates what Hitler has done almost as much as we do. He is a good man."

"So? Good for him. What does that have to do with coming here?" Tears started to form in her eyes. She knew the answer. She hated the answer. She didn't want to believe the answer.

"You said it yourself, my love. We can't bring a baby into this. I swore to keep you and our baby alive."

"No. Not like this. I'd rather die."

"No!" Max shouted through gritted teeth. "Never say that." He ran his fingers through his hair and then firmly held both of Gerda's shoulders, as tears streamed from his eyes. "I could not tell you while you were carrying him or while you were delivering him. It would have been too cruel. But you know this is best for our boy. This war will end. Hitler will end someday, and we will find each other, all of us, if that is God's will."

"All of us? What are you saying?"

"I'm saying I will keep my wife and baby alive, even if I have to give my own life."

Gerda's knees buckled and Max lowered her gently to the floor, slipping the baby from her arms. He walked over to the tall balding man who gently took the baby.

"My cousin is a wonderful woman. She could have no children of her own, but she will care for this child like her own." He was speaking in the direction of Gerda, who had her head turned away, refusing to look.

Max nodded. "Thank you, my friend. As agreed, I will not say your name here and you will not say your cousin's name. If it is God's plan that we reunite, we will find him, but for now, the risks are too great for everyone."

The men embraced. As the man turned to leave, Gerda said, "His name is Max. My baby's name is Max."

* * *

The group of Jews in the cellar were silent all morning. No one dared speak. Karin wept in the corner, consoled by Ursula. Gerda just stared at the wall. Max paced nervously and looked at the door to the cellar.

Otto approached Max and drew him in for an embrace. He leaned close to his ear to speak with no one else hearing him. "You did what I could not. Ullie would not have forgiven me if I sent Karin away, but by keeping our baby here, I fear I may have condemned her to death. You are a brave man."

Max squeezed Otto tightly. "That means a great deal to me. I wish I felt brave. My heart is broken." He paused, looking over to Gerda. "But the pain is only beginning."

Near noontime, there was another set of knocks indicating a friend on the other side of the door. A short, clean-shaven, slender man stepped in. He wore a suit and tie covered by a new-looking trench coat with a single button cinched.

Max held a hand up, signaling the man to stay by the door, then walked over to Gerda.

She braced and shook her head, "No. Don't you dare."

"Listen to me, then you decide. OK?"

Gerda tossed her head and did not respond.

"I swore I would keep you alive. Now, more than ever, that must be so. You will live through this war so you may go to find our son."

Her look softened as she realized Max did not expect to survive himself.

"You have met Manfred. He is the salesman for Steiff we dealt with at the store. He sold us such beautiful stuffed animals, the best in the world." Max attempted a smile.

"Of course I remember," Gerda responded stiffly.

Max lowered his voice to a whisper. "You know he is—um—different. He is thirty-six and has no wife, no girlfriend." Max glanced back at Manfred and waved to signal he needed more time. "I spoke with him because I know he sympathizes with us. I also know that the current times can be just as dangerous for men like him as they are for Jews."

Max put his hands over his face, unable to look at his wife while saying his next words. "I asked a printer friend to make these." He pulled papers from his pocket and handed them to Gerda.

She took the papers and unfolded them slowly, but she knew already what they were. Certificate of Marriage—Manfred Adler and Erika Adler. Tears streamed from her eyes.

"I also have identity papers for you with that name." Tears wet his cheeks fully now, with beads of saline gathering at the upper edges of his beard. "If you and Max don't live, my life will have been wasted. Please."

Gerda kissed Max long and firmly, both of them in tears. She felt as if this were simultaneously the greatest act of love and the greatest betrayal she had ever known. She looked at her husband and he briefly met her eye, then looked down. "I guess they really can take everything," she said as she stashed the papers in her coat and walked up the stairs with her new husband.

CHAPTER 27
DIE STRASSE: THE ROAD
1944

After washing Friedrich in the sink and putting a clean set of clothes on him, Josef took what food was in the apartment and filled his pack. He led Friedrich out through the broken door of the apartment, positioning himself between the child and Renate's body that lay under the blanket.

"Where is Mutti?"

"She had to leave. I'm sorry. She made me promise to protect you, and I will."

Josef's heart beat loudly in his chest. He did not have a plan when he killed Hans. He had simply decided in that moment that it was the only way to protect the child, and for reasons he did not understand, protecting this child was now the most important thing in the world to him.

As they descended the stairs, Josef saw Herbert Van Doren peering out of the window and ignored him. He placed

Friedrich in the passenger seat of the Kübelwagen and walked around to get in the driver's door. Van Doren had now emerged from the store.

"Is everything in order?" he said timidly.

Josef thought quickly. "Yes. My counterpart left with Frau Brunst already." He saw the small man frown, likely knowing they had not come down the stairs. "The apartment is an official SS crime location now. No one is to enter, under penalty of death." He hoped this would buy him some time before Hans was discovered. "I am ordered to bring the child to the camp in Düsseldorf. Thank you for your service to the fatherland, Herr Van Doren."

Josef started the engine and set off, but he did not know yet where to. He turned to Friedrich and asked, "So, where would you like to go?" He did not expect an answer but thought engaging the child would keep him from crying.

"To find Mutti," Friedrich squeaked out through a trembling lower lip as tears fell. Even after all of the horror of the past years, this was the saddest sight Josef could recall. But it gave him an idea of where to go.

"Well, Friedrich. You have given me an idea, but it is a long way to go. If I get you to a place where you will find your Mutti and have other children to play with, will you go a very long way with me?"

Friedrich looked up at Josef, sniffed, and nodded.

Munich was over six hundred kilometers away. It would take all night to drive there but Josef knew he must move quickly. The body of his partner would be discovered soon, and the SS would be searching for him within a day or two. The chaos of the war being lost was his ally, but the level of his treason was so great that even in this chaotic time, they would hunt him. Before leaving, Josef removed the flag from the front of the vehicle, so it would blend in with all other military vehicles, versus standing out as SS or Einsatzgruppen. He checked his map for the best route, avoiding populated areas, turned the vehicle south, and began to drive.

An hour into the drive Josef stopped to get fuel. He could not chance fueling the vehicle at a military base, so he stopped in Jüchen, a small town south of München Gladbach along the rural, lightly traveled route he had chosen. He pulled up to the only petrol fueling station in town. He figured he would have to fill once more along this journey. There was no reason for caution yet. Josef assessed that it was highly unlikely that Hans had been found, and even if he had been, they would not have communicated his treason broadly yet.

An older man, thin, with baggy clothes and his belt cinched tightly so the pants and shirt bloused above and below it approached the Kübelwagen. He was waving his hands in front of his chest and shaking his head. Josef rolled the window down.

"There is no fuel. I'm sorry, son. We've had none for a week and I don't expect any for some time."

"Where can I get some then?"

"Only at the base, I'm afraid, but that won't be a problem for you. It's the locals who can't drive now."

Josef frowned. "And what about the next towns south?"

"No one has fuel right now. Only the military." The man looked puzzled. "Why don't you just go to the base?" He bent and looked at Friedrich in the passenger seat. "You have a child in there."

"Yes, I'm aware," Josef responded tersely. He had to alleviate this man's suspicion now. "He is the son of a senior officer. I am transporting him back to his mother after visiting with his father in Düsseldorf. There are no convenient military bases on my route, which is why I stopped here."

"I see. Where are you headed?" the man asked. His question sounded like a blend of suspicion and curiosity.

"You wish for me to tell you the address of a senior official?" Josef laughed. "I'll just need to take a new route so I can fuel at a base. Good evening."

As he pulled away, the man waved, and Josef felt he had successfully avoided suspicion well enough that the man was unlikely to place a call. But he had a bigger concern. His fuel would only take him another fifty kilometers. That would leave him more than five hundred kilometers from his destination. To walk that distance, lugging a child along, would take weeks. There would be a manhunt ensuing, likely within a few days. He decided the best course for now was to drive as far as they could go with the fuel they had.

They drove south for about thirty minutes. Josef looked at the passenger seat and saw that Friedrich had fallen asleep. He was cradling Bärli in his arms. The fuel gauge was close to zero. There was too much risk of stalling in a location where they would not be hidden, so Josef decided to find a place to hide the Kübelwagen. They were just south of the small town of Zieverich. He had driven past the petrol station there, hoping, but did not stop because a sign in front had Kein Benzin (No Fuel) hand-painted onto a plank of wood, leaning against the pump. He had, however, stopped at a shop in town and used his uniform and position to secure a bag of food that would last them a day.

The rural route they now rambled down was lightly wooded on both sides. Josef found a footpath into the woods that was wide enough for the Kübelwagen to pass through. The path took them fifty meters off the road before it became too dense and narrow to continue. This, Josef thought, would provide adequate cover for the evening. Even with the sparse foliage of November, the distance from the road made it almost impossible to see them. He turned off the engine. The steady rumble turning to silence roused Friedrich.

"Did you find Mutti?"

"No, Friedrich. Remember what I told you. This will be a long journey." *Even longer now*, Josef thought. "We will sleep here tonight. In the morning, we will start to walk. It will be a great adventure that you will remember forever."

Friedrich pulled his coat tighter around himself and turned to his side, closing his eyes again.

* * *

Morning came and it was cold in the car, even with the top up and windows closed. As they slept, Friedrich had sprawled across the narrow gap between the two front seats and lay with his upper body on Josef's lap, arms hugging himself against the cold. Josef nudged the boy awake.

"We are going to eat something and then walk. You can go behind a tree to do your business, OK?" The boy stared blankly back at him. "Have you ever gone to the toilet, but in the woods?" Friedrich shook his head, no. "Well, it's the same as the toilet but without one. You just squat down."

Friedrich returned and confirmed he was successful. Josef was relieved, not wanting to have to be involved with that process on this long journey. They ate a portion of the block of cheese, loaf of bread, and strips of cured meat that Josef had procured the prior day, then stashed the remainder in his pack.

Removing a military-issue compass from his pack, standard for all members of the German military, Josef found due south and began walking through the sparsely wooded area. He decided they would stay off the road as much as possible. As they walked, his mind went back to Hans frequently. He could see his face with bulging eyes as he had squeezed his neck. The look of confusion, his flailing arms, that sickening crack as Josef felt his thumbs crush his partner's larynx. He wondered when the body would be discovered, when he would become a wanted man. If the piano store owner had not seen him leave with the boy, there may have been a chance that Josef's superiors would assume he met with foul play as well.

Josef's mind came back to the present and he realized he was not watching Friedrich. He wheeled around to see if he had left him altogether. To his surprise, the boy was right on his heels, half jogging to keep up with Josef's long strides.

"Are you doing alright, little man?"

Friedrich nodded.

"You are fast for your size, but I will slow down a bit."

The boy nodded again.

"You don't talk very much, do you?"

Friedrich shrugged, not intending the humor that Josef found in the act of a nonverbal answer to that question.

Josef laughed, "Well, maybe just not to me, and I cannot blame you for that. You have had quite an ordeal." He stopped and knelt down in front of Friedrich and put his hands on the boy's shoulders. Friedrich looked panic-stricken, and Josef realized that a day earlier, the boy had watched him do that very thing to Hans before strangling him. He pulled his hands back. "I will tell you again, Friedrich. I promise to protect you. I will never harm you. You have Bärli now. I protected him for twelve years and now you protect him, so that means I protect you. Do you understand?"

"Yes," Friedrich answered softly.

"There, we are talking now."

* * *

They walked all day. It was remarkable how Friedrich kept moving and never complained. *He is a German through and through, following orders and not complaining,* Josef thought. He thought back to his time at the Adolph Hitler School, the time spent learning about the physical and moral inferiority of Jews. While he did not believe everything he was told, some of the teachings must have bled through because this boy surprised him at every turn. He stayed hidden in a wall for nearly eight hours. He had walked nearly twenty kilometers today.

"I never asked you how old you are, Friedrich. Will you tell me?"

Friedrich lowered his pinky and ring fingers, staring at his hands as if he was mentally guiding his fingers to the right position, then held up his thumb, index, and middle fingers on his right hand.

"No. I can't believe it. You are just three?" How long ago was your birthday?"

Friedrich shrugged.

"Do you know the month?"

Renate had made a point of telling Friedrich his birthday many times and made him repeat it back. "March ninth."

Again, the boy had surprised Josef. He was four months

shy of his fourth birthday, and he was smart enough to know the exact date.

Throughout the day, they were able to stay mostly off of the roads, but now they were in a more heavily populated area. They were to the west of Köln, a major city. Josef had decided they would stay to the west of the city, head due south, then move southeast toward Munich. They had weeks of travel ahead. The easiest part would be the first days, before the discovery of Hans's body, when he would be hunted.

The food supply from the prior day was depleted, so Josef decided to head to town in uniform to take supplies from a store that would be obliged to comply.

They settled in a patch of pine trees, and he sat Friedrich down. "I already know you are very good at staying hidden. This is a dangerous journey we are on. To keep you safe, you must stay hidden. I will be back here before it is fully dark. Don't move." Friedrich nodded, so Josef got up and strode toward town.

It was easy to find the main road in the small western suburb of Köln and just as easy to locate the primary store for provisions. Josef entered the store and nodded at the man at the counter, a stout, round-faced man with octagonal glasses. "I'll need some cured meat, cheese, and bread—oh, and some milk."

"You guys have cleaned me out. Are you with the group that came through an hour ago? They have plenty for you."

News of a military group unnerved Josef, but he knew he could not show it. "I am with the Einsatzgruppen, reporting to the SS. I am not with any other group that was here. My partner and I root out Jews, and he is staked out at a home nearby. We need provisions. I am sure you have something for me." Josef leaned in. He knew his size intimidated most men.

"Of course, my apologies. I-I just assumed, never mind."
He hurried to the back, walking with a waddle, returning a
few moments later with a wooden crate filled with the supplies
Josef had asked for. "I added a bottle of beer for you too, sir."

"I thank you, as does the fatherland."

Josef hurried back with his supplies, keeping careful watch
for any military vehicles or personnel. He saw none and found
Friedrich sitting quietly, exactly where he had left him. *German
through and through*, he thought again.

* * *

By the third day of the journey, it was clear that there was a
glaring flaw in the plan to walk for weeks to Munich. That
flaw constantly surrounded them and reminded them of its
existence, especially at night. It was the encroaching cold. The
first night in the Kübelwagen was tolerable, with their body
heat trapped, at least partially, inside the drafty vehicle. On the
second night, Josef wrapped his coat over Friedrich, who also
wore his own wool coat, but Josef shook so hard he could not
sleep. Last night they found a remote spot and Josef built a fire,
using the flint in his small field kit. It was standard issue and
stuffed in the bottom of his pack, though never used prior to
that night.

It was only early December; the real cold was still to come.
Josef knew that something would need to change. He sat by the
remnants of a fire, feeding it small sticks to keep some warmth
alive, while he glanced around, fearful of being discovered due
to drifting smoke or someone watching. He puzzled over the
best way to get Friedrich to his destination. By now, there was
a good chance that he had been discovered as a traitor, that
Hans's body had been found. The trains would be watched

closely by the SS. He could steal a car, but there was no fuel to be had. They would only make it as far as the fuel already in the tank and it would alert the authorities to their location when the theft was reported.

There was no clear solution, so he shifted from the longer-term plan to immediate needs. They needed shelter for that night. He studied his map and decided they would walk until dusk before he would try to get them lodging.

As they trudged along, Josef asked Friedrich questions in an attempt to discover his past while also distracting the child from the laborious hike. It was obvious that Renate was not his mother but that she was keeping him safe. *Safe from people like me*, Josef thought. But it seemed that the boy had been with Renate a long time. He knew nothing of any other life. To Friedrich, she was his mother, his Mutti. This solidified Josef's plan to go to Munich.

* * *

After another full day's travel, they were south of Bonn at the small town of Röttgen. They remained to the west of the Rhine River. They would need to cross to the east side at some point. Bridges would represent a high risk of being discovered, but that would be a problem for another day. Now, he needed to find food and shelter for the night. The cold was already biting, and the wind had picked up more than prior evenings. They could not stay outdoors.

He positioned Friedrick behind a garage that appeared to be abandoned. A few junk vehicles sat in front of it, missing parts and rusting. The house on the property sat fifty meters to the south, with the garage blocking any view to where Friedrich was positioned. The wind blew from the south, so the garage provided a break in the wind, making this spot feel warmer than they had felt all day.

"I will go into town to find a room. If the area is clear and I am able to get the room, I will look for a way to sneak you in." He rubbed his hands together briskly, back and forth, creating friction and heat, then quickly put them on Friedrich's cheeks. The boy looked surprised and then smiled. Josef grinned back and said, "You see? That's what we need, some warmth. I will be back soon."

Josef found his way to the central road in town and a small provisions store that looked like it had rooms above. The town felt remote and would likely be a safe place to stay the night. He exhaled, stood straight to present an air of confidence, and strode toward the front door. Just before entering, he noticed, out of the corner of his right eye, a familiar sight—a small red flag with a swastika, waiving in the steady breeze. It was affixed to the front of a Kübelwagen with the customary black crosses on each door.

Panic grabbed hold of Josef, and he was turning to walk away when the front door opened and an SS officer emerged. He was a large man, not quite as tall as Josef, but perhaps Hans's size. He was thick in the midsection with a waist wider than his chest. He wore a thick mustache that matched bushy, black eyebrows. As he exited the store, he had already taken a bite out of a block of cheese that he had removed from the bag he carried.

Josef decided that his best course was to continue forward. He stepped toward the door, saluted, and loudly proclaimed, "Heil Hitler."

The SS officer looked carefully at Josef and with a mouth

full of cheese, mumbled, "Yeah. Heil Hitler," with little enthusiasm. He took a step past, then turned as Josef was opening the door to the store. "Hold there."

Josef stopped and turned. "Sir?"

"What is your name?"

Thinking quickly, he said the first name he could think of that was not his own. "Günter Kimmich, sir." That name was always on his mind.

"Hmm. You are a big man, like the description I was given of a Josef Zohren. He might be traveling with a child though." He looked up and down at Josef. "I'd best see your papers."

"My papers?" Thoughts raced through Josef's mind as he tried to buy time. All personnel had papers. Even citizens were required to carry papers proving their identity. "Of course, sir. They are in my vehicle in the back."

"I should radio the base," the officer said, speaking slowly, as if thinking through the words as he spoke them. He took a step toward his vehicle.

"The vehicle is right here, sir. Just around the corner. I will clear this up for you." Josef looked at him with a level gaze, his piercing blue eyes serious and steady.

"Very well." The officer pulled his sidearm with his right hand and pointed it at Josef, while still holding his provisions with his left. "I will follow you."

Josef walked around the corner of the building. He thought of Friedrich. If he were caught now, he had not instructed Friedrich to leave that spot. The dutiful German boy who feared fairy tales and demons would wait there until he froze to death.

The light was fading in the early evening, and the shadow

of the building made it slightly darker as they rounded the corner to the left of the front door. As he crossed the line of that shadow, it took a split second to adjust and see the landscape at the side of the building. The officer was two paces behind him, so Josef stopped after one step, counted for another step, and then spun around and lunged for the gun.

He missed the gun but caught the large man's right wrist with his own right hand reaching across. He was able to hold the arm and gun pointed away from his own body and get his left hand over the hand holding the gun; then he squeezed with all his strength. He heard the man let out a squeal of pain as he dropped his bag of provisions and struck wildly at Josef with his left hand. Josef squeezed the right hand even harder. There was a crack as a bone in the SS officer's hand snapped and he roared with pain. Josef spun him around and put his arm around the man's neck as the gun fell from the broken hand. He pulled his choke hold tight, hearing nothing but gurgling sounds from the officer's throat. Josef recalled training at Grafenwoehr on this very type of chokehold.

He whispered, through gritted teeth, "You people taught me this," as the man's body went limp.

* * *

A Kübelwagen rumbled up to the abandoned garage where Friedrich sat, frozen with fear. The door opened and heavy footsteps approached. He hid his face and then heard Josef's voice.

"I didn't find a room for us to go to, but I brought one here." He led the boy to the vehicle, and they drove off to find a remote location to sleep. Josef knew he would not be able to drive that vehicle the next day. In fact, he would not be able to wear his military uniform again. He was discovered and now, the hunt was on.

They drove about fifty kilometers to put some distance between them and the SS officer's body where the search for them would be centered. Josef pulled down an old dirt road and parked behind an abandoned barn. He moved a suitcase off of the back seat, as well as the bag of provisions the SS officer had dropped when Josef choked him. He had picked up the bag before taking the vehicle. They moved to the back seat and laid down. Friedrich laid on top of Josef for warmth. Exhausted, they both slept until morning light.

As morning broke, Josef woke with a start. He had been dreaming about Liesel, though not like he used to. This was not a dream about he and Liesel making love, or even in love. In this dream, she hated him. She spoke to him with venom in her words, telling him that he was a demon.

Friedrich roused and opened the door to exit the vehicle and do his morning business. It had become normal for him to do it outside now. Josef began to plot their next move. He knew he could not drive the Kübelwagen any farther. It would draw too much of the wrong attention. He also knew he had to change out of his uniform. His eyes landed on the suitcase. He grabbed it and unclasped the top, flipping the lid of the hard-sided case up. It was a treasure—men's clothes.

The SS officer must have been headed for a day back home with his wife, or to visit a mistress, for he had packed clothes to change out of his uniform. There was a gray wool coat, brown sweater, beige corduroy pants, two T-shirts, and two pairs of socks. Josef removed his official issue M44 military slacks and pulled the corduroy pants up and on. They were several sizes too big around the waist and too short on his legs, but they would have to do. He slid his belt through the loops and cinched it tight around his waist. Stepping out of the vehicle, he felt somewhat ridiculous with the baggy pants, looking like a fireplace bellows under the belt. But the sweater fit, and the coat covered the pants well enough. The new clothes would give them a chance of not being spotted as easily.

They abandoned their second vehicle of the week and began to walk. They were on a rural road, headed southeast. Josef knew they were not far from the Rhine River to their east. They would come to a town soon, as small towns were speckled along the edge of the Rhine. Based on the map, Josef calculated they were about ten kilometers north of Weissenthurm. There was a bridge there, the Hermann Göring Bridge, and this may be his last and best chance to cross the Rhine before the hunt intensified even more. If the SS officer was found this morning, it would take the better part of the day to organize a grid search for them, and they could have traveled in any direction, making the search area quite large.

"We must make Weissenthurm by midday, Friedrich, so we will start walking now. We can eat while we walk, OK?"

The boy nodded. He reached into the food bag and broke off a large piece of cheese. He pretended to feed a little to Bärli, whose lower half was stuffed in the pocket of his wool coat with his head and arms sticking out.

"You are taking excellent care of him, Friedrich." Josef tussled the boy's hair.

It was a crisp, cold day, but the wind had died down overnight making the walk more bearable. There were wispy clouds in the blue sky that made their presence felt when the sun ducked behind them, robbing them of a few extra degrees of warmth. The rural road they walked down was sparsely settled, with an occasional farm. Only a few vehicles passed, two military transports and one civilian car. Each time they heard the rumble of an engine, they ran from the road and hid in some bramble or long grass.

Clothes are a funny thing, Josef thought. *I am wearing another man's clothes, the pants do not fit well, and yet I feel more at ease than any day I can remember.* Being out of uniform gave him a sense of freedom. He would be able to blend in with anyone on the street when they reached town.

CHAPTER 28
DIE BRÜCKE: THE BRIDGE
1944

J osef and Friedrich arrived at the outskirts of Weissenthurm by eleven a.m., taking the normal, slower pace Josef had perfected over the past days to maximize speed without wearing Friedrich out. The boy spoke a bit more frequently now, observing birds or trees or clouds. He also asked about his Mutti less frequently. He was still intent on finding her but was starting to comprehend that the trip would be long.

With no more military clothing, Josef would not be able to demand free provisions. He had not worked that problem out yet, but the priority was to get across the bridge. He decided not to hide Friedrich this time, as they were both dressed as civilians. They could be brothers, or an uncle with his nephew. It should not arouse suspicion just walking together. At least not yet, he hoped.

Ahead in the distance they saw the Hermann Göring

Bridge. It was a steel structure of large beams in triangles stretching over three hundred meters down each side of a road that spanned the mighty river. It connected Weissenthurm on the west side to Neuwied on the east. It was an important passage for those headed to Frankfurt or Munich.

An engine rumbled in the distance behind them. Josef looked back and noticed it was a civilian vehicle. Friedrich squeezed Josef's hand and looked up at him with a furrowed brow.

"We don't need to hide from the cars here, Friedrich. We are just two men out for a walk." Josef gave him a smile and nod of assurance that seemed to satisfy the boy.

As the car rumbled past, Josef noticed a man in the driver's seat. He looked to be in his forties and wore a suit and tie. He had a thin-brimmed hat on his head that gave him a look of importance. His black car, a German-made Mercedes Benz, was spotless. The man watched them as he passed and even slowed down slightly. Josef held his breath, *had he been wrong about whether they would arouse suspicion?* But the car kept on moving.

As they walked on and came closer to the bridge, Friedrich's face registered the awe he felt looking at the mass of metal rising up above the earth. He also gazed at the river and its flowing waters. Josef thought it was likely the boy had never seen such things. Perhaps all he had ever known was the small square where they lived. Renate would have kept him close to home, hoping no one would identify him as a Jew.

There were two military vehicles by the bridge. Two uniformed men were leaning against one of the vehicles. They looked to be no more than fifteen or sixteen years old. Both were small and looked so young. Josef wondered if he had looked like such a child back in early 1941 when he began his service at just fifteen. He was assessing the situation, looking in every direction, and deciding how he might get past the two servicemen when he noted the man in the black Mercedes again. The car was parked now at the side of the road about fifty yards behind them. He must have circled back behind them, but for what purpose? The man had rolled down his window and appeared to be watching them.

Unnerved, Josef squeezed Friedrich's hand and pulled him to the left to walk north down the road that ran along the riverside. They would have to address the bridge later when there were no prying eyes. For now, they would walk into the center of town to find a way to get food, perhaps an unattended cart, or Josef might need to steal from a store.

As they turned the corner onto the main road, Josef saw two Kübelwagen parked at the roadside. Three members of the Einsatzgruppen that he did not recognize were walking along the storefronts, peering in windows. He quickly ducked back around the corner, pulling Friedrich off of his feet but catching him again before he fell to the ground. He was surprised that they were here already. It felt like terrible luck that they would be in this small town when there was a one-hundred-kilometer-diameter search area. Was it the bridge that they assumed he would head for? Then he thought of the sharply dressed man in the Mercedes. He must be connected. He must have called them in.

They circled to the back of the building. Josef crouched down and tried to think of a way out. The bridge was too great a risk now. It was likely known that they were in this area. Only more troops would come. He had now killed two members of the Nazi police: his own partner, then an SS officer. He reflected that just an hour earlier, he had felt free, dressed as a civilian, as if shedding the uniform had transformed him. Now, they were trapped, and he could not come up with a plan of escape. He looked into Friedrich's eyes. The boy obviously sensed his fear and was trembling.

"I'll find a way out. I promised to protect you." He stood and looked in each direction. "We must leave this town, head away from the river." With that, he took the boy's hand and walked north. His idea was to get away from the center of town, which encompassed primarily one road, then head west before turning south again. They traveled more than one hundred meters and saw no one. Josef started to feel that they had a chance. Then he heard a shout from behind them. "*Stop!*" He looked back to see a single member of the Einsatzgruppen giving chase. It must be the fourth member of the group, he thought, as they always traveled in pairs.

They could not outrun him. Friedrich had proved himself strong for a child, but his short legs would not keep up. Josef scooped the boy up in a swift motion and ran, carrying him over his shoulder. It quickly became apparent that this was not much better than letting the boy run on his own. Josef was large and strong but was not a fast runner. With a child added to his shoulders, he ran so slowly that their pursuer closed half the distance between them in just thirty seconds.

Josef turned a corner, hoping to find a place to hide. A shiny black Mercedes was pulling up that block and stopped. The well-dressed man with the hat began to step out of the car. Josef had to think quickly. Behind him was one pursuer, but the other three would follow quickly. Ahead was one slim man, and he had a car they could use. He lowered Friedrich to the ground and charged at the man.

"Wait. I'm here to help you. Get in the car, quickly."

Josef stopped, stunned by the claim. It didn't make sense.

"Josef Zohren. You have few options right now. I promise you, I am your best hope. There is no time to explain. Get in quickly or all will be lost. When that soldier turns the corner, you will be beyond my help."

The man had kind eyes, and what he said was true. There was no other option. So, Josef trusted a gut instinct, grabbing Friedrich's hand and jumping into the back seat.

"Get down so you are not seen." The man sped off, turning sharply.

"Did he see us?" Josef asked, still lying in the back of the car, with its fine, hand-stitched leather seats.

"He saw my car, but you had already ducked down when he turned the corner."

"They will be looking for your car then?"

"No." The man let a small laugh escape. "They know my car well. I'm helping them look for you." He paused. "In fact, I am the reason they are here. I called them."

Josef sat up quickly. "So, you are a liar and you do mean us harm." He pulled the sidearm from his bag and pointed it at the back of the man's head. "But now you are alone with me. I'm afraid you've made a mistake."

"Calm down." The man held his right hand up, still steering with the left. "And for God's sake, stay down where you can't be seen. I did not lie to *you*—I lied to *them*. Please let me explain."

"Keep driving and speak." Josef didn't know why he instinctively trusted this man, but he did. He kept his pistol in his right hand and listened hopefully.

"My name is Antoni Schuyler. I am what is often called a *sympathizer*. Your prior unit would have called me a traitor." He turned slightly and smiled at that word. "I believe what we have done to the Jews is immoral and that Adolf Hitler is a criminal."

Josef could barely believe the words he was hearing. No one had ever said such things in his presence. Loyalty to the Fuhrer was absolute and unquestioned in Germany. This man had just casually spoken words that were punishable by death. "I don't understand. How do you know my name? Why would you turn us in if this is true?"

"You see, most of the sympathizers you have met in your profession are hiding from the Nazi regime, hiding from the SS. In my estimation, this is their mistake."

Josef shook his head, bewildered by what he was hearing.

"My father was a very successful man, rest his soul. He taught me many things, too many to recount, but one was that you keep your friends close and your enemies closer." Antoni turned his head again to share a wry smile. "The Nazis are my enemy. In fact, I hold them as the enemy of all real Germans. So, I keep them close, very close."

Having cleared the town area, Antoni pulled onto a dirt drive and stopped the car. Josef held the gun in plain view as Antoni turned to face him and Friedrich in the back seat. "I am a man of considerable wealth. Mind you, I did not earn this wealth, my father did. I just had the good fortune to be born to a wealthy family and inherited the money when my parents passed—tragically young."

His honesty and humility were surprising. Most men of wealth or power, particularly senior officers in the military, glorified their rise. This man was openly admitting he had not earned his fortune. Josef was intrigued by him.

As Schuyler continued, his face showed excitement about what he was about to share. "I have used my considerable wealth to make powerful friends inside the Nazi party. I throw extravagant parties and invite top political figures to my home. And yes, I feed them information to prove my loyalty." He paused and thought. "Well, I guess more accurately, I should say *to fake my loyalty*. At the same time, I am harboring Jews in my own home. They never suspect me because I feed them information from time to time, and even if they did suspect me, they would never dare search my home because of my high-placed friends."

Antoni pointed at Josef and shook his finger. "Now, you have been up to some mischief, young man. One of my high-ranking friends called me yesterday to share that you had killed two military men and were harboring a Jewish child." He shook his head and gave an exaggerated *tsk, tsk, tsk*.

"So, when you saw us today, you suspected I was the soldier on the run with the child?"

"Well, your description is not too difficult, you know. You are enormous and obviously not a Jew, with your blond hair and blue eyes, and you travel with an obviously Jewish-looking child. You were not difficult to spot, my friend."

"But you turned us in? Why would you do that if you are a sympathizer with the Jews?"

"Well, I must confess it did not work out as I planned." He shook his head. "I saw an opportunity to help you and make some points with the Nazis at the same time. After I drove past you, I thought I could notify them but get to you well before they arrived. I did not know you would head straight to the bridge and be in view of two military men. I was forced to wait, then the Einsatzgruppen arrived, and I thought I may have doomed you. I do apologize."

Josef absorbed all of the information and nodded. He believed this man and lowered his pistol, stowing it in his pack again. "What is the plan then?"

"I could ask you the same. What has been your plan?"

"I need to get this child to Munich."

"I see. And your plan is to walk there, with the SS hunting you, in winter, with no food, shelter, or money?" Antoni looked at Josef out of the top of his eyes, emphasizing the obvious flaws in Josef's plan.

Josef turned red and shrugged. "The plan changed when I ran into the SS officer. I had to protect Friedrich."

Schuyler gave an appraising look at Josef. "Indeed. There is nothing more important than protecting an innocent life." He turned to Friedrich. "I now have an important question for you, young man."

Friedrich looked up with wide eyes and nodded.

"Who is that in your pocket?"

"This is Bärli. It is my job to protect him," Friedrich responded with a smile, while patting the small bear's head.

Antoni smiled, reaching over the seat back to place a hand on Friedrich's head. "So, I have found two protectors today. This is a fortunate day indeed."

CHAPTER 29
DAS SCHLOSS: THE CASTLE
1944

The Mercedes rolled up a secluded drive in the mid-afternoon. A large home loomed ahead. Josef knew now that at least this man had spoken the truth about his wealth. Hopefully, he truly meant to help them. Josef had grown up in Freising, a suburb of Munich. His family was well off compared to most. He had seen larger homes owned by the wealthiest of the Munich community, homes built to show off wealth in the midst of an urban environment. He had never seen anything like the property that lay before him. The three-story home sprawled across a secluded landscape. The Rhine River flowed behind it as if the river itself was in Schuyler's private backyard.

The roofline was like a mountain range, jutting up and then cascading down over and over. A turret on the right front corner of the house was half as wide as a grain silo with windows on all three levels. The deep red brick had ivy crawling up its left half, almost reaching the roof. There were no other homes in view. A large patch of land was cleared of trees around the front of the home, perhaps two or three acres, and beyond that on each side were old-growth trees. Josef thought of *Grimms' Fairy Tales*. This looked like a place from those stories. If it were, that would mean Antoni Schuyler was some witch or demon and they were willingly walking into his trap. He glanced down at Friedrich and saw that his eyes were wide as he stared and took in the surroundings. Josef wondered if the same thoughts of fairy tales had entered the boy's mind.

"We are here, men. Let me show you where you will be staying." Schuyler opened the door and stepped out of the car.

Where you will be staying echoed in Josef's ears, it felt too permanent. "Sir, we will not be staying long. I need to get this boy to Munich."

Schuyler looked at Josef and seemed to weigh his words. "Josef, please call me Antoni." He paused and placed a hand on his chin. "I know you are eager to care for Friedrich, and that is admirable. You, of course, may go at any time, even right now if you wish, but I still don't know how you would travel in the winter. I could give you better coats and a food supply of as much as you can carry, but even if you evade capture, you would starve or freeze long before you reached Munich."

Josef thought about Schuyler's words and could not argue with any of the logic. "So, Antoni, are you suggesting we wait out the winter here?" He said it halfway jesting but immediately saw on Schuyler's face that this was exactly what he was saying.

"It's up to you, of course." Then he held his hands open, gesturing at the sprawling home before them. "It's not such a bad place to wait, is it?"

The idea was jarring, a full turn from everything Josef had planned. They had been on the run nonstop for days. He had imagined this journey moving forward consistently until he reached his goal. Now, could he really just wait here? His mind raced as they walked toward the house. His goal with Friedrich was important but was it actually urgent? Did a few months matter if it made them both safer? Might the war even end in that time? It all began to make sense to him.

As they reached the steps, Antoni turned, looking thoughtful. "Now, Josef, you understand you will be hiding with Jews, yes?"

Josef stared back blankly. He had heard the words but somehow had not fully considered this fact. His mind raced back through all of the apartments, cellars, barns, attics, and bombed-out buildings where he had found Jews, often living in filth. Was this his fate? "I understand."

"I hope you know that you have been told many lies about the Jews. They are just people, no different than you and I."

Sympathizers had said things like this before, but Jews were different. Josef had learned so many things about the Jews during his training: how they were corrupt and how they destroyed the economy with their inherent greed. But this belief that they were equal was even more difficult to contemplate when he saw the faces of the people he had killed. They couldn't be equal. He did not argue, but his face showed the doubt he had in Antoni's words.

"Don't you see it, Josef, in this boy? He is a Jew."

"Friedrich is exceptional." As Josef said it, he realized he was proud of Friedrich, as one would be of a brother or a son. "He is not like other Jews."

"Josef." Schuyler shook his head. "I have no doubt he is exceptional, but the point is, he is a boy. It doesn't matter if he is a Jewish boy. You obviously saw that when you decided to help him, decided to risk your life." He reached up and put a hand on Josef's shoulder. "You will see the good in the people here as well, I am sure."

* * *

They were greeted at the door by an elderly man wearing a suit and tie. He had wavy white hair and a serious face. "This is Heinrich. He has served our family for almost fifty years. He is a close friend."

"Good day to you, gentlemen. Please come in. I would take your coats, but I'm afraid you will need to bring everything with you to your room."

As they walked through the home, Antoni led the party and Heinrich followed behind. It was difficult to keep track of the names used for each room. Josef had never been in a home that had a room other than the living room, kitchen, or bedroom. They had passed the study, library, sitting area, wine cellar, and pantry. The pantry was larger than Josef's bedroom back in Freising and was loaded with loaves of bread, wheels of cheese, and cured meats. After they toured the upstairs with its seven bedrooms, it appeared they had seen the entire house.

Antoni led them back down to the main level, stopping in the library. It was a large room, lined with bookcases, packed with hundreds of books. A model of the solar system hung from the ceiling, as did several model planes. A fine Persian rug, with angular burgundy and brown shapes, intricately woven, covered the floor from wall to wall. In the center of the room, a rectangular table of dark wood had a large globe of the earth on it. Friedrich was staring at it, so Antoni pulled a chair from the side of the table and picked the boy up to stand on it. "Go ahead and spin it."

While Friedrich played with the globe, Antoni spoke with Josef. "You see, my father made his fortune on imports. Most of what he imported was completely legal, but for those things that may have been, shall we say, "in a gray area," he added a feature to his house that allowed him to store them without fear of being discovered." He nodded to Heinrich and the two of them went to the end of the room. Three bookcases covered the back wall. The two men each went to either end of the middle bookcase. Antoni moved a book from the end of the top shelf of the left case, where it abutted the middle case. He then felt the inside of the case and pulled out a wooden dowel that slid through a hole, pinning the two cases together. Heinrich did the same on the right-side bookcase. They repeated this process on every shelf. In all, there were eight wood dowels, four per side, that pinned the cases together.

The two men then peeled the rug back from the bookcases, which revealed scuff marks on the floor where the middle case would slide forward. They proceeded to slide the case forward about one meter, so there was just enough space to pass behind it. This was much more elaborate than any hiding place Josef had seen. He imagined he and Hans finding this place. He would be going in with his gun drawn now. Instead, he was going into his new temporary home.

Antoni entered the room behind the bookcase first. Josef followed, holding Friedrich's hand, and Heinrich stayed behind, presumably to keep watch in case the room would need to be closed up quickly. The room was long and narrow. It ran from the front of the house to the back, about fifteen meters, but only about five meters from the wall with the bookcases to the far wall of the room, which was parallel to the bookcases and would have been the right side of the house from where they had driven up to it outside. There was a window on the short wall to the right, which faced the front of the house and a matching one on the short wall to the left, which faced the rear. There were no windows along the long wall, which was the side of the home. Both windows were covered with thick curtains.

It was an ingenious design, Josef thought. No one would put windows in a secret room. The evenly spaced windows that covered the front and back of the home all looked uniform. Unless you counted them outside and then recounted inside, one would never know that the library ended short of the final window. The house was so large and had so many rooms, it felt impossible to keep your bearings. In fact, until they walked into this room, and he realized the long wall must be the side of the house, Josef had completely lost his sense of direction.

There were four chairs in the room that did not match each other. One was wood and three were padded fabric chairs. A large, rectangular wooden table sat at the center of the space. In each corner of the room there was a narrow bed with a mattress, all of which had been made up neatly. There was a sink in the far left corner, just beyond a makeshift partition. Josef assumed that a toilet was added in that corner and the partition erected after Schuyler started harboring Jews.

There were four people in the room, and all looked intently at Josef. He was used to the reaction he got from people the first time they saw him. His size would either intimidate people or interest them. This felt different. He felt he was being judged.

There were three women and a young boy, maybe twelve or thirteen years of age.

The oldest of the women was slim and hunched. She wore a brown frock and had long silver hair and glasses. Her hands moved with a small tremor, not the type caused by fear but by old age. She looked to be at least seventy. The next woman looked to be in her fifties. She was short and plump with jet-black hair. She wore a black blouse with gray linen pants. The third woman was taller than the other two by a full head. She had darker skin and shoulder-length brown hair. She was attractive and reminded Josef vaguely of Günter's mother. She had slippers on her feet and wore a black robe, which looked expensive. It looked as if she were ready for bedtime. The young boy had sandy-brown curly hair and was slim. He was about the height of the oldest woman and likely weighed no more than her. He wore a knit gray sweater with a white bird on the front. The two older women and the boy were staring at Josef. The younger woman stared at Friedrich and smiled.

"Hello, my friends," Antoni began. "We have some new guests who will stay here." There were darting looks between some of the Jews. "I found these two in town, on the run from the SS. This wonderful boy here is Friedrich, um …" Antoni looked at Josef silently asking if there was a known surname. Josef shook his head. "Well, just first names for us all is best anyway. This is Josef. He is Friedrich's protector. The child is Jewish, and Josef here was fleeing the SS when I found them."

The short, round woman began to speak, clearly having questions, but Antoni held up a hand. "Let's finish the introductions, shall we? He motioned to the woman he had silenced and said, "This is Erna. She has been here the longest. Her husband and children were taken while she was out of the house three years ago. I have not had success in locating them through my contacts. Our seniormost resident is Sidonie." He held up a hand, motioning to the older woman. "She has been here almost as long. I found her wandering the street when her home had been burned." Pointing to the youngest woman, he continued, "Amalie joined us two years ago. Tragically, her husband was shot as they fled from the trains. She managed to escape. Then Micha, our brave boy, hid in the woods for two weeks after his parents were taken." Schuyler patted Josef and Friedrich on their backs. "Welcome to you. I am sure the group will be very kind to you. Heinrich will see to another bed, and we will bring some food in for supper." With that he walked out of the room but left the passage behind the bookcase open.

Josef stood facing the group of Jews. He felt exposed, naked. They would surely ask about what he had done. Erna immediately confirmed his fears. The short, round-faced woman took two steps forward and leaned toward Josef, as if to get a better look. "You are no Jew, that is for certain. How did you avoid military service? All young men are required to serve, especially now that the tide has turned. Why are you helping this boy? Are you a spy coming here?" the questions were rapid fire and Josef stood frozen, glancing around the room for help. His eyes landed on Amalie, who was smiling.

"Let's let them settle in, Erna," Amalie interjected, seeing Josef's pained expression. "There will be plenty of time to get to know each other now. What I really want to do is get this boy cleaned up. The poor little man has had an ordeal, no doubt. We will bathe him and wash his clothes." She knelt before Friedrich, placing her hands on his cheeks as if she had known him all his life. "You are a precious boy, Friedrich. I have a blanket that I knit just for you. We will wrap you in it while your clothes dry." She then reached down and took Bärli from his pocket. "May I?"

Friedrich nodded.

"My, my, what a wonderful bear. Someone made this with a great deal of love. She examined the cellulose structure, seeing the missing eye and concave head. Then she turned the bear around, looking closely at the buttons up the back of his outfit and the fine, symmetrical white and gold stitching. "This is remarkable. Far beyond my skill. You must be a very special boy to have such a bear." She kissed the top of his head, and Friedrich walked willingly over to the sink, holding her hand.

Erna still stared suspiciously at Josef. Micha came closer for a better look. "I think you are the biggest man I have ever seen," he said, looking up at Josef. "What is it like to be so big?"

It was a genuine question, Josef could see in the boy's eyes. It always puzzled him how people saw his size as such a gift, how they viewed him as so fortunate. He had always seen it as something that created an expectation of who he was inside. He saw the disappointment on coaches' faces when he did not overmatch opponents on the Fussball field or wrestling mat. Since joining the military, he had learned to use his size as an advantage to amplify force with aggression. He shrugged to Micha. "I guess it's OK." He could see in the boy's face that the answer was a disappointment.

In the corner of the room by the sink, Friedrich was undressed. Amalie was wiping him with a cloth when she exclaimed, "You have a Nebenwarze." The two other women ran to the back and looked at Friedrich's chest.

Micha turned to Josef with a question on his face and Josef shrugged. So, he asked the ladies, "What is a Nebenwarze?"

"It is an extra nipple," Amalie responded. "Some people say that people with a Nebenwarze have supernatural powers. We have an exceptional boy with us!" She tussled his wet hair and he laughed. Josef realized he had never heard Friedrich laugh until this moment.

Heinrich returned with a large tray of food. Friedrich sat on Amalie's lap, her arms wrapped around him. He was swaddled in a blue knit blanket with yellow stars speckled across it. They looked like mother and son, both glowing from the affection of the other.

"Josef, we would like to hear of your journey," Sidonie said softly as she took a piece of cheese and an apple from the tray. It was the first time she had spoken since the new, larger group was formed. "You are among friends here. You can speak freely." All of the faces in the room were fixed on Josef. Only Erna's face wore a skeptical scowl. The others looked blankly, expectantly.

"I found the boy in München Gladbach. We have been on the run for four days now. Herr Schuyler found us in town with soldiers closing in and brought us here."

After a short pause, Erna chortled, "That's it? That's what we get?"

"Erna. Let's wait, please." Sidonie put her shaking hands together in a prayerful position. "Josef, can you tell us a bit more from further back?" She paused. "You don't have to. We are not here to interrogate you."

Interrogate—the word pained Josef. Did she use it on purpose? Does she know what he did—what he was—what he is?

Seeing the pain and conflict on Josef's face, Sidonie spoke again. "Let's not speak more of the past tonight. We are celebrating new friends." The group ate in silence.

The silence was broken by Friedrich, who casually said, "We are going to find my Mutti. Are you all coming?" and then took a bite of bread. The three women looked at Josef. His flushed face and searching expression told them the truth. They all looked sadly at the child but did not answer him.

* * *

It was evening and a few candles flickered on the table in the center of the room. Heinrich had added a bed along the wall behind the bookcase. Josef settled down to rest, exhausted from the constant fear and flight that had consumed him for the past four days. Only now did he realize how much weight he carried now that he felt safe. The irony was not lost on him that he now hid with Jews in the very type of place, albeit more luxurious, that he would previously have been charged with rooting out. The genius of Schuyler's plan awed him—*hiding in plain sight*, he said to himself.

The bookcase moved and Josef swiftly reached under his bed and put a hand on his pistol, though he did not remove it from the pack yet. It was Antoni. He nodded to Amalie, who left her bed, where she was stroking Friedrich's head, and walked over to him. "I think I will stay here tonight with the boy, my dear."

"I understand." He kissed her lips softly and slipped back out.

Amalie looked at Josef, who was just a couple of steps away. He looked away, pretending not to have noticed their kiss. "It's not how you think, Josef."

"It doesn't matter what I think."

"It does to me." She knelt down by his bed. "My husband was a wonderful man, and I loved him with all my heart. I did not expect to love again. Antoni also lost his wife and his unborn child during birth. I had been here a year before I told Antoni how I was feeling about him, and it turned out he felt the same way about me." She paused and looked back at Friedrich, lying in the bed in the far right corner of the room. "I think it is amazing how God puts different people together at the moment they need it most, don't you?"

CHAPTER 30
GEBEN: GIVING
1944

Hanukkah began on December 10. Amalie had been knitting in her corner day and night for the past week. She had left the room for only two evenings with Antoni. Even on those evenings, she returned within a few hours so she could sleep by Friedrich. Micha had taken to following Josef and asking him questions. He would eat the same food that Josef ate and even try to match the quantity. He had made himself sick on the third day when trying to eat as much cheese and bread as the giant man.

There was a sense of calm and harmony in this group. Other than Erna's occasional attempt to press Josef for more information, there seemed to be no ill will amongst any of them. They talked to each other at times but also seemed comfortable in silence: Amalie knitting quietly, Erna and Sidonie reading in a chair.

As the sun set, Heinrich brought in a tray of assorted foods. Sidonie lined up nine candles in the center of the table, her shaky hands struggling to place them in a straight line. "Would you help me here, Josef?"

Josef felt unsure. He knew this was some sort of religious ritual. He was taught that the Jews had strange ways and beliefs. He wanted no part of it, but he could not refuse an old woman with shaky hands. "Of course."

"Just line them up straight, if you would. We have no Menorah to hold them, so the table will have to do." He lined up the candles. Heinrich placed an expensive looking lighter on the table and left the room. "Would you light the candles, Josef?"

Micha and Erna looked quickly at Sidonie, and Josef noticed their questioning looks. It was clear that this had some meaning. "I don't think I should."

She smiled. "It won't make you Jewish, my boy. You are the oldest man in our group, and I would like you to light the candles. Just the taller one in the middle and the one on the end. That's all."

He looked around the room at each person there. Erna frowned. Amalie gave an assuring nod. He lit the two candles.

After they ate, Amalie went to her corner and grabbed an armful of knitted goods. "I had the other gifts ready but had to put some extra time in for our new friends. She handed Erna and Sidonie shoulder wraps and said, "So you have warmth during the winter chill." They hugged and thanked her. She handed Micha a sweater with a hawk on it "Do you know the hawk weighs just a few pounds and is one of the fiercest animals in the world?"

He gave her a long hug.

She turned to Josef and Friedrich and gave them each a scarf. "It would have been a sweater with more time." She laughed. The child's scarf bore a lion, while the larger scarf for Josef had a lamb neatly knitted into one end.

Friedrich laughed at his lion and took the scarf to show Bärli. Josef puzzled over the meaning of his gift but simply said, "Thank you."

* * *

The eighteenth of December came, and the last candle was lit. They had blown out the candles each night after an hour so they would last the full week. Throughout the week, more presents were exchanged. Micha had drawn pictures of each of them and handed them out. Josef was taller than a tree in his drawing.

On this last night of Hanukkah, they let the candles burn all evening until they formed a conjoined puddle of wax on the table and a few flickering flames remaining. Antoni slipped into the room and nodded to Amalie. She ran excitedly to the corner of the room and retrieved a small box. She returned and handed it to Friedrich. "It was my hope to complete this gift for you while you slept, but you keep quite a fierce grip on your little bear. You are a good protector."

Friedrich pulled the top off of the box and removed a spool of cellulose fiber. He reached in again, retrieving two black buttons. He looked quizzically at Amalie.

"Herr Schuyler was able to find these supplies and I am going to fix your bear for you. Would you like that?"

Friedrich's brow furrowed and he replied, "Yes, but ..."

"What's wrong?"

"Bärli is missing only one eye."

"I see, but we could not find the exact button, so I was planning to replace both eyes."

Friedrich shook his head. "You can't take his good eye."

"It is settled then. I'll fix his head a little bit so he feels better, and I will add one eye." She smiled at him and then at Antoni.

Josef marveled at the care taken with each gift, the love between these people. He felt uneasy in the conflict between what he had known before coming here and what he had witnessed. All of this made his past deeds even more unforgivable. Are these Jews exceptional, or had he killed people just like them?

The gifts had concluded, and Schuyler slipped back out after a hug from Friedrich and a kiss from Amalie. Each member of the cobbled family made their way back to their beds. Josef began to breathe heavier. His hands were shaking and his eyes filled with tears. With a sudden urgency he spoke. "I have a gift to give." The words caught in his throat and everyone in the room noticed and stopped what they were doing. They slowly worked their way back to the middle of the room, watching him.

"I was given wonderful gifts. Thank you." His voice came out in ebbs and flows as he struggled to take in enough air to speak. "But I have given nothing. So, I have something for you all." He paused. "Perhaps it is mostly for Erna." He looked directly at her with tears beginning to tumble down his cheeks. She was caught off guard and did not know how to react. She looked away briefly but then met his eye again and nodded as if she knew what was coming.

"You know nothing about me, and I have hidden things because they are terrible." His eyes shifted to Friedrich who stared up with a look of concern, not too different from the adults in the room. "I was about twice this child's age when I got Bärli for my birthday. It was at a toy store owned by Jews. The woman there made him. I don't think I was that much different than Friedrich then. I think I was good." Now the floodgates opened, and he sobbed loudly. "But I am no longer good."

He looked back at Erna. "Yes. I was in the military. In fact, I was in the Einsatzgruppen. I hunted for places like this, for people like you. I was the one who found Friedrich and his Mutti." Josef dropped to his knees. "I've done things I cannot even say out loud. I can only tell you that I will never be able to repay what I have stolen."

The room was silent. The three women looked at each other, searching for any answer to what they heard. Micha walked over to Josef and put an arm around him as Josef's back heaved with sobs.

Erna stepped forward and stared at Josef with a level gaze. She began to speak through gritted teeth. "Truth is a difficult gift to give, Josef. But you must understand it is equally hard to receive. Men like you took my husband, my two boys. I don't know if they are alive or dead. Perhaps it was even you who took them." Her hands balled into fists, and she shook her head, her cheeks reddening quickly. "Micha's parents were taken as well, and we know your people killed Amalie's husband. So, I hope you are under no illusion that your confession here today, or even rescuing this boy, changes any of that. Let me tell you something my grandfather told me when I was young. I was feeling badly because I had hurt someone I cared about, said some terrible things." She paused, wiping her own tears now. "I told him I was going to make it up to my friend. He told me what I am going to say to you now. He said, *There is no hope of creating a better past.*" She reached down and grabbed Josef's chin, forcing him to look her in the eye. "Do you understand that, Josef?" She added with her voice cracking. "That is my gift of truth to you, Nazi."

It was the last gift of that evening.

* * *

It was New Year's Eve, almost two weeks after the end of Hannukah. The room had been quieter since that night. Josef stayed mostly on his side of the room, sitting on the corner of his bed by the back of the bookcase. He even took his food back to his bed to avoid the discomfort of sitting close to the people who now knew his truth, knew his past. He mostly avoided looking in Erna's direction, but the few times he glanced toward her, he found her looking back at him. Sidonie kept to her reading and said little. Amalie would make a point of occasionally engaging with Josef in obvious ways. She would ask if he wanted more bread or a book, just to break the silence. Even Micha stayed away, as he likely feared a reprisal from Erna.

The bookcase began to move and soon after, Heinrich stepped in with a platter of food and tea. Antoni followed and addressed the group. "As you know, tonight there will be a party here. It is important that I keep up appearances, and I have not held a party for the Nazi elite in several months. The supplies I bring in to feed eight people under this roof would surely garner attention if it were not for the parties. Plus, I may learn valuable information. We all see what is happening.

The war is going very poorly for Germany and the end seems imminent now, perhaps only a few more months. At least that is my hope." He looked around the room, looking forlorn, no doubt having heard about the tensions as he spent nights with Amalie. He made eye contact with each person in the room, in turn. "I don't need to tell you how imperative it is that there be no lights and no noise this evening. We will have more than twenty senior officials here tonight, plus some wives, and a few mistresses. I was surprised I could get such attendance in the current circumstances." He paused, looking like he wanted to say more, then turned to leave. As he reached the opening between the wall and the bookcase, he stopped and turned. He pointed to Friedrich, while looking at Erna and said, "I believe everyone in this room wants the same thing for that boy. Let's remember that, shall we?"

The evening came with the sound of car engines, opening and closing doors, talking and laughter outside. The voices soon moved into the house, with music added as background. At the edges of the curtains, the six occupants of the secret room could see the glow of the waning moon, just two days past full. The sounds of merriment grew in the house. A giggling woman was just on the opposite side of the bookcase, removing books and calling out titles in a loud, drunken voice. At one point, when she apparently stumbled, the bookcase shook, causing everyone in the room to hold their breath for a moment.

The tension of the past two weeks paled in comparison to the weight that hung in the air this evening. Josef listened to the sounds of frivolity coming from just a few meters behind him, people laughing and singing, as he looked upon the dark room filled with five frightened, silent people before him. It was all at once incongruous and perfectly symbolic of the world he now knew.

A loud roar from beyond the bookcase told the group in the hidden room that the clock had struck midnight. It was 1945 now, hopefully the year the war would end. More than an hour later, the last car door closed. The low rumble of an engine came to life and then rumbled into the distance. No one in the room, except for Friedrich, had slept. Friedrich was sound asleep on Amalie's bed as she stroked his dark curly hair. Josef rolled onto his back and stared at the ceiling. The thin strips of moonlight from around the curtains filtered through the room just enough to allow shapes to appear. A moment after he laid back, the round figure of Erna loomed over him. It startled him, but he just tensed his body and waited.

"Are you sure, Josef?" she asked.

He paused, waiting for more, then replied, "I don't understand the question." He tried not to sound afraid but felt that he failed, as his voice squeaked out.

"Are you sure which side of the bookcase you belonged on tonight?" She did not wait for a reply, walking back to her bed, fading into the darkness as she reached her bed.

CHAPTER 31
DER KELLER: THE CELLAR
1957

Hubert and Ria Schiffers spent hours detailing the events of the early 1940s. They shared stories about all of the Jews illegally housed in their cellar. They even demonstrated the hidden hatch where they would drop food and supplies into the cellar.

They, of course, spent the most time on Max and Gerda, two people they showed obvious affection for, going back to the days when they were still operating Biermann Toys. But when the subject of their whereabouts came up, it appeared to be another dead end.

"I'm afraid I don't know what happened after they left here," Hubert said, shaking his head. Gerda left the same day you did. It was the day after your birth. Two men came, one for you and one for her, but I only knew one of them. He was a fellow tradesman, Franz Brunst, as you now know. I did not know the other man, but I am confident it would have been someone your father associated with through his store. That is how both Franz and I were connected to him."

"Your father was taken by the Einsatzgruppen a few months later with the others. He was a smart man, your father. He saw the path to keeping you and Gerda out of harm's way. I suspect your father is dead, I am sorry to say, because I would have heard from him. Of the five people in our cellar—well, six including you, you are the third I have heard from. Ullie and Karin Eisen both survived the camps, but Otto did not. Ullie was able to find out the date of his death from the archive in Arolsen."

This was a revelation. His mother was not with his father when the Nazis took him. Perhaps he had sent her away in the same fashion Friedrich himself was sent—for safekeeping.

"So, you have heard from neither of my parents. They must be assumed dead," Friedrich said, as if he was confirming for his own mind. He didn't like to admit it, but he still held a faint hope.

"I would assume so, but I will say this. I did not know your mother before all of this. It is possible that she stayed hidden. She may not have come back here even if she survived."

Dieter leaned forward and asked, "Herr Schiffers, may I ask how *you* survived? I assume the Nazi soldiers who came here would have arrested you for treason, such as it would have been called then."

Ria and Hubert exchanged glances, then she spoke. "It was the strangest thing. Max convinced one of the two young men, Nazi Einsatzgruppen, that the Jews were here without our knowledge." She scoffed. "It was a ludicrous idea. No one could believe it. We had essentially admitted to it before going down to the cellar. Then that young man, a massive boy, a giant, really, decided to let us go." She looked at her husband and gave a sad smile. "We have talked about this a thousand times. I don't think we will ever understand it."

Friedrich looked at Sigrid and nodded. His giant had emerged again. "Thank you. May I go to the cellar, please, Herr Schiffers?" Hubert nodded in agreement.

The cellar was dank and dark, with a low ceiling. Friedrich's hair grazed the rafters as he walked. He stood with eyes closed in the center of the small space, hoping to feel his parents there. He imagined what it must have been like to live in these confined quarters with five people. His mother gave birth to him right here, no hospital, no medical staff, just a group of Jews in hiding from the Nazis. He felt no spirits. He heard no echoes of the past. But he did feel somehow closer to his parents, closer to his past. He had now stood again in the place he was born. He also left with a glimmer of hope that his mother could still be alive.

As they left and thanked the Schiffers, Hubert handed Friedrich a small framed picture. "We found this in the cellar after everyone was gone. I want you to have it."

It was a bride and groom on their wedding day. The picture was old and faded. Time had washed out some of the detail, but the smiles were clear. Friedrich looked up at Hubert, wide-eyed. A smile and nod confirmed, these were his parents.

CHAPTER 32
DAS ARCHIV: THE ARCHIVE
1957

The archive in Arolsen would take multiple trains and require an overnight stay, so Dieter requested a government vehicle on loan and drove the three of them north, on the trek of over five hundred kilometers. Friedrich was endlessly amused on the ride as Sigrid asked questions of Dieter repeatedly and actually got him to talk more than anyone had in memory. It was evident that his father was growing fond of Sigrid.

A few hours into the ride, Sigrid fell asleep. She always slept soundly, wherever she slept. She lay across the back seat with her head propped on an armrest and her mouth hanging open. Dieter said, "She is like a puppy, that one. Boundless energy when she is awake but then sleeps like the dead."

Friedrich let out a loud, involuntary laugh, partly because it was genuinely funny and partly due to who said it. He could not recall the last time his father had joked about anything.

As they arrived in the city of Arolsen, it was already dark. They had arranged for two rooms at a small inn near the archive location. They ate dinner at the inn, then retired to the rooms with Dieter and Friedrich sharing one. There was only one bed, so Friedrich slept on the floor.

As he lay awake. He imagined looking at his parents' death notices the next day. How would he feel? He did not know these people, but they had created him and, in their way, protected him. It was difficult to think about the end of this journey, but it felt like tomorrow would be that end.

"Papi," Friedrich whispered in the dark room. "Do you think there is any chance they are alive?"

"It's probably too much to hope for, Son."

* * *

The archive was a large brick building with a gable roof on a tall three-story structure along the right side and a two-story offshoot to its left. An arched sign at the gate read Allied High Commission for Germany – International Tracing Commission. Walking into the entry hall, there was an instant feeling of solemnity, as if they had entered a place of worship. Friedrich instinctively folded his hands together, then noticed that Sigrid had done the same.

It was just after eight o'clock in the morning, and already dozens of people were in line ahead of them, waiting to talk with volunteers at the archive. The war ended twelve years earlier, and still, so many people searched for loved ones.

Looking around the room, most of the visitors were older and dressed in black. If people made eye contact with one another, they would nod and give a partial smile with lips pressed together. It seemed everyone who entered felt that same solemnity. Within thirty minutes, they were at the front of the line, and a young woman in her twenties offered help. She wore a name tag that said Marianne with a Swiss flag on it. Her accent would have given her away as Swiss anyway. She was tall, with blonde hair just past her jawline and a pleasant smile.

"We have two people we are seeking. We know that one was brought to a camp, but we are not sure about the other," Friedrich said.

"We have areas for different camps. Do you know which camp it might have been?"

"No, but he was taken in Munich in 1941."

"You should start with Dachau. It is the most likely one. I can guide you."

They followed her back to a file room and it was immediately apparent why the building looked so tall for only three floors. The ceiling was more than three meters high, with rows of metal shelving from floor to ceiling so tightly packed that an adult could just barely walk down the aisles without turning their shoulders to the side.

Dieter let out a gasp and said, "All these people. Our national shame."

Sigrid had not spoken since they exited the car. The weight of the moment seemed overwhelming to her. She tugged on Friedrich's sleeve to pull him down to her level, then got on her toes and whispered in his ear, "Whatever you find out today, just know that I love you."

It was the first time either of them had said those words. They had known each other for less than a month and yet the gravity of what they had experienced together made it feel much longer. He smiled softly at her, closed his eyes, and leaned his forehead against hers.

Marianne guided them to the middle row and said, "We are still adding more records every day. We are organized by year and alphabetically within that year. To the left we start in the 1930s, so you will be able to start right where we are standing and work to the right. This is 1941. I will be back in front, and you can come ask me anything. Please do not remove any files. You may look here and place everything back where you found it."

They walked into the first aisle and looked around. It was overwhelming. Tens of thousands of records. Dieter said, "Let's see where we are." He pulled a file out and announced the name, Adelsdorf. He slid the file back in, moved a step down the aisle and pulled another, Ahlberger. They all looked at the hundreds of files stacked from the floor to the high ceiling that lay between Adelsdorf and Ahlberger. Sigrid began to cry at the thought of the magnitude of people, of lives, this all represented. Friedrich felt numb.

They took several long strides down the aisle, and Friedrich pulled a file. "Balcke," he called out. Another stride brought them to Bendik. When they homed in on Biermann, they found a single file—Otto Biermann, age fifty-two at the time of his death in 1941. They moved on to 1942.

There were no people named Biermann who died at Dachau in 1942, but the grim reality they saw was that they had to take more and larger steps between letters in the alphabet. It was as if they were walking the path of escalating Nazi cruelty. In the 1943 section, the *B*s took up several sections of metal shelving. There were five files with the last name Biermann. The fourth file belonged to Max Biermann, age thirty-five at his death.

Friedrich sat on the floor before the shelf and looked at it as if it were his father's final resting place. There was no body, no grave, just this shelf. After a few moments, he wiped his cheeks, slid the file back in place and said, "Let's find my mother now."

They completed the Dachau files, and no Gerda Biermann appeared. They then looked through each of the other large camps. They split up after lunchtime to cover more ground, but by the time the archive was ready to close at five o'clock, they gathered back together and no one had found her.

"I can take another day from work, so we can return tomorrow if you would like, Friedrich," Dieter offered.

Friedrich looked thoughtful. "She went into hiding with a man that Max arranged to take her. It is possible she changed her name. I don't think we will find her here with the information we have. We need to go back to investigate the toy shop. We must find the man she left the Schiffers' cellar with. We have made it so far. This will not end until we know the full story of Gerda Biermann."

CHAPTER 33
DER STURMANGRIFF: THE ASSAULT
1945

S hafts of light streamed into the room in slivers around the curtains of the front window, which faced east, as it did each morning. It was late April and even with closed curtains, it was clear from inside the hidden room that it was a beautiful morning outside. The temperature had moderated enough by the end of March for Josef and Friedrich to continue their journey, but the news of the advancing allies and an imminent end to the war prompted patience.

Heinrich brought a tray with assorted bread and tea for breakfast. Friedrich sat on Amalie's bed with her, playing a guessing game. Sidonie and Erna read books, and Micha was painting. Antoni brought him an easel and painting supplies after seeing the potential in his drawing, which had become more detailed and proportionate over time.

Josef sat on his bed, watching the room. He knew he had

to leave here soon. He hoped for an end to the war and safe passage with Friedrich. He knew this place was not reality, that the storm of war raged outside. He knew that somewhere, Captain Schmidt and others like him were hunting and killing Jews and so-called *traitors* still, like the people in this house. He knew this time would end soon. But for the moment, he was at peace, a temporary and artificial peace, but peace nonetheless.

Schuyler walked into the room—they usually left the bookcase open most of the day now. They had become lax, knowing the German military had bigger problems than a room full of Jews in a mansion. The brilliance of Schuyler's plan still seemed intact as he regularly had tactical updates from his contacts with information the general citizen would not know. The Nazi government still tried to project confidence in their ultimate victory, but even the casual citizen without inside intelligence would have to see the signs of the imminent fall. Even the newspapers could not fully hide the truth behind propagandist headlines. In the early years of the war, the paper glorified the handful of German soldiers killed with large obituaries proclaiming their valor. Now, the obituaries read like a census document with lists of names and dates by the thousands.

Antoni sat at the table and folded his hands. They all knew his body language now. He had news, and it felt significant. Everyone gathered close. He poured a cup of tea and took a sip as if he intended to build suspense. "The world armies have crossed onto German soil." He took another sip, letting the magnitude of that statement sink in. My contacts expect that Germany will be overrun within weeks." He smiled. "The war is ending."

There were no cheers or shouts, too many had been lost for

that, but the joy in the room was unmistakable. They hugged one another. Erna and Sidonie cried tears of joy. Antoni stood and faced Amalie. He took both of her hands and they each leaned forward with their foreheads resting together. "Someday soon, we will go for a walk in the open, my love."

That simple statement made Josef contemplate all that had been lost. The lives lost were foremost, but the simple things lost were a tragedy all their own. These two people in love had never been able to walk outdoors together. The image of them walking outside snapped his mind out of reflection and into the danger of the situation. He called out to Antoni. "What news of the SS and Einsatzgruppen? What are their orders?"

"That was not part of my conversation, why?"

"They will move to exterminate all Jews in and out of the camps."

The room fell quiet. The moment of joy was over. Erna asked, "Why would they do that if they have lost? How could you know this?"

"It is how they think. They will want to finish the job." Josef paced as he spoke. "Early on, we were ordered to evacuate Jews to the camps. Later, when there was no room, we were ordered to just kill them." There were gasps in the room, but he pressed forward. "Now, with the German army fighting on their own soil, they will put more resources into finishing the job. This will be a very bloody month until the war ends." He looked up, looking at each of them in turn. "*Blut und Boden* will be their purpose."

Antoni nodded slightly. "I'm afraid you may be right. I need to learn more from my contacts. I'll make some calls." He kissed Amalie and walked quickly from the room.

The room was quiet again but not peaceful. Josef sat on his bed and reached into his pack. He removed his pistol and checked the ammunition—four bullets. For a while it had felt like he could leave his past behind. The group had accepted him. A month prior, they had celebrated Friedrich's fourth birthday, singing songs and playing games. He pretended to be a horse and gave Friedrich a ride. Micha jumped on his back too. He was part of this family thrown together by the war. But today he reminded them, and himself, of who he was. The past would never be behind him.

* * *

The next morning, Heinrich came in with breakfast. As he left, he leaned in next to Josef and said, "Follow me, please. Herr Schuyler needs a word." Schuyler was at a desk in the study. His hair was uncharacteristically disheveled. He appeared to be wearing the same clothes as the prior day, with his shirt rumpled and unbuttoned. He had a glass of liquor in front of him, a hand pressed to his forehead.

He looked up and gave Josef a half smile. "I think we have made a grave mistake, Josef." The corners of his mouth curled down as his eyes became glassy. "It has been months since our last party. I simply could not get anyone to come, with the state of the war. Supplies have been so hard to come by, gas, food." He put his head in both hands. "I should have cut back on the food, but we have so many mouths to feed here, and I love these people. Heinrich was stopped and questioned on his last supply outing, and ..." He stopped short but his look said everything that needed to be said.

"When will they be here?" Josef said levelly.

"I don't know. I suppose it could be any time. But I have little doubt they will come."

"Then I must get you ready."

Schuyler looked at him with surprise. "Ready? How can I be ready for this?" His hands shook. It was clear to Josef that this man, who had been so brilliant in his strategy to avoid conflict, had no idea how to win in an actual conflict.

"First, Heinrich should not be here. There is no need to endanger more people." Josef spoke firmly and the two men nodded. "When they come, they will demand that you take them to the hidden room. You must do so with no argument."

"I won't let them harm my friends. I can't ..."

"Listen," Josef interrupted. "You will see when I am done." Josef pulled a chair from the corner and sat across from Antoni to look him in the eye. "They will assume you have a secret knock to notify the Jews that it is you entering the hidden room. We don't have that here, but you will let them believe that we do. When you get to the bookcase, they will have a gun to your head and will order you to knock. I want you to knock as many times as there are soldiers with you. This will tell me what I am dealing with. Do you understand?"

Antoni stared back intently and nodded.

"I need you to say it."

"I understand, Josef."

"Rather than pull the bookcase toward you, as you typically do, I want you to push it into the room and I want the right side, as you face it, to come in, so it swings like a door." Josef nodded as if he were listening to his own instruction and understanding the plan better himself. "It is important that you do not look to your left. I will be there, and I don't want their eyes to follow yours to me. As soon as the last of the soldiers enter the room, I will need you to drop to the floor and stay there. I don't want the man behind you to even accidentally pull the trigger when the gun is pointed at you."

Schuyler swallowed. Beads of sweat had started to form on his brow. "What about the others?"

"We could put them in another part of the house, but it wouldn't matter. If I fail, they will all die. I think they will need to be in the room with me. It will divert attention from me, if even for a second, and give us all a better chance." He sensed Schuyler's reluctance and saw him shake his head almost imperceptibly. "Antoni." Josef grabbed his hand and looked at him steadily. "I won't fail."

* * *

When Josef returned to the room, he did not speak but began to look around. He stood at the door and pretended to walk in. The others stared at him, trying to decipher his actions. Heinrich came in after him and brought several boxes of food. Then he hugged each person and walked out without saying a word.

"What is happening?" Amalie asked as Antoni entered the room.

Josef looked at Antoni and nodded, indicating he should be the one to share the news. Antoni began, "I'm afraid we may be raided." Erna gasped. Friedrich looked like he was about to cry, most likely reacting to the mood in the room more than the words. "Josef has a plan to keep you all safe. I am to lock you in now and not return until we know for sure." He moved to Amalie and embraced her. "I'm sorry I can't stay. It's the only way."

When the bookcase slid into place, all eyes were on Josef. He looked back at each of them in turn. "I will not let any harm come to you. That is my promise. I swore to protect Friedrich and now I swear to you all." He spoke firmly but without emotion. There were no tears now, just a level gaze and a determined voice. "When I would enter rooms filled with hiding Jews, they would all be clustered together. You will be spread apart, making it more difficult to shoot at you." He could see Micha trembling. "Micha, I will need your help. When the time comes, I will ask you to make sure each of the ladies is on their bed, then you will go to yours. That will put you all in different corners. Can you do that?"

Micha straightened his narrow shoulders and nodded. Amalie flashed the hint of a smile at Josef and nodded her approval for how he engaged Micha.

"I want to place Friedrich behind the partition in the corner. We will push it against the wall." He took Friedrich by the hand and led him to the corner. "I'll need you to hide one more time, OK? Let's just try it now to check if I can see you." He placed Friedrich against the wall and started to slide the partition in front of him, pushing it tight to create only a narrow gap. As Josef slid the partition into place, Friedrich let out a startlingly loud scream. It shook everyone in the room. No one had heard this boy yell or scream before.

"What's wrong?" Josef responded, quickly pulling the partition back to see if he had hurt the boy.

"I can't go back in the box," he cried.

"Of course. I am so sorry." Josef imagined the trauma of the child's eight hours hiding in the narrow gap behind the wall in Renate's apartment. He realized that Friedrich's past may never be behind him either. "We will have you sit on Amalie's bed with her when the time comes."

The rest of the day and evening were quiet. Few words were spoken as they listened for sounds of trouble outside. All they heard was the rush of the Rhine from behind the house. Erna and Sidonie read their books but rarely turned a page. No trouble came that night. Josef stayed awake for most of it but drifted off in the early morning when Micha awoke.

Light broke through in narrow beams around the front window. They could hear birds and the river as they took bread for breakfast. It felt like a normal morning other than the unspoken tension that hung over the room like a looming shadow. Josef dared to hope that Antoni had overreacted to his feeling that suspicions were raised. Then, above the muted roar of the Rhine came the rumble of a vehicle engine, followed by doors opening and closing. Josef stood. "You all know what to do."

The next moments felt like hours. Micha dutifully walked the circumference of the room, assuring everyone was in the right place, while trying to hide his shaking hands. He made eye contact with Josef and nodded to convey that everyone was ready. Muted voices inside the house came closer. Josef looked around the room into each corner. All eyes were on him. He stepped to the edge of the bookcase that would act like a door hinge and planted his foot against the edge to make sure that corner did not slide into the room and reveal him earlier than he wanted to be seen. His pistol was drawn.

Schuyler's voice could be heard, but only Josef was close enough to make out the words. *I am letting you in willingly. Please do not hurt anyone.* The knocks at the bookcase began: One, then a second. Josef held his breath and prayed for no more, then a third knock came. There was no fourth knock before the bookcase began to move. He knew he had three armed men to deal with, which he assumed would be a captain, supervising two members of the Einsatzgruppen.

The back of the bookcase pivoted into the room exactly as Josef had instructed. As it reached a forty-five-degree angle, it stopped. From their point of view, the soldiers would see only Amalie and Friedrich until they stepped into the room. The first figure to step beyond the end of the case was Schuyler. He was shaking and sweating so much that beads of moisture dripped onto the floor. An arm was extended behind him, holding a pistol touching the center of his back and urging him forward. He took another few steps and three men stepped into the room behind him, the first being the soldier who held a gun to Schuyler's back. The next two were standing side-by-side. The one standing closer to Josef also had a pistol drawn. The captain stood to the soldier's right. Josef's mind flashed to Schmidt. He was thankful this was not him. This Captain was smaller than Schmidt and had not, as of yet, drawn his pistol. The three men were looking to the back of the room at the people, sitting quietly on their beds. Confusion registered on their faces.

Schuyler threw himself forward onto the ground and let out an involuntary yell as he did. Josef fired a shot, striking the unsuspecting soldier who had held the gun on Schuyler in his left temple. He fell without firing a shot. The closer of the two remaining men wheeled and fired wildly in the direction of the shot he had heard at the same time that Josef aimed and fired at him.

Josef simultaneously saw his bullet enter the soldier's throat and felt a searing burn in the right side of his own chest, just

below the shoulder. It felt as if a glowing fireplace poker had
jabbed inside him. His arm went numb instantly, and the gun
in his right hand clanked loudly on the floor. He winced but
kept his eyes forward and saw the stunned captain reaching
for his Luger pistol. Josef let out a guttural scream, sounding
like a wounded animal, and ran forward. Everything felt like it
was moving at half-speed. He could hear the echoing clank of
his gun as it struck the floor, see the two lifeless bodies before
him, and hear the muted, distorted screams from the others
in the room. A beam of light pierced through a gap in the
curtains, illuminating the captain's wide-eyed panic as he raised
his gun to fire.

Their bodies met before the gun was fully raised. Josef
realized he could not move his right arm, so he wrapped his
left arm around the captain's back in a swift motion and kept
driving his legs forward. After two more steps, they started to
tumble with Josef on top of the captain. He let his full weight
come down on his foe and felt the air blow out of him like a
burst balloon. Josef sat up and started punching with his giant
left hand. One blow, then another, he punched until he was
exhausted. There was a loud crack as the last of his powerful
blows landed and he fell forward onto the captain again and
lay there. There was silence in the room. After several minutes,
Josef sat up to look at the destruction he had inflicted. The
captain's face was unrecognizable. There was no breath from
the mangled flesh where his mouth had been.

* * *

An hour passed, and Josef was still shaking with a mix of fear
and adrenaline. He heard voices but could not make out any
words. Amalie knelt before him and held both of his cheeks,
directing his gaze at her face. "Josef, we must go now. Please."

He stood and shook his head as if his confusion was a layer of dust to be shaken off. "Yes. Of course. I need to take Friedrich now." He said slowly, as if in a daze. "You all need to hide someplace else."

"No, Josef. I want to keep Friedrich with me," Amalie begged. "I think he belongs with me."

Schuyler walked up and placed a hand on Amalie's shoulder. "It will not be safe with us. Friedrich has a better chance with Josef." He waved his hand at the carnage all around, the bodies on the floor. "I think that much is plain."

"No. I won't allow it," she cried.

"Josef," Schuyler added while looking at Amalie. "Tell us where you are taking him, please."

Josef shook his head again and collected himself before answering. "My partner killed the woman he called his Mutti. I promised to take him to find his Mutti. I knew it was a kind of lie because it was not what he meant, but my plan was to take him to the Munich Orphanage. I thought that would be the place he would find his Mutti, even if it is a new one." He put his bloody left hand on Amalie's shoulder. "But I do think he found a wonderful Mutti already."

Antoni sighed, "I agree with Josef of course, my love, but it is not possible now. The war is almost over. The allies will be here within a month. If we survive this next month, we may be out of hiding then, perhaps even be allowed to marry. I promise that the moment we can be out of the shadows, we will go get Friedrich. But our road will be perilous. I would take comfort knowing that Friedrich is with Josef."

Amalie walked away silently. She agreed that Friedrich would be safer with Josef but could not speak the words.

Antoni turned to Josef. "I will be heading east. I have a friend that the SS does not know about and will not connect me to. If we can get there, we have a chance to stay hidden. I have a second car, older but it runs well. I stocked up with fuel in cans that you can pack in the trunk. It should get you most of the way. I suggest you approach Munich from the north. All eyes of the military are south and west of there right now. Good luck and thank you. We all owe you our lives."

Erna approached and said, "Josef, I think you are forgetting something."

He did not know what she meant and immediately felt embarrassed and even afraid, as he often felt when confronted by this small, round woman.

"You were shot, you big oaf. Let me look at you." It was true, Josef had forgotten even though the pain below his right shoulder throbbed. She pulled his shirt down carefully over the shoulder. "It went out the back. I suppose that is good, though I don't know much about these things. The blood is already clotting in the holes on both sides. We should wash and bandage it before you go since I doubt you will be stopping at a hospital." She gave him a smile and then leaned close with her round face close to his. "Do you remember the words my grandfather said to me about trying to make up for the past?" Josef nodded and swallowed, fearful of her next words. She gave a sad laugh, shook her head and said, "*There is no hope of creating a better past*, he said. At the time, Josef, I thought he only meant that what I had done was irreversible and since I could not undo it, I should feel the full weight of my actions always. But as I have gotten older, and perhaps just a little wiser, I think there was another meaning he intended. He wanted me to focus on what

I could do going forward, wanted me to do better. What was done was done, but my actions from that point forward would be all I could control. I cannot forgive what you have done. I can leave you with that gift though."

* * *

Within an hour they had all packed light supplies, including a change of clothes and enough food for a few days. Schuyler's black 1944 Mercedes Benz 770 was fueled and ready for travel. Fortunately, Heinrich was sent ahead the prior day, as the car would be tight with Antoni, the three women, and Micha.

Josef's wounds were cleaned and wrapped. Supplies were arranged for him, as he still had little use of his right arm. They cleaned his shirt as best they could. None of Schuyler's clothes would fit, so he would need to wear a blood-stained shirt with bullet holes in the front and back of the right shoulder area.

The car from the garage was an older model, identical to Antoni's new car. The 1932 Mercedes Benz 770 was also black but had faded a bit over time. It was rarely used now and wore a layer of dust, but the engine fired up when called upon.

Inside, they had closed the secret room, leaving the three bodies hidden there. The Kübelwagen that had brought the three members of the Einsatzgruppen to their door was driven to the back of the home and pushed down the bank into the Rhine River. They hoped that this would buy them time before they were hunted again.

All the preparations were complete, yet no one knew how to leave. They looked at each other with both cars packed, fueled, and running. Micha gave Josef a long hug then ran to the back seat of the shiny new car. Antoni Smiled at Josef and said, "Sometimes words are not adequate, and some debts can never be repaid. Whatever life we have left, we owe to you."

Erna and Sidonie came to each side of Josef, hugged him gently, then reached up to touch his cheeks. "I believe you have goodness left in you," Sidonie said softly. They each then leaned over and kissed the top of Friedrich's head as he was already wrapped in a long embrace from Amalie.

Amalie stood and wiped her tears. She smiled at Josef and asked, "Do you know why you are the lamb?"

He shook his head. He wanted to speak but couldn't without breaking down. Antoni's and Sidonie's words had already moved him so deeply.

"Friedrich is the lion, which is a symbol of bravery and strength. You, Josef, are the lamb. The lamb represents redemption in our faith."

Now, whether he spoke or not, his tears could not be held back. They streamed from his eyes. He did not feel redeemed, but these people had all forgiven him. "I promise that I will get Friedrich to Munich. He will be waiting for you there."

CHAPTER 34
DIE LIEFERUNG: THE DELIVERY
1945

Driving a Mercedes Benz, even an older model, was quite different from Josef's only other driving experience—the loud, shaking, rattling Kübelwagen. This car rode smoothly. The leather seats were worn, but the quiet, smooth ride felt luxurious. Friedrich clutched his bear and lay on the back seat to stay out of sight.

When they crossed the Hermann Göring Bridge, it was unguarded, a further sign of the trouble facing Germany. The signs of defeat were everywhere. Having been locked away in a mansion for months, Josef was unprepared for the magnitude of damage that had rained down on every town they drove past. Months earlier, sitting in Schiller Platz outside of Renate Brunst's apartment, two buildings in the square had been bombed. Now, in the larger towns they passed, some roads did not even have two buildings standing.

In the safe confines of Antoni Schuyler's estate, well outside of town, they would hear the sounds of war, bombs, and anti-aircraft guns firing in the distance. Those sounds felt now like a small echo of the hell that had poured down on the country. Josef's thoughts went to his parents and the Kimmich family. Did Freising take this type of beating? Were they all still alive?

The kilometers fell away behind them and there was no resistance. No one stopped them. Few people even looked up when they passed. On a remote stretch of road between Frankfurt and Stuttgart, Josef stopped to add fuel to the tank. He removed two ten-liter cans from the trunk and began to pour them.

Friedrich sat up to watch, then asked, "Will we find my Mutti now?"

Josef stopped pouring. He had feared this question because he doubted his capacity to lie to the boy any longer. He tipped his head back and looked at the afternoon sky, mostly blue with a handful of puffy white clouds. "No, Friedrich, we will not. I am sorry."

The boy looked questioningly at Josef. He did not look surprised but rather seemed to be working out a problem. "Will I see Frau Amalie again?"

What an amazing boy, Josef thought. He had worked out already that they were not headed to the woman he thought of as his mother, but he knew that he was loved by Amalie. "I think you will, Friedrich—and I very much hope so."

* * *

Evening was starting to fall, and still, their luck held, no stops and no sign of the SS or Einsatzgruppen. They were, however, very low on fuel and the last of the cans had been used. They would not reach Munich but could get within fifty kilometers. Since they were approaching from the north, as Schuyler suggested, they could potentially even reach Josef's hometown of Freising, north of the city.

The car sputtered to a stop just north of Freising. They would be left with about forty kilometers to Munich. Josef felt confident they could move fairly easily until they reached the edge of the city. He grew up in Freising and knew the roads well. It would be easy to take a route down the west side of town to pass his home. He thought of his mother, she could have been planting in the garden today. The thought of her pained him. He had worked hard not to think about his parents. There was no doubt that they knew of his treachery to the fatherland. He was sure that his mother would hate him for it, just as he was certain that his father would hate him for what he had done to so many helpless Jews.

With the pain of regret heavy in his chest, Josef led Friedrich down the east side of town, away from his home.

* * *

They slept in an alley by a bombed bakery. There seemed little chance of being disturbed there. They had been able to cover twelve kilometers during the night before Friedrich was so tired he stumbled to the ground. Josef carried him another three kilometers to where they slept. They were about twenty-five kilometers from their destination. Josef planned to reach it by nightfall.

It was May 1, 1945. The streets were quieter than Josef had expected. He felt an eerie calm in the air, no sounds of activity, no soldiers. He took some bread and cheese from his pack. They had enough left from Schuyler's house for several more meals. He broke off a piece of each and handed them to Friedrich as they began to walk.

On what he hoped would be the last day of their journey, Josef considered for the first time that he had no plan past dropping Friedrich at the orphanage. The German army wanted to kill him for treason and the allies would likely kill him for his crimes. He shook his head and thought about Friedrich instead, this boy to whom he had pledged protection. He would miss him terribly.

"Friedrich. The place we are going will have other children to play with."

The boy looked thoughtful. "Will they be like me?"

"I don't think there is anyone quite like you, Friedrich."

"I mean, will they be looking for their Muttis?"

Josef's mouth fell open. He thought being raised in war must advance you beyond your years. It made him sad for the boy. "Yes. They will."

They rested in the afternoon and then pushed on. The final stretch was ahead. They had reached the edge of the city, still with no resistance. No one even paid attention to them. There were few people on the street. The level of destruction was even greater than what they had seen on their drive. Munich was clearly a primary target for the Allied armies. On one road they traveled, every building for a full kilometer had been either damaged or completely destroyed. A thought came to Josef that had not previously: *What if the orphanage is gone?* He quickened their pace.

Ahead, they heard the sound of vehicles and a commotion of yelling and occasional gunfire. Josef pulled Friedrich behind a fallen cement building facade that lay across part of the road.

He peered over and saw a procession of military vehicles with soldiers walking beside them. They were headed toward them. Josef tried to plot the best escape route. He could not go back to where they came from as the orphanage was ahead of them. If he looped around, he was unsure if he could bypass this caravan, which sounded large and may stretch through the entire city. He couldn't make sense of why the German army was marching here. He sat with his back to the concrete barricade, thinking desperately as the sounds became louder.

"Why do they sound so funny?" Friedrich asked with a puzzled look.

"Give me a moment, Friedrich. I need to think now."

"Listen. They sound funny."

Josef looked at the boy and then listened. The soldiers were speaking English. He could even understand some of the words, recalling his time at the Gymnasium school. He was not sure whether to be relieved or even more frightened. He had to get Friedrich to the orphanage, and he could not make it through either army, German, or Allied. Then a thought struck him—the Germans would kill them both. The Allies would only kill him.

He removed his pistol from his pack and looked at it—two bullets. He felt foolish that in his haste to leave Schuyler's house, he had not taken ammunition from the men he had killed. He peeked over the barrier at the approaching line of men and trucks. There was even a tank at the front. They were fifty meters away now. He had to wait just a little more.

He turned to Friedrich and held his cheeks in his hands. "You are so smart. You remembered your exact birthday when you were just three. I need you to remember a few more things, OK?"

Friedrich nodded. "You will tell the people at the place you are going that you are waiting for Frau Amalie. And you will tell them that you came from München Gladbach, Kaiserstrasse on Schiller Platz, OK?" The boy nodded. "You need to say it all back to me."

"I am waiting for Frau Amalie and I come from München Gladbach, Kaiserstrasse on Schiller Platz."

"Good boy." Josef then raised his gun with his left hand in the air and fired a single shot.

The commotion behind the barricade quieted and a loud, forceful voice yelled something in English. Josef discerned that he was demanding he throw down his weapon. He placed the Luger pistol on the ground in front of him and raised both hands. Recalling his English classes, he said, "A child here. Don't shoot."

He motioned for Friedrich to stand. He hugged him tightly with his left arm and kissed his forehead. Josef stood, lifting Friedrich in his left arm. He held his right hand open and raised it as much as he could to show he had no weapon. Friedrich clung tightly to Bärli.

The Allied soldiers had guns trained on them and stood silent. The tank and armored vehicles had rumbled to a full stop now. Josef put Friedrich down and pushed him forward. The boy looked up, confused. "You must go to him." Josef pointed to the nearest soldier who he assumed was the one who had spoken to him. Friedrich walked forward.

Struggling to recall his English, he addressed the soldier again while pointing into the distance behind the line of Allied vehicles. "He goes there. Waisenhaus."

The soldier held his hands up, not understanding, while sounding out the German word "*Vasenhouse?*"

"It means orphanage," another soldier added. "It was on the road we just passed."

Josef nodded to the soldier, who acknowledged the request with a return nod.

CHAPTER 35
ZURÜCKVERFOLGEN: RETRACING
1957

Two weeks had passed since the trip to the Arolsen Archives. Researching Max Biermann's business acquaintances was proving difficult. Most of the stores along Kaufingerstrasse, where Biermann Toys had operated, were either gone, driven out by the war, or under new management. Records from before 1938 were thin. It had been nineteen years this month since the Nazi government had ruled it illegal for Jews to own businesses and had taken Max and Gerda's store. In the time since, war ravaged the country, and millions died. Magda had provided as much as she could, and Dieter even called in favors within the government, but they were coming up empty.

Friedrich and Sigrid were pouring over a box of papers that Magda had provided, spreading them out on the living room floor in the Beckers' apartment when Dieter returned from work.

"Sigrid, I'm glad you are here. Something was troubling me today. Thinking back to when this all started, you told Friedrich there were two applications for his adoption, yes?"

"That's right. There were two. That isn't uncommon. I paid little attention to the other, as we know you were awarded him."

He looked thoughtful and rubbed his chin. "The thing is that there would have been no time for another application." Dieter walked to his favorite blue fabric chair and sat, without removing his coat. "I had connections with the government. It was wartime and I worked in a munitions factory. I was held in some esteem for that, I am ashamed to say." He paused and shook his head. "Minna and I were unable to have children, so I used my position to be put to the front of the line for any new young boys available for adoption. We wanted a boy under the age five. Minna wanted to teach our child mathematics and piano. Anyway, this is why it happened so quickly. I was called the very day Friedrich arrived. He was immediately awarded to us. We picked him up as soon as we were able to make our home ready."

Friedrich looked puzzled and asked, "Why would someone apply to adopt me if I were already adopted?"

"That is what troubled me all day. I don't know why I had not thought of it before."

Sigrid stood. "I'll go now. No one will be in the records room at this time. I will come back here tonight.

* * *

The clock moved slowly while Sigrid was gone. Dieter had not turned a page of his newspaper for some time, and Friedrich suspected that his father felt the same anticipation that he did.

Sigrid entered without knocking, held up a paper, and

blurted out, "I think you will owe me a whole cake, Friedrich." The three of them hustled to the kitchen table where Sigrid placed the application. The application date was July 10, 1945, two months after Friedrich was already placed with the Beckers.

"Why would someone fill out an application for me months after I was adopted? It makes no sense."

"Look," said Sigrid. "Here. Your first name, Friedrich, is written in the same writing as the person filling this out. They knew you before." Sigrid was bubbling over with excitement. "And have you read the names yet?"

"Antoni Schuyler and Amalie Schuyler," Friedrich read out, slowly realizing the significance. "My intake form. You said I told them I was waiting for Frau Amalie." He looked excitedly at Sigrid, then quickly became puzzled again. "But we know my mother's name is Gerda. Who is Amalie?"

Dieter pointed to the paper, his finger landing on the address listed for the applicants. "Weissenthurm—I think we will go to find out."

* * *

As they pulled into the secluded driveway on the north end of Weissenthurm, the three of them held their breath. None of them had seen a house this large. Beyond the house, the mighty Rhine River flowed. It was a spectacular view on this crisp, clear November day, with blue skies and only a few puffs of clouds to be seen. As they opened the doors of the government car that Dieter once again took on loan, the steady murmur of the river could be heard above the sound of the breeze in plentiful beech trees.

No other house could be seen through the trees, and they suspected that even if the landscape were barren, it would be a kilometer in any direction before any structure would appear. They were obviously on the property of someone important, someone of great wealth.

"Your castle, Friedrich. Just as you remember," Sigrid said, placing a hand on his back.

The front door opened and a slim man with neatly trimmed gray hair walked down the steps and approached them. He was wearing black dress shoes that looked freshly polished and a sharp, tailored gray suit with a white shirt but no tie. "May I help you?" he asked. He had an easy smile and seemed genuine in his offer.

Friedrich stepped forward, offered his hand to shake and asked, "Are you Herr Schuyler?" A woman emerged from the house and walked toward them.

"I am indeed," he replied, shaking Friedrich's hand. He did not let go immediately and gazed up into Friedrich's eyes. "I know you, don't I?"

"I think so, sir. My name is …"

"Friedrich," the approaching woman shouted excitedly. "My god, it's Friedrich." She was an attractive woman at least ten years younger than her husband. Tears sprung to her eyes, as she rushed forward and wrapped her arms around Friedrich, completely ignoring the two other visitors.

"You are Frau Amalie?"

"Yes, you remember me?"

"Well," he paused, "I remember this was a good place, a place I felt safe. At the orphanage, I told them I was waiting for Frau Amalie. It was on my papers there."

Two children walked out the front door, appearing curious about the commotion in front of the house.

"Please, all of you come in. My name is Antoni, and you know that this is Amalie, my wife. We have three children. Micha, whom we adopted after the war. He is grown and lives in Frankfurt now. Here we have our two that Amalie delivered a year apart from each other in 1948 and 49. The older is our Friedrich." He turned and looked up at his guest, "I hope you don't mind. We loved you so. Then, our little girl here is Sidonie. There is so much for us to catch up on."

* * *

The group spoke for hours. The entire history of 1944 and 1945 in the hidden room behind the library was revealed. They toured the room, which was kept almost like a museum, with the beds still in place.

As Friedrich walked around the room, the rest of the group stood quietly watching him. "That bed there." He pointed to the far right corner of the room. "I slept there with you, Frau Amalie." She nodded. He turned to the only bed that was not in a corner. It sat against the wall behind the secret bookcase. "He slept there, didn't he?"

Amalie nodded. "Do you remember him, Friedrich?"

He looked at Sigrid, who nodded, urging him to say what he could remember. "I remember a giant who traveled with me. I know it sounds strange."

Dieter looked stunned, having never heard this memory. "You never spoke of this, Son."

"It seemed like a dream. A giant with blue fire in his eyes, and a castle. I convinced myself it was from a fairy tale."

Amalie smiled and ran her fingers through Friedrich's hair. It should have felt overly familiar, but it didn't. It felt natural. "I don't know if he was a giant exactly, but he was one of the largest young men I have ever seen." Her face became serious. "He risked everything for you, Friedrich, and he kept his word to get you to that orphanage. I'm sorry we were too late."

Friedrich turned toward Dieter, answering Amalie while looking at his father. "I was raised by two wonderful parents. I don't think you were too late. I think it happened exactly how it was meant to." He saw the emotion creep up in his father, who cleared his throat and nodded to his son. Turning back to Amalie, Friedrich asked, "What became of the giant?"

Antoni and Amalie exchanged looks. "Sit down and we will tell you what we know about Josef."

CHAPTER 36
DER VERKÄUFER: THE SALESMAN
1957

For weeks Friedrich and Sigrid searched for clues to who the mystery man was who left with Gerda in March of 1941. Max Biermann had trusted two other people, Franz Brunst and Hubert Schiffers. Both men had done work at the toy store and each of them helped compile a list of all the other workers they could recall from that time. They met with more than a dozen tradesmen, but none had any information. Most could not recall working at the store.

They canvassed the neighborhood of the old store, which had ceased to exist in 1940, just two years after it was taken from Friedrich's parents. The few businesses that remained from before 1938 had no useful information.

Sigrid and Friedrich sat on the wall in front of the orphanage on a Friday after school. They were in the exact spot where they had spoken for the first time. It was December and the air was cold. It was an overcast day but there was little wind. They each wore wool coats, Friedrich's brown and Sigrid's a faded red.

"I'm not sure where to turn, Sigrid. I'm losing hope that we will find out what happened to my mother."

"We will solve this, I know it, but think of what you have accomplished. You found your father in the archive, your caretakers in Mönchengladbach and Weissenthurm, your giant and your castle. We have seen your tiny box in the wall and your secret hideout in the castle. We even found the hideaway your parents stayed in and their wedding photo. I doubt you imagined this much success when we began."

"You're right, of course. I suppose I've become greedy for more. I have to know what happened to her. I just have to."

"Something else to remember. You are up to four mothers now. You collect women who love you like they are coins." Sigrid laughed, then turned more serious. "You have so many who love you."

There was a wistfulness in her voice, this girl who no one wanted. Friedrich turned to her and said, "You know that you are loved too, don't you? I love you more than I can put into words. You have been my first and best friend if we don't count my mother and a stuffed bear." He smiled. "I even think my father is pretty fond of you now, and he doesn't like many people."

* * *

Saturday, at six o'clock in the morning, there was a knock at the door of the Beckers' apartment. Dieter went to the door in his housecoat with Friedrich behind him, wiping sleep from his eyes. The knocking started again just before Dieter opened the door. Sigrid stood on the other side with her hand still raised with a fist, ready to knock more.

"I'm sorry, but I waited here in the cold since five thirty and could not wait anymore." She rushed inside rubbing her arms to get warm. "I've had an idea."

The two men looked at her expectantly without responding.

"We have focused on workers because Herr Brunst and Herr Schiffers were tradesmen who did work at the store. What if our mystery man was someone who worked with them in a different way?"

Dieter and Friedrich, still groggy from leaving their beds, looked at her blankly.

"I think we should go to other toy stores, especially ones that were in operation back then, and describe the man Herr Schiffers saw."

Understanding crept over Dieter's face. "He may have been a supplier or salesman. Yes. Very good. We will make a list of toy stores to speak with. They won't open for several hours, so let's have some breakfast first." As he walked to the kitchen, he turned back and said, "Friedrich didn't think of this. Perhaps we should have adopted the girl." He winked at Sigrid, who laughed and gave Friedrich a playful shove.

* * *

The first store they visited had been in operation for only five years. They did not have any suppliers matching the vague description given—a neatly dressed, slim man with dark hair. The second store, called Bahnhof (Train Station), had been in business for twenty-eight years, but the original owners sold the business ten years prior, in 1947, and retired. No one at the store could recall anyone matching the description. They did, however, provide an address for the original owners, David and Sylvia Schein. It was an apartment in Munich.

Sigrid and Friedrich went in search of the Scheins while Dieter went to explore the next store on the list. As they walked through Munich, they held hands and talked, sometimes about their quest but often about their lives before they met. Sigrid shared the comings and goings of friends she made through the years at the orphanage while Friedrich mostly listened, occasionally sharing something about his school or some memory with Minna.

As they arrived at the address for the Scheins, Sigrid turned to Friedrich and said, "It's selfish of me, but I have to admit that I'm sometimes glad when a lead doesn't work out. I even hope sometimes that no one will answer when we knock on a door." She looked down and shook her head.

"Do you think this will end if we find out what happened to my mother?" Friedrich took his hand and lifted her chin to see her face. "You think I am using you for your investigative skills." He gave her a playful smile.

"I just …"

Friedrich interrupted her, adding, "The investigation will end. We will not." He leaned down and kissed her.

The apartment building on Emdenstrasse was a shabby-looking two-story box-frame building with five equally sized units on each floor. Each unit had a door and a single window facing the street. The unit they were seeking was second from the left on the first floor.

They rapped on the door and heard a loud, gravelly cough from inside. The door opened and an old woman stood before them. She was short and stooped with a mop of unkempt gray hair. She wore a dirty white nightgown. As she opened her mouth to speak, she revealed several missing teeth in front. "Yes. What is it?"

"Hello, Frau," Sigrid began, bending down slightly to be seen by the hunched woman. "We are looking for David and Sylvia Schein.

"I am Sylvia, but people call me Sylvie. My husband, David, passed three years ago."

"I'm so sorry. May we ask you a question about your toy store. Well, about someone you may have known there?"

Sylvie nodded and waved them inside. The apartment was as disheveled as her own appearance. Dirty clothes lay on the floor in piles and used dishes sat on almost every flat surface. She moved some dirty clothes off of the couch and motioned for her guests to sit.

Friedrich said, "We are seeking a man who you may have done business with at the store. He was very slim, and he dressed likely in a suit. He was clean-shaven with dark hair."

"That's not much of a description," she said, letting out a hacking cough. "I suppose that could have described many people. I don't know."

Sigrid looked thoughtful, then said, "Can you tell us who your favorite suppliers were, or salespeople? Someone you liked and trusted?"

Friedrich smiled at the brilliance of Sigrid's line of questioning. Max obviously liked and trusted this person, so it was logical that other people would have felt the same about their mystery man.

"Let me think." Her face was serious and then she smiled, showing her few scattered teeth. "Oh, I always enjoyed that man from Steiff. The finest stuffed animals in the world, you know. Made right here in Germany. He was a slim fellow, always so nicely dressed and kind. My David just loved him too. Such a fine young man, so friendly and thoughtful. We were so pleased that he finally got married. You know people talk when a man of a certain age has no lady friends."

"Do you remember his name or where he is now?"

"Manfred. Yes, Manfred Adler. But where he is, I couldn't say. I heard he went east somewhere when he married. That must have been around 1940."

"Might it have been 1941?" Friedrich asked.

She thought a moment, then replied, "Could be. It was a long time ago."

* * *

Magda stepped into the café at Marienplatz wearing a broad smile. Friedrich and Sigrid sat at the same table where they had met with her before. The café was bustling. They sat with three cups of tea and three slices of Bienenstich awaiting Magda's arrival.

As Magda sat, she was noticeably excited. "I have found your Manfred Adler. He used to work for Steiff, but he left there when he moved to Straubing in 1941. It is to the east but still in Bavaria, so I have full access to the records. I have his home and work address on this paper. I think you will find the work location quite interesting." She gave Friedrich a knowing smile, then took a folded piece of paper from her pocket and slid it across the table.

As Friedrich unfolded the paper, Sigrid let out a gasp and grabbed his arm.

CHAPTER 37
DER RIESE: THE GIANT
1945

As Friedrich hugged his bear and began to walk, as instructed, to the Allied soldier, he turned back with tears in his eyes. "Goodbye, Josef," he said through trembling lips.

Josef dropped to a knee and pulled Friedrich back. He looked into the boy's eyes and saw nothing but purity and love. It stung his heart, knowing he did not deserve it. He recalled Günter's eyes, hopelessly searching for any way out. Then Hans's eyes appeared to him, bulging as he was being strangled by a man he called brother. He imagined his mother's eyes now, narrowed and bitter in disgust for her son's treason and his father's eyes cast down in sadness and shame for the atrocities committed by his own flesh and blood. He glanced down and saw Bärli, his oldest friend, cradled in Friedrich's arms. With his new, larger button for a right eye, and his old, smaller left eye, the bear gave him a questioning look. Even Bärli knew what he was now.

"Do you remember, Friedrich, the first thing you asked me?" The boy shook his head.

"In the apartment, when you emerged from the wall, you asked me if I was a demon." Josef smiled, but tears streamed down his cheeks. "Well, I never answered you, did I?" He gritted his teeth as the tears flowed freely now, fully wetting his face. "I am a demon, Friedrich. I am a demon. But you know what? Even a demon can love someone very much." He hugged the boy tightly, kissed his forehead, and then pushed him forward toward the Allied soldier.

Josef stepped back behind the barricade of fallen cement and sat down. He heard frantic yelling from behind him as the soldiers shouted warnings, demanding he show himself again. He picked up his pistol in his left hand, with its one remaining bullet, and guided it under his jaw. He thought of Günter and positioned the gun so that the bullet would travel the same path as it did for his friend. He could feel the smooth metal of the trigger under his index finger. He wanted to press down, but his hand would not follow his brain's command. He thought of his small friend, what he must have felt in that moment when he pressed the trigger of the K98 rifle, the strength it took to kill one good person in order to save many more. For all his size and physical strength, Josef could not compel his finger to place enough pressure on the trigger to fire his weapon. He lowered the gun and shook his head. The shouts behind him grew more intense and he heard the bolt action of rifles preparing to fire. He looked down at his pistol, pulled the chamber open, and removed the lone remaining bullet. Gritting his teeth, he switched the gun to his dominant right hand, sprang to his feet and spun toward the Allied soldiers while raising his wounded right arm as high as he could. He screamed, "There is no hope of creating a better past," as a hail of bullets penetrated his body.

CHAPTER 38
DER KREIS HAT SICH GESCHLOSSEN:
FULL CIRCLE
1957

On the train to Straubing, Friedrich felt the familiar angst he had felt so many times over the past months. He recalled his trip to Mönchengladbach, feeling the devastation of believing he had found his mother, only to lose her again moments later. How naive he felt to have believed the journey would end there so easily. Perhaps he was being as naive today, but he didn't think so. The information Magda shared would require too large a coincidence to believe that this trip would be in vain, but exactly what he would find, he did not know.

He turned to Sigrid, pressing his lips together in a smile that begged a question. She complied with a nod, asking him without words to tell her whatever he needed. "I want to tell you about my mother—my real mother—before we find—" He paused and shrugged slightly. "Whatever we find in

Straubing. She was my closest friend. I know that's not what a man should say."

"I think it's a wonderful thing to say."

Friedrich nodded, then dropped his head, his eyes half closed as if he were falling into a trance. "When her hands lay on mine, teaching me the keys of the piano, I could feel her guiding the notes but just barely." His hands instinctively went in front of him as if playing invisible keys. "At first, she was basically playing the melody through me, pressing my fingers down as if they were an extension of her own hands. In time, she pressed more lightly. I could feel her impulse before her finger even moved and I would play the note. We played Beethoven the most. Her favorite song was "Für Elise", and we would finish each lesson with it. When I was eight, I sat on her lap one day, and we played that song from beginning to end. As we finished, I realized that her hands were not touching mine at all and yet I had felt them there the whole time." A tear rolled down his cheek. "She was a good Mutti. Sometimes, I still feel her hands."

As the train crept to a slow, grinding stop, and the steward bellowed, "Straubing Station," Friedrich put his face in his hands, wiped his tears, and exhaled. He reached for Sigrid's hand and noticed she, too, was wiping away tears. They walked off the train together. It would be a short walk, as the address they sought, Herr Adler's work location, was listed on the paper as 702 Bahnhofstrasse (Train Station Street).

They stepped out of the station onto Bahnhofstrasse, looking for numbers to guide them left or right. It was sunny and clear. The day was crisp and cold, a perfect December day. Straubing had a quaint downtown area, marred by a few ghost buildings, hollow shells of structures ravaged by bombs during the war. Somehow, though, it didn't dampen the Bavarian charm of this small city, with its sharply pointed roofs and flower boxes on windowsills.

The small Platz in front of the station was covered with the pale green hue of dormant winter grass. The smell of coffee and baked goods filled the air from the bakery adjacent to the train station to their right, number 812. They looked at each other with a mix of fear and anticipation, realizing that they were less than a block from their destination.

After a few steps in that direction, Friedrich stopped and took both of Sigrid's hands. "I'm nervous," he said with a forced smile.

"Whatever we find, it will be fine." She tilted her head up, rose to her toes, and kissed his lips softly. They arrived at 702 and looked in the window. A model train circled the display, running around mountains made of papier-mâché. Model airplanes hung from the ceiling. A selection of Steiff animals that would have made a zoo envious were arranged on a table just behind the window display. Each animal wore a meticulously hand-knit outfit. One bear stood out, as it wore an identical outfit to the one on Bärli. They both noticed it immediately and looked at each other with shared wonder and confusion.

They walked under a sign that matched the paper Magda had given them. It read, Max's Toys. They opened the door, and a bell jingled, announcing their arrival. A woman behind the counter rose and put her knitting down. Her dark eyes flashed as they landed on Friedrich.

*   *   *

AFTERWORD

As I began the process of selecting the setting for my second novel, I kept coming back to Germany in World War II. Aside from being a tragic period in history, full of powerful, emotional stories, my own ancestry drew me there. Before I continue, I should make clear that the story of *The Threads Remain* is fictional. The surrounding events are real, but the characters are not.

My parents formed a most unlikely couple. To say that my very existence was a long shot would be an understatement. I'll start with my father's side of the family, which were Ashkenazi Jews who immigrated from Russia to America. My great-grandfather helped establish one of the first synagogues in Western Massachusetts. The living members of my father's direct line of ancestors were all in America at the time of World War II, so they did not suffer the tragic fate of so many European Jews. However, they did have extended family overseas who were more directly impacted by the war.

My mother was born in Germany in 1941 at the height of the German war machine's power. Her father and two of her uncles were killed during World War II while fighting on the German side. My maternal grandmother went into labor with my aunt, my mother's younger sister, the day she learned her husband had been killed at the Russian front. My mother was three years old when her father, a German officer, was killed. She has no memory of him.

My mother did, however, retain some small fragments of memories during the war. She recalls air raid sirens blaring and the panic in her family as they rushed to the bomb shelter in the basement of their apartment building. One specific memory she retains is of her uncle going back upstairs to their apartment during an air raid to retrieve her cellulose bear that she had named Bärli, in order to calm her from crying. So, I suppose Bärli is the only character in the book who is not fictional. In fact, we still have the little bear, which sits in a glass case in my granddaughter's bedroom. My mother, who is eighty-four at the time this book is being published, is thrilled to see her childhood toy bear, made by her grandmother, still having a place in our family. In that way, those real *threads remain*.

Returning to the unlikely set of circumstances that led to my parents becoming a couple and giving me life, I take you to 1956. My fifteen-year-old mother is preparing to move to the United States with her mother and younger sister. Her mother was moving the family because she fell in love a second time, twelve years after her husband was killed in the war. That love was a US citizen, and he was African American, a rare match in 1956.

If my grandmother's second marriage was not unusual enough for the time, let's move to my Jewish father bringing his new girlfriend home to his devout Jewish parents. I'm sure my Nana and Grandpa had more than a little hesitation about the German Catholic daughter of a World War II German officer. Obviously, my mother, born in 1941, had no knowledge of Hitler or the atrocities of the Nazi regime while it was happening. The war ended shortly after her fourth birthday. Nonetheless, I know it was a match my grandparents had to adjust to.

I share all of this to say that this complicated family history weighed heavily on my choice of subject and setting. I have long studied and imagined what people went through in one of the darkest periods in human history.

GLENN SHAPIRO was born and raised in New England. He is a lifelong writer of poetry and short stories, but made the leap to novels as part of his "second act" after retirement. His first novel, the gold rush era historical fiction *Cold Spring*, met with acclaim from both critics and readers. He is the son of a Jewish father and German-catholic mother who was born in Germany during the war and raised there, post-war, through her adolescence. For his second novel, *The Threads Remain*, he tackled that tragic time in history through characters inside Germany before, during and after the war.